MATCH MADE IN COURT

BY
JANICE KAY JOHNSON

MILLS & BOON

First published in Great Britain 2011
by Mills & Boon, an imprint of Harlequin (UK) Limited,
Eton House, 18-24 Paradise Road, Richmond, Surrey TW9 1SR

© Janice Kay Johnson 2010

ISBN: 978 0 263 88875 1

23-0411

Harlequin (UK) policy is to use papers that are natural, renewable and
recyclable products and made from wood grown in sustainable forests. The
logging and manufacturing processes conform to the legal environmental
regulations of the country of origin.

Printed and bound in Spain
by Blackprint CPI, Barcelona

Matt hadn't had such a good time in years.

Hadn't laughed like that in years either, he realised as they started towards Linnea's house.

"It was a fabulous idea," Linnea said in a quiet voice, her gaze warm. "Hanna was happy. She hadn't been since…" She swallowed. "I'd better get her some clean clothes and take a quick shower myself before I start lunch."

"You need it." His voice came out huskier than usual and he touched a mud streak on her cheek. His fingertips tingled, and it was all he could do to withdraw his hand. It curled into a fist at his side.

She went very still at the fleeting, soft touch. Her eyes darkened as she stared at him. Then, without a word, she turned and hurried from the room.

Damn it, damn it, damn it! What was he *thinking*?

Something about her drew him in a way he hadn't experienced in years, maybe never. Her air of fragility, coupled with a spine of steel. Yeah, all that, and her slender, graceful body, her generous breasts, the tiny tendrils of pale hair that curled against her nape. The whole package. He couldn't understand how he'd been so blind all these years.

Matt wished he was still blind. He and Linnea had been on opposite sides in the courtroom last week, and they'd keep b⋯⋯⋯⋯⋯⋯⋯⋯⋯⋯aim to Har⋯

And th⋯

Dear Reader,

Whenever I peruse newspaper articles about domestic violence cases that end in tragedy, I tend to think about the families. More is split asunder than a couple. What about the grandparents on both sides who have become friends and who love any children? Sisters and brothers, in-laws and cousins who have all swirled together to become one family, but who now must take their places on opposite sides of a courtroom?

Don't we all believe that romantic love can transcend any obstacle? But as Shakespeare showed us in *Romeo and Juliet*, family opposition can be one of the most heartrending obstacles of all.

When in the course of a tempestuous argument Finn Sorensen kills his wife, Tess, their young daughter, Hanna, in essence loses both her parents. She's lucky in one way—Tess's brother Matt Laughlin wants her, and so does Finn's sister Linnea. But Linnea's family has never liked Matt, and he despises them. Facing off in a bitter custody battle is a rocky way to begin a romance…

I hope you're as fascinated as I am by the emotional tangles wrought by our childhoods, by family and by our ability to always understand why our hearts lead us so powerfully to make choices that don't seem sensible.

Enjoy!

Janice Kay Johnson

The author of more than sixty books for children and adults, **Janice Kay Johnson** writes novels about love and family—about the way generations connect and the power our earliest experiences have on us throughout life. Her 2007 novel *Snowbound* won a RITA® Award from Romance Writers of America for Best Contemporary Series Romance. A former librarian, Janice raised two daughters in a small rural town north of Seattle, Washington. She loves to read and is an active volunteer and board member for Purrfect Pals, a no-kill cat shelter.

CHAPTER ONE

LINNEA SORENSEN HATED being interrupted by phone calls during dinnertime.

This was why she not only had caller ID, she had an answering machine instead of voice mail. She could not only tell *who* was calling, she could find out what that person wanted before she decided whether to answer.

This morning, she'd put chicken paprika to cook in her slow cooker. Thank goodness because she was starved. She'd worked a full day at the library, then on her way home had had to walk the Millers' two Irish setters, rain or no rain. Having been bored all day, they were thrilled to go outside, which meant they bounded and dove into the neighbor's shrubbery and got tangled with each other. Her shoulders ached from the dogs' straining against their leashes. Of course, she had to go back before bedtime, but this time she could stand on the stoop and let them out in the tiny yard for a last chance to pee.

Wet, tired and chilled as she was, Linnea showered the minute she got home. She reluctantly put on a sweatshirt and jeans instead of her pajamas, dried her hair and then gratefully dished up dinner. She was just inhaling the glorious aroma and picking up her fork when the damn phone rang.

Of course it was her parents' number that appeared. She was *not* talking to her mother right this minute.

Except that the distraught voice she heard hardly sounded like her mother.

"Linnea? Are you home? Something terrible has happened. Finn just called and—" She made a ragged sound that might have been a sob. "He says Tess is dead. That—that she fell and hit her head and…"

Linnea dropped the fork and grabbed the phone. "Mom?"

"Oh, thank goodness! You are there!"

"Tess is *dead?*" Honestly, Linnea liked her sister-in-law, Tess, better than she did her own brother.

"Surely he's wrong, but…he was dreadfully upset. He says the police are there, and he wanted me to come and get Hanna. Your father isn't feeling well. Can you possibly take her home with you tonight, Linnea? Until we know what's happening?"

"Well, of course I can. He'd already picked her up from after-school care?"

"He said she's there. I pray he's kept her in her room so she doesn't know what's going on. Will you go now?"

"I'm on my way. I'll call you when I know something." Hands shaking, Linnea dumped the food back in the slow cooker and put the lid on. She slipped her feet into rubber clogs, grabbed her coat and purse and went out the door again.

Although she and Finn both lived in Seattle, it might as well have been in different worlds. His four-thousand-square-foot faux-Tudor home, which boasted a media room and five bathrooms, was in upscale Laurelhurst; her own two-bedroom cottage was in a blue-collar neighborhood in West Seattle. With the dark night and wet streets, the drive to Finn's took her over half an hour. The entire way, her anxiety kept her hands tight on the wheel and her thoughts bouncing off each other, never settling.

Could Tess really be dead? Just from stumbling and hitting her head? What had she hit it on? A corner of the kitchen counter? Or their raised slate fireplace hearth? Mom had worried so about that hearth when Hanna was little. But people didn't die that foolishly and…meaninglessly. Did they? And why were the police there? Did they always come when the death wasn't something obvious and expected, like an eighty-year-old with coronary disease having a heart attack?

Poor Hanna! Linnea adored her six-year-old niece, who—she sometimes swore—took after her more than either her mother or father. Not that Hanna was timid, exactly, but she was quiet and thoughtful. She often daydreamed, which annoyed her father no end. Finn was brilliant and ambitious, impatient with woolgathering and anyone whom he deemed "dense." Tess, a successful interior designer, was creative but also tempestuous. In her own way, she had as strong a personality as Finn did. Hanna, it often seemed to Linnea, was a bit of a changeling.

Linnea saw the flashing lights when she was still a couple of blocks away from her brother's house. The street was blocked at the corner, although officers were removing the barricade to let a fire truck lumber out. As she hesitated, the lights atop an ambulance went off, and it, too, started up and followed the fire truck.

Her heart constricted. Was Tess in the ambulance? But it definitely wasn't speeding toward a hospital, which must mean Finn had been right. By the time he got home, it must have been too late to save her. Linnea hated the idea that he and Hanna had walked in the door and found Tess on the floor. She had a heartrending image of the little girl crying, "Mommy!" and running to her mother's still, prone body.

People gathered in clusters on the sidewalks, all staring as if hypnotized toward Finn's house. Neighbors? They were weirdly lit, seemingly by strobe lights—red, blue, white. Blink, blink, blink.

Linnea stopped at the barricade and rolled down her window when the uniformed officer walked up to her car.

"Ma'am, do you live on this street?"

"No, I'm Linnea Sorensen. That's my brother's house? Finn? He called me…well, really he called my mother…" *He doesn't care.* More strongly, she finished, "I'm here to pick up my six-year-old niece. She shouldn't be here with…with whatever's happened."

"One moment, Ms. Sorensen." He stepped away and murmured into a walkie-talkie. When he came back, he said, "I'm going to let you through."

She gave a jerky nod and rolled up her window. When he pulled the barricade aside, she drove through the opening. People's heads turned as her car inched forward until she stopped behind one of—*oh, God*—five police cars. Why would there be so many, just because Tess tripped and hit her head?

With trepidation Linnea got out and went toward the house. Almost immediately, another uniformed officer stopped her, then passed her forward. She was walking up the driveway when the front door opened and her brother appeared, police officers on each side and behind him. With shock she realized that he was handcuffed.

Finn Sorensen was a big, fit, handsome man, his dark blond hair sun-streaked. He had such charisma other people tended to disappear in his presence.

Linnea most of all.

Still wearing dark dress pants and a white shirt, he'd shed the tie and suitcoat, probably when he got home earlier. He was in a towering rage, she saw, storming down the front steps as if he were dragging the two officers behind. In comparison, they were stolid and uninteresting, their faces very nearly expressionless.

Finn was halfway to the street when he saw Linnea. He stopped, his angry gaze making her feel about two feet tall.

"As you can see," he said in an icy voice, "these idiots have jumped to conclusions. Tell Mom and Dad I'll call Nunley as soon as I get to the jail. They don't need to worry about it. I'll be out before morning and filing a lawsuit against these cretins before they start chowing down their noon fries and burgers." His tone was scathing, dismissive. The two men listened with no apparent reaction.

"Is—is Tess really dead?" Linnea asked.

"Yes. She fell." His lips drew back in a snarl. "As I keep trying to explain."

"I'm so sorry, Finn."

"You'll take care of Hanna," he snapped, as if her obedience was a given, and walked past her with the two men each gripping one of his elbows.

Oh, Lord! Had Hanna seen her father arrested on top of the awful discovery of her mother's body? Linnea rushed up the steps, stopped inside by a plainclothes officer. He wore a rumpled brown suit, his badge clipped to his belt. She could see that he had a gun in a black holster at his side, too.

"Ms. Sorensen?"

"Yes. I'm here for Hanna."

"Your niece is upstairs in her bedroom. A female officer is with her."

Hanna must be terrified.

She bit her lip. "It's true? My sister-in-law is dead?"

"I'm afraid so," he said, with surprising gentleness.

"She hit her head?"

"In the course of an argument with your brother. Did they fight often, Ms.— I'm afraid I didn't catch your first name."

"Linnea," she told him. "And it's true that Finn and Tess had arguments, but that's all they were. They yelled, then made up. Finn never hit her or anything like that." At least, she thought privately, that she knew about.

"I'm afraid they won't be making up this time."

She went very still. "Is she—her body, um, has she been taken away yet?"

He shook his head, his eyes uncomfortably watchful. "No, but if you go straight upstairs, you won't see her."

A shuddery breath escaped her. "All right." She hesitated. "Do you know... Did Hanna see her?"

"We don't think so. She says that she heard Mommy and Daddy yelling and she doesn't like to listen."

Linnea actually shuddered at the image that conjured. How often had Hanna huddled in her room trying not to listen to her parents screaming at each other? At the same time, Linnea was hugely relieved to know that Hanna hadn't seen any of the final, violent scene.

"Does she know?"

"That her mother's dead? Yes, insofar as a child her age can understand."

"Okay." She closed her eyes for a moment, girded herself, then started up the stairs.

At the top, she could see into the master suite at the end of the hall. She could make out a corner of the bed, smoothly made. It might be that neither Tess nor Finn had gotten this far; both were workaholics who rarely walked in the door before six or seven in the evening. They might have started arguing the minute they got home.

Hanna's door was closed. Linnea rapped lightly, then opened it. A uniformed woman sat on the bed. The six-year-old was on the floor, back to the bed, her knees drawn up and her arms hugging her legs tightly.

"Pumpkin?"

Her niece leaped to her feet and flung herself at Linnea. "Aunt Linnie! They said Grandma was coming, but I wanted you!"

They hugged tightly, Hanna's arms around Linnea's waist. "I was so scared," she mumbled.

"I know, honey. I know."

It was several minutes before Hanna drew back, face wet. Linnea crouched to be at eye level.

Hanna sniffed. "Officer Bab—Bab—"

"Babayan," the dark-haired young woman supplied.

"She says Mommy is dead."

Grief clogged Linnea's throat. She had to swallow twice before she could say, "That's what they told me, too."

"That means…she won't ever come home again?"

Linnea hated having to be the one to make her beloved niece understand how final death was. "No. You remember when Confetti died."

Hanna bit her lip and nodded. The family's tortoise-shell cat had been twenty-one when she'd failed to wake up one morning.

"You saw her."

Another nod.

"Whatever made her Confetti wasn't there anymore. She'd left her body behind and…" Linnea hesitated only very briefly. She had doubts about what happened after death, but she wouldn't share them with Hannah. "She'd gone to heaven. Well, your mom has gone now, too. It wouldn't surprise me if Confetti was waiting there to get on her lap."

"I want Mommy here!" Hanna wailed. "I don't want her to be in heaven!"

Linnea pulled her into another embrace. "I know," she whispered. "I know. Oh, honey, I love you."

Eventually Hanna recovered enough to ask where her daddy was. Linnea explained that he was having to talk to the police about what happened. Hanna only nodded. Linnea had noticed before that she didn't go to her father with the uncomplicated trust she ought to feel for a parent. Finn loved his daughter, Linnea didn't doubt that, but he lacked the patience to be unfailingly gentle even for her sake.

"You're going to spend the night with me," she told Hanna. "Let's pack your suitcase right now. Just in case, why don't we take enough for you to stay for a couple of days?"

The police officer gave her a small nod of approval.

Hanna's small suitcase, thank goodness, was on the top shelf in her closet. Linnea packed enough clothes for three or four days, while her niece gathered favorite toys and games. Then while Linnea collected her toothbrush from the bathroom, Hanna put on her shoes.

"I'm ready," she said stoutly, looking very slight and terribly young. Her twin ponytails sagged, one lower than the other, strands of blond hair escaping to cling to her damp cheeks.

Ignoring the wrench at her heart, Linnea smiled at her. "Good. We'll have fun."

Officer Babayan followed them downstairs. Linnea steered Hanna straight for the front door, pausing only long enough to collect her pink coat from the closet in the entry. She noticed that the female police officer had very casually moved to block any view that Hanna might have of the great room where the Sorensens mainly lived.

Where Tess must have died.

Hanna almost gulped. Maybe she *had* hit her head on that sharp-edged hearth.

On the front porch, Hanna stopped in her tracks. "Why are there so many police cars here?"

"When they get a call saying someone is hurt, any officers who are near come rushing to find out if there's anything they can do. I guess there must have been a bunch of them this time."

Holding Hanna's hand, carrying a duffel bag of toys while Hanna pulled the pink wheeled suitcase, Linnea hurried her down the rainy walk and past several of those squad cars to her small compact. She put everything in the trunk, helped her niece buckle in and started the engine. She didn't like the fixed way Hanna stared toward those flashing lights and the open front door of her house with people going in and out.

As she backed out and drove up the block, Hanna's

head swiveled so she could keep looking back. Linnea hated that she saw the neighbors clustered, staring.

Then the same officer pulled a sawhorse away to let Linnea's car through, and she was able to accelerate up the street until the flashing lights vanished from her rearview mirror.

MATTHEW LAUGHLIN HAD barely risen from bed and was padding barefoot and shirtless to the small kitchen in his rented Kuwait City house when his phone rang.

Damn it, there had to be a problem on the job site; the offices weren't open yet, and it was currently late evening in the U.S.

He picked up the phone. "Laughlin."

The hollow quality of the long silence told him this call was originating in the United States after all. He relaxed; Tess did sometimes call at this god-awful hour. She was a night owl, and knew when to catch him at home.

But it was a man's voice he heard. "Mr. Laughlin? My name is Neal Delaney. I'm a detective with the Seattle Police Department."

Matt groped behind him for a stool and sank onto it. His hand tightened on the phone until the plastic creaked. "Tess? Tell me my sister is all right. And Hanna." God, Hanna. Had they been in a car accident?

Waiting out the silence stripped his nerves raw.

"I'm afraid I have bad news. Your sister is dead."

"How?" he asked in a hard voice. "What about Hanna?"

"Hanna is fine. She's with her aunt, uh, Linnea Sorensen." This time the pause seemed not to be a consequence of international telecommunications, but rather a hesitation. Perhaps reluctance to tell him the bad news.

"Your sister died of a blow to her head. We have arrested your brother-in-law for her murder."

Son of a bitch. Rage pummeled him, as dangerous as the Kuwaiti cloudbursts.

He had disliked Finn Sorensen from the first time Tess introduced them. Tried to talk his sister out of marrying Finn, hidden his unhappiness when he failed. God knew she'd always stood up for herself, or so Matt had tried to believe. Later he'd worried most about Hanna, a quiet, sensitive child who regularly saw her father throw things when he lost his temper. But murder... That was something else again. It ran deeper, hotter, than Finn Sorensen's childish inability to withstand frustration.

Matt heard the detective talking, caught only the end. "...other family?"

"No," Matt said. "Our parents are dead. I'm Tess's only family." His decision was already made. "I'll catch the first flight I can get on. Today, I hope. I'll be in Seattle..." Hell. The complexity of time changes defeated him for the moment. "Give me your number. I'll phone when I get into Sea-Tac."

He wrote down Detective Delaney's number, gave his blessing—if you could call it that—for the autopsy, then ended the call. Even as he left a message for George Hanson, the project supervisor for the port facility they were building at Shuwaikh, Matt was already going online to check for flights.

If he could pack and be out of here in half an hour or less, he could catch a direct flight to Washington, D.C., then, after a two-hour layover, another leg to Seattle. With a flick of his finger, he confirmed that he wanted to buy the ticket.

He didn't have that much to pack, really just his clothes and toiletries, plus a few gifts he'd picked up for Tess and Hanna. Those gave him pause. His jaw muscles tightened, but he couldn't let himself think. Not yet. He dropped the presents he'd planned to take home to Seattle for Christmas into his suitcase, then zipped it closed. Laptop in its case, passport and wallet in his back pocket, he walked out of the house where he'd lived for nearly a year now, knowing he wouldn't be back.

Hanna needed him.

The airport was only fifteen kilometers south of the city. He left behind the wide boulevards, parks and towering skyscrapers of a city that had looked futuristic to him when he first arrived. He turned in his rental car at Avis, checked his bags at the airline counter and boarded the plane with minutes to spare.

Not until the plane had taxied down the runway and taken off, banking to allow him one last glimpse of the aqua-blue gulf, the surreal silhouette of the Kuwait Towers and the dry tan landscape of the Middle East, did he close his eyes and allow himself to feel the first stunning wave of grief for his little sister.

His face contorted and he turned his head toward the window so that no one could see.

Tess. God, no. Not Tess.

THE PROBLEM OF WHERE he would stay didn't hit Matt until he was tossing his suitcases into the trunk of the car he had rented at Sea-Tac Airport. He slammed the trunk closed, then stood there feeling stupid.

He guessed he must have dozed in the past twenty hours, off and on. But he hadn't been able to get a first-class seat on either leg of the flight, and he was too big a man to ever feel comfortable in coach. He'd reached a point where his mind seemed to be slogging through heavy mud. It didn't want to be diverted, didn't want to think about anything new. *Trudge, trudge.* See Hanna, go home, drop onto a bed until he felt human again.

As human as he could feel, considering the man his sister had loved had murdered her.

God. He rubbed his face hard, scrubbing away the snarl that had drawn his lips back from his teeth.

The trouble was, home had been Tess's house these past few years. Whenever he was in the States long enough, he'd stayed there. Had his own bedroom. It gave him a chance to spend time with her and stay close to Hanna.

Home was currently a crime scene.

Okay. Check in to a hotel, see Hanna. Tomorrow he'd look into renting a place, somewhere she would feel at home. He knew for the moment she was safe enough with Finn's mousy sister, but by God Tess's daughter wasn't staying long term with anyone related to her killer.

He got in the car and took out his cell phone and the slip of paper where he'd written the cop's phone number. He reached Delaney, who agreed to meet with him the next morning. Then he drove to Seattle, trying to recall any particular hotel from memory. He didn't want to be downtown. Where did Finn's sister live? Matt couldn't remember and didn't really care; she was a nonplayer as far as he was concerned. Oh, Hanna was fond of her; she often mentioned her aunt Linnie when they spoke on the phone and recently when she'd learned to write well enough to e-mail. The sister was probably the best of a bad lot. Matt didn't like Finn's mother, either. The father was too quiet to have made much impression on Matt.

He finally settled on the Silver Cloud Inn on Lake Union. Once in a room, he called directory assistance for Linnea Sorensen's phone number. There were three L. Sorensens, he discovered. He took down all three numbers, then dialed until he recognized her voice on the message.

"You've reached Linnea and Safe at Home Petsitting. Please leave a message and I'll get back to you as soon as possible."

"Matthew Laughlin. I'm in Seattle. I'd like to see Hanna." He gave his cell-phone number, then sat down heavily and stared blankly at the wall.

He finally stripped to his boxers, set his cell phone on the bedside table and crawled under the covers.

NOT SURE IF SHE WAS DOING the right thing, Linnea had decided to keep Hanna out of school the rest of the week. Fortunately, she had the two days after Tess's death off from work, so she and Hanna went to the library, to the beach and playground at Lincoln Park and to the several petsitting jobs she currently had.

The Miller dogs had a little girl of their own, so they were thrilled to see Hanna. When their long pink tongues slopped over her face, Hanna actually giggled, the first sound of genuine happiness Linnea had heard from her since that awful night.

Mostly, she remained painfully subdued. She watched TV or played a game when Linnea suggested it, and she tried to pretend she cared what they had for dinner, but she only picked at the food. Linnea sat with her every night, gently rubbing her back, until she fell asleep.

Hanna didn't once ask when her daddy was coming to get her or if she'd be able to go home. Linnea was glad, because, although Finn was out on bail, he hadn't even called to find out how Hanna was doing. Linnea wouldn't have known he was out of jail at all if her mother hadn't told her.

Charges had *not* been dropped.

"They can't possibly believe a man like Finn killed his wife," Linnea's mother had said incredulously during one of their phone conversations. "Why on earth would they pursue something so ridiculous and put all of us through this?"

What kind of man did her mother imagine Finn was *like?* Was she referring to his success?

Linnea wished she could share the belief there was no way on earth her brother had killed Tess. But, unlike her mother, she'd been aware of how much anger Finn harbored. Linnea had always been a little afraid of her brother. It wouldn't surprise her if he was arrogant enough to believe that, as a prominent attorney at a major law firm, he was immune to police suspicion.

Well, he'd been wrong. He might not be convicted, of course; she could imagine a jury refusing to believe that a man that compelling, that handsome and charming and successful, would have committed such a crime.

"He says she fell and hit her head on the coffee table," her mother reported with bewilderment. "I don't know if they think he pushed her... But even that's hardly murder!"

No, it wasn't. But they had charged him with second-degree murder, not negligent homicide or battery or whatever they normally charged men whose wives died during an argument that had become physical with.

They clearly thought he'd done something much worse than push Tess.

What Linnea did know was that she was going to argue if he tried to reclaim Hanna too soon. There was no way he could give a child the reassurance and routine and gentle affection she needed right now. Especially when he was caught up in the fight against this charge. No, she would do more than argue, Linnea decided despite some inner quavering; she would simply refuse to let him take his daughter.

After coming home from walking the pair of Irish setters, she saw the red light on her answering machine blinking. People seeking a petsitter didn't usually call so late in the evening. She sent Hanna to brush her teeth and get ready for bed, in case the message was from Finn or even from her mother, who didn't always think to watch what she said in case her granddaughter was listening. Not until Linnea heard water running in the bathroom did she push the play button.

The voice was terse and hard. "Matthew Laughlin. I'm in Seattle. I'd like to see Hanna." Except for the phone number he added on at the end, that was all he said.

Her heart sank. Wasn't Tess's brother supposed to be in Saudi Arabia or Dubai or Kuwait or somewhere far away? He was a civil engineer for a major international construction company that built everything from off-shore structures to transit facilities and dams. She hadn't met him more than half a dozen times in all the years since Finn married Tess because he was so rarely in Seattle. He had been present for a few holiday celebrations, but otherwise Finn hadn't gone out of his way to include his parents and sister at dinner parties when

Matthew was in town. Linnea suspected the two men didn't like each other very well.

She hadn't liked Matthew Laughlin.

No surprise. He was too much like Finn.

Not angry, necessarily. She sat looking at the phone number she'd written on a notepad, analyzing her reaction to him. No, she'd never heard him raise his voice or even make the kind of slashing gesture Finn used so powerfully to convey his impatience and disdain. Tess's brother was much more…contained than Finn. Almost, she thought, more unnerving because of the lack of bluster. But, like her brother, when Matthew Laughlin spoke, he expected everyone to listen. She could imagine that he was used to giving orders and being obeyed. Tonight's message was typical. He probably didn't even want her to call; it was Hanna he expected to hear from.

And that, she admitted, was another of the reasons she didn't like him. From the first time he'd set eyes on her, he'd dismissed her. She wasn't worthy of his time. Linnea doubted they had exchanged ten words with each other. His gaze seemed to skate over her. And, okay, she knew she wasn't beautiful. But she wasn't *nothing,* either, of so little consequence his behavior was acceptable.

It bothered her how well she could picture him. He was nearly as tall as Finn and broader in the shoulders, more powerfully built, as though he did actual physical labor rather than computer-aided design. He wasn't beautiful like his sister, or like Finn for that matter. Matthew Laughlin's features were blunt, pure male. He kept his dark hair short, as if he didn't want to be bothered with it, and his eyes were dark gray, rather like the steel girders on the projects he designed. Whenever she was around,

she was painfully aware of him, almost—but not quite—
as if she were afraid of him. She could have her back
turned and know when he walked into a room. But she
wasn't afraid of him, and she didn't understand why she
reacted to him the way she did. And, no, that wasn't his
fault, but she didn't have to be fair, did she?

Well, she wasn't going to let Hanna call him until she
knew better what he wanted. Hanna did like him, Linnea
knew; his gentleness with her and even with Tess was his
most appealing quality in her opinion. She'd seen the way
Hanna's face lit with delight after he murmured in her ear,
and how he touched his sister's arm after Finn had been
carelessly cruel. Just a quick grip that turned Tess's flash
of anger into a rueful smile for her brother. Unlike Finn,
who went at the world as if he were a bundle of dynamite
with a lit fuse, Matthew was quite good at *de*fusing. A
couple of times, after seeing his smile or a light, perfectly
timed touch, Linnea had had a sharp pang of something
uncomfortably like envy even if she didn't like him.

But she still wasn't letting him talk to Hanna until
she'd heard what he had to say first.

"Aunt Linnie!" her niece called. "I'm ready to be
tucked in."

"Hop into bed," she called back. "I'll be right there."

Taking a deep breath, she picked up the phone and
dialed the number he'd given. It rang five times, then
went to voice mail.

"Laughlin," his voice said curtly. "Leave a message."

"This is Linnea Sorensen returning your call. It's—"
her gaze sought the clock "—eight-ten. I'm tucking
Hanna into bed right now, but if you call back in the next
few minutes I'll get her up to talk to you. Otherwise, we

won't be home tomorrow because I have to work. I'll try you again tomorrow evening." She hung up quickly, as if he might still pick up. She hoped he didn't call back tonight, that at least she had a reprieve until tomorrow evening. She wasn't looking forward to seeing him again, especially under the circumstances.

And she was wary of finding out what kind of relationship he imagined having with Hanna, who hardly knew him given the rarity of his visits. Probably he only wanted to see her a few times while he was in Seattle to bury his sister, after which he'd go back to…wherever it was he'd come from.

What scared Linnea was that…if he disliked Finn as much as she thought he did, and was convinced that Finn actually had killed Tess, how would he feel about Hanna being raised by her father? Linnea knew how *she'd* feel.

How she did feel.

If Matthew Laughlin was angry enough, would he try to take Hanna?

"Over my dead body," she whispered, then went to sit at Hanna's side until the little girl fell asleep.

CHAPTER TWO

"YEAH, THEY FOUGHT," Matt told Detective Delaney. "Finn is a son of a bitch. I tried to talk my sister out of marrying him. She didn't listen."

The two men sat in a small conference room at the police station. Matt reserved final judgment, but his first impression of the investigator was of competence and dispassion, both of which struck him as positives. He was pissed enough himself to keep the pressure on. He needed a smart cop investigating his sister's death, not one who jumped to conclusions.

Neal Delaney had risen from his desk in the bullpen to meet Matt. He was a big guy, maybe fifty, with steady brown eyes, a firm grip and a tie he'd already tugged loose at ten in the morning.

Matt hadn't objected when Delaney wanted to start by questioning him. He was happy to tell anyone who would listen what he had thought about his brother-in-law.

"I could never understand how he hid his temper at the law firm," he admitted. He'd disliked the idea that Finn saved his nasty streak for the people who loved him most.

"I don't think he did," Delaney said, then looked sorry he'd opened his mouth.

Matt raised his brows.

After a moment, Delaney shrugged. "The partners are shocked. His secretary isn't. An intern told me Mr. Sorensen flayed him alive when he made a mistake."

Being fair stuck in his craw, but Matt finally said, "Not the same thing as killing someone."

"No, but interesting." The investigator cleared his throat. "Had he been physically abusive to your sister?"

Matt frowned. "If so, she wouldn't admit to it. I had my suspicions. A couple of bruises she laughed off. A broken wrist she claimed she got by slipping on an icy sidewalk. Broken collarbone that was supposed to be a ski injury."

Delaney scribbled in his notebook. "We'll follow up. I haven't had a chance to talk to her doctor yet."

Matt braced himself and asked, "What does Hanna say?"

"A female patrol officer spoke to her while they waited for Ms. Sorensen to come get her. The little girl says Mommy and Daddy yelled a lot and sometimes things crashed. She apparently scuttled for her bedroom whenever they started to fight. She was pretty scared, and Officer Babayan didn't push it. I'll need to talk to Hanna myself, maybe with her aunt present so she feels comfortable."

"Or heads off any honest answers."

Delaney sat back in his chair, contemplating him. "That your impression of her?"

Matt was ashamed of how little impression he actually did have of Linnea Sorensen. "No," he said finally. "But it stands to reason she'd want to defend her brother."

"Maybe." His eyebrows pulled together. "I saw her when she arrived at the house as Mr. Sorensen was being taken out in handcuffs. She didn't exactly rush over to hug him, and he talked to her like she was the family maid. Not real warm and fuzzy."

Matt thought back to those Christmas and Thanksgiving dinners when they'd all been in that ugly, ostentatious house that was Tess and Finn's pride and joy. Offhand he couldn't remember brother and sister ever talking; in fact, he'd seen her quietly slide from a room when Finn entered it.

Okay, maybe she didn't like him, either. That would be a point in her favor.

"I don't know how they feel about each other. His parents think he walks on water, I can tell you that."

Another note.

"When did you last see your sister?"

"Thanksgiving a year ago. I was here for a week. Finn was midtrial and hardly home. Tess took the week off and she and Hanna and I did tourist things. Rode the ferry, went up the Space Needle. We'd intended to ski, but there wasn't enough snow for even Crystal to open."

Delaney nodded. The previous winter had been wet but warm, a disaster for winter sports businesses.

"Finn was cordial enough when I saw him. We both… tried. For Tess's sake." Finn, Matt sometimes thought, disliked him in part *because* he felt obligated to be on his best behavior when his brother-in-law was in residence. Tess told him he was imagining things.

"I'd like a few answers, too," he said, voice implacable. "You say Tess hit her head on the coffee table. What makes you think she didn't stumble and wham into it wrong?"

"The medical examiner says there was too much force applied. Her skull was shattered."

God, Matt thought. *I didn't want to know that.*

He frowned. Yeah, he did. He owed it to his sister to

find out the worst. He hadn't been able to protect her, but he could be sure justice was served.

"He's going to bring in an expert to testify that if she was hurrying when she stumbled she could have flown forward and hit hard enough."

"Uh-huh, but here's the compelling part. If you fell, you'd hit the top edge." Delaney ran his hand along the rim of the conference table. "Right?"

"Yeah," Matt agreed.

"Your sister didn't. Tissue and hair embedded in the wood shows that the force of the blow was along the side and the sharp edge at the *bottom* of the tabletop rim. The only way that could happen is if she rose up from beneath the table and hit her head—"

"In which case there isn't enough force."

"Right. The alternative…"

"Is if somebody lifted the whole coffee table and swung it at her," Matt finished softly.

Tissue and hair. Goddamn it.

"You got it." The two men looked at each other, and Matt saw pure determination in Delaney's eyes. He wasn't going to let Finn walk.

Reassured, Matt held out his hand. "Thank you."

One shoulder jerked. "Just doing my job." But they shook, and Delaney walked him out. "Where can I reach you?"

"The Silver Cloud on Union Bay. I'm going to look at rentals today, though. I figure I'll be staying in Seattle, at least through the trial. I intend to have Hanna with me."

Those eyebrows rose again, but Delaney didn't comment. "I'm going to ask you to stay away from Mr. Sorensen."

"I have every intention of doing so." Matt's tone hardened. He'd been furious to find that Finn had walked out on bail within twenty-four hours of killing Tess. "Unless he tries to take Hanna home with him."

Matt had been relieved by Linnea's phone message, which made it clear that she still had the six-year-old. He was annoyed at himself for apparently sleeping through the ringing phone last night, but God knew he'd been exhausted. He'd see Hanna tonight. With a little luck, he'd have a house to move into within the week.

Normally if he'd planned to be in the area for a few months, he'd have gone for a condo. Why take on mowing and weeding? But a child should have a yard. A swing set, a playhouse, someplace to kick a ball. His ideas were vague. He didn't actually remember seeing Hanna play outside in the yard in Laurelhurst. When he and she kicked around a soccer ball, they'd walked down to a nearby park.

His guess was that Hanna hadn't had many opportunities to hang out during the day at home. Both her parents tended to work six days a week minimum and, except during the summer, probably picked her up from after-school care and got home after dark. She'd told him once that she was practically always the last kid picked up. She had sounded wistful, but when he tried to talk to Tess about it, she rolled her eyes and said, "Have you *seen* her day care? It's an amazing facility with great teachers. Saturdays they go on field trips, and the rest of the time they do art and put on plays. She's learning to speak Spanish and about architecture from walking tours and…"

She'd gone on and on, extolling the virtues of this

Rolls Royce of day-care centers. His guess was that a kid who'd been in school all day probably didn't want to then go straight to language lessons or be organized to put on a play or do anything else supervised. That was not how he and Tess had grown up. They'd had a stay-at-home mom. Sometimes they'd been in organized activities— Little League for him and dance lessons for her. But mostly they'd been able to get off the school bus, have a snack then go to a friend's house or read or watch TV. Their entire lives hadn't been organized the way Hanna's was.

But he also knew that Tess's interior-design business had been her dream. It was important to her. What was she supposed to do? Close it down until Hanna was a teenager? She'd actually gone to part-time Hanna's first year and had sounded restless the entire year, Matt remembered thinking. When he asked her once if she and Finn intended to have another baby, she'd shaken her head emphatically.

"We adore Hanna. How can we not? But look at us. We both love our jobs. We thrive on pressure, on being busy. Especially Finn. He was next to no help when she was little. And did I tell you how much I hated being pregnant?"

She had, although he'd forgotten.

"No." Another shake of the head. "Hanna's going to be an only child."

He'd been dismayed, maybe because he remembered how important he and Tess had been to each other after their parents died in a car accident. He'd been in college and his sister a sophomore in high school, but he had managed to keep her with him. He hated to think how much more devastating the loss would have been if he hadn't had her.

His jaw tightened at the realization that she was gone now. She'd been the one person in the world he knew loved him, always and forever. Until Finn Sorensen's temper got the best of him.

Was the bastard even sorry? Did he wish he could call back the burst of rage that had him lifting the whole coffee table and slamming it into his wife's skull?

Or was he self-serving enough to blame her because she'd provoked him? Or even to convince himself it had happened the way he was trying to tell police, that Tess was ultimately to blame because she'd somehow slammed her *own* head into the table?

Despite having been related to him by marriage for eight years now, Matt had no idea how Finn really thought. Despite Tess's exasperation, they'd both resisted playing a round of golf together or even sitting down with a beer. Eventually, he'd thought, she'd become resigned to the fact that her husband and her brother would never be friends without really understanding how deep the chasm was.

Matt bought a *Seattle Times* in front of the station and took it to his car. He'd look at online classifieds later, when he got to his hotel, but he could start with what was in the newspaper.

Sitting in the parking garage, he worked his way through the rental section, making a few appointments to check out places.

By dinnertime, he'd seen a dozen, but nothing that struck him as perfect. He wished he had a better idea how important staying in the same school was to Hanna. Did she have good friends? He'd have to ask her tonight.

At five-fifteen, he called Linnea's and a woman picked up. "Hello?"

"This is Matt Laughlin." He'd pulled to the curb and set the emergency brake, even though he hadn't expected her to be home quite yet.

"Oh," she said softly. "You didn't call back last night."

"I'd had a long flight. I conked out and didn't hear the phone ring."

"Oh," she said again. "Matt, I'm so sorry about Tess."

He forced out a thank-you. "How is Hanna handling this?"

There was a small silence. He wished he could see her face. "I'm not sure. She's so quiet. I've been trying to keep her busy, even though I don't know whether that's the best thing to do or not. Maybe I should be encouraging her to grieve. I just don't know," she said again.

"Busy sounds smart to me."

"Do you think so?"

For God's sake, wasn't that what he'd just said? He reached up and kneaded the back of his neck, where tension had gathered. "Yeah. I do." He paused. "I'd like to see her."

"I assumed you would." He could all but feel her gathering herself. "I'm going to ask you not to...to say anything negative about her father. Not right now. I...haven't even told her he's been arrested."

"How the hell are you explaining his absence, then?" *Oh, shit.* "She isn't seeing him, is she?"

"No." The single word was firm enough that he momentarily pulled the phone away from his ear and gazed at it in surprise. Interesting. Maybe Delaney was right that she didn't much like her big brother. "Finn hasn't even called," she said. "Mom tells me he's out on bail. He must know he isn't in any state right now to be comforting Hanna."

Uh-huh. What father wouldn't want to be the one to explain to his small daughter what happened to Mommy? To hold her and dry her tears and do his damnedest to make her world feel safe again? Matt couldn't imagine that not being his first priority.

"Maybe," he suggested, every word dropping with a distinct clunk, "the bastard has enough conscience that he can't look Hanna in the eye."

Crap, he thought immediately. That wasn't the way to assure Linnea's cooperation.

But after a very long silence, she said only, "I doubt he's figured out what to say to her."

Huh. Did that mean she believed her brother was guilty?

"Have you had dinner yet?" he asked. "Can I take you and Hanna out?"

The offer was an impulse; he wanted to spend time with Hanna, not Linnea. But it made sense. His niece hadn't seen him in almost a year. Despite their e-mails and phone calls, they always had to ease into their friendship. Besides…he found himself more curious than he'd expected to be about this sister he'd scarcely noticed in the past. What was the saying? *Still waters run deep.* Did hers, or was she the mouse he'd guessed her to be?

After another discernible pause, she said stiffly, "Yes, if you mean it. I haven't started dinner yet, and I know Hanna would love to see you."

"Have you told her I called last night?"

"No, I wanted to talk to you first."

Tone silky, Matt said, "To make sure I wouldn't rant about her daddy."

"Um…something like that." She sounded embarrassed, but had enough spine to add, "I don't really know you."

"No. We never bothered, did we?"

"You didn't seem very interested."

So. She had teeth. Maybe saying *we* never bothered wasn't quite accurate. He'd automatically extended his dislike of Finn to Finn's family. So no—*he* hadn't bothered.

"You may have guessed that your brother and I didn't much care for each other."

She didn't comment.

After a moment, Matt said, "Is this too early? Can I come by now?"

"Now is fine. We eat early. Um…do you need directions?"

"I got them off the Internet last night." He couldn't even remember why he'd had her address. Presumably Tess had given it to him, God knew why.

"All right," Linnea said. "We'll be ready."

The drive took him longer than he expected. It was interesting, he thought, that she'd chosen to live so far from either her brother or parents, without having actually left Seattle. Maybe deliberate, maybe a job had determined where she rented or bought. He knew from what Tess had said that she worked at a library. Obviously, from her phone message, she had some kind of petsitting service, too.

Her house turned out to be a tiny, midcentury bungalow in a blue-collar neighborhood in West Seattle. It was on a fairly steep side street, the single-car garage essentially in the basement beneath the house. He pulled to the curb, cranked the wheels and set the emergency brake before turning off the engine. He got out and surveyed Linnea Sorensen's tidy home. Rented, he presumed, but she did maintain it. Leaves on the Japanese maple in front had mostly fallen and been raked up. Grass was sodden but carefully mowed. The house had been painted a warm chestnut-brown and trimmed with deep rose, a surprisingly warm and cheerful combination. The front door was seafoam-green.

No doorbell, he discovered, but a shiny brass knocker made a deep thudding sound when he lifted and dropped it.

The door opened immediately and he had a moment of sharp surprise. His first sight of the woman who'd answered the door disconcerted and unsettled him; funny, she didn't look like he remembered. It hadn't been *that* long since he'd seen her.

On the heels of his surprise came disappointment because Hanna was hovering shyly behind her aunt, peeking out at him as if he were a stranger.

He smiled at her. "Hanna Banana."

She whispered, "Uncle Matt? I thought... Mom said..." That made her look stricken. "You were coming for Christmas."

Keeping his gaze on her small, distressed face, he said gently, "When I heard about your mom, I came right away. You and she are my only family, you know."

Not *are—were.* Now he had only Hanna. He wanted to hug her. To lift her up into his arms and take her away.

"Oh," she breathed, sounding alarmed, and buried her face in her aunt's leg.

Ease into her life, he reminded himself, tamping down his frustration.

He lifted his gaze to Finn's sister, ready to figure out why he'd felt that odd shift inside at first sight. Damn it, he'd remembered her as colorless, washed-out, her hair and skin pale, her eyes—who knew?—her body so slight she could fade into the woodwork.

Either she'd changed, or he hadn't looked at her before. Or, hell, she had been cast into shadow by her brother and his sister, both vivid personalities, both larger than life and impossible to ignore. Even so, he liked to think of himself as observant, which meant there was no way he should have failed to see that Finn's sister was beautiful.

Because what he saw now was a lovely woman. Slight, yes, but in a leggy, slim-hipped way. She could have been a dancer or a runner. Although her breasts, he was jolted to realize, were generous enough to have been a nuisance for either. How had he escaped noticing breasts so lush and perfectly sized to fit a man's hands?

Her hair was a pale, ash blond—moonlight where her brother had rich gold hair. Straight instead of wavy like his. His eyes were bright blue, hers a softer blue-gray. Her features were fine, even delicate, as was her bone structure in general. The hand that squeezed her niece's shoulder was long-fingered and slender. With deft use of makeup and the right clothes, she could be stunning.

Feeling stupefied, he was also angry at himself. What was he *doing,* evaluating her as a woman? She was Finn's sister. Enough said.

Frowning slightly, he realized that she was assessing him in turn. Had she ever really looked at him before, either? He couldn't help wondering. Or, in her case, was this more of a review?

"Ready for dinner?" he said. "You'll have to suggest a place. Anything from pizza to gourmet French is fine by me. Except—" he smiled at his niece again "—I seem to remember that Hanna Banana was a little bit picky the last time I saw her."

She squeezed tighter onto Linnea's leg. Linnea laughed. "Well...definitely nothing gourmet. *All* six-year-olds are picky."

Finn, of course, had been irritated by her refusal to eat mushrooms, broccoli, anything new, anything too mixed together to separate into components. Tess had laughed and said pretty much the same thing Linnea had.

"Then how about that pizza?"

Now Linnea smiled at him, lighting her face. "I take it somebody wants pizza."

A soft, sympathetic smile didn't change anything. Except—damn, he was pretty sure he'd never seen her smile before.

He heard himself admitting, "Yeah, it's the one food I miss when I'm abroad. I can find it, but it's never quite the same."

"Then pizza it is. Let me grab my purse." She gently disentangled herself from Hanna, who froze in place, her gaze darting to his face before she ducked her head.

"Thank you for e-mailing me," he said quietly. "I liked hearing from you."

She whispered something. He hoped she'd liked getting e-mails from him, too, and, even though she'd needed Tess's help with spelling, hadn't been sending them under her mother's orders.

A sharp stab of pain reminded him of Tess. The truth that she was gone hadn't really hit him yet. Mostly he still felt anger. But because he saw her only intermittently, for a week here or there, her absence didn't yet seem real. For Hanna, though, it must be very real.

Or was it? he wondered, troubled. She hadn't seen her mother's body, hadn't talked to her dad. She had probably, in the past, stayed with her aunt Linnie for a few days. Did she really grasp the fact that her mom was gone for good?

Fortunately Linnea returned immediately. She locked the front door, took Hanna's hand, and walked ahead of Matt down the concrete steps to the sidewalk. He asked about her booster seat, but Linnea said that she hadn't thought to get it from Hanna's house, and anyway she was getting almost tall enough to do without. His niece looked tiny to him, but he didn't know that many children and it made sense that she was taking after her parents, both tall.

Linnea sat beside him in front, her purse clutched on her lap. Although she leaned back, her spine seemed very straight. She stayed quiet unless he asked her a direct question or she was telling him where to turn. He was a lot more conscious of her than he liked being, maybe because he kept catching an elusive scent that made him think of baking. Vanilla, maybe?

The pizza place was nearly empty, this being a weeknight. They ordered: half cheese to accommodate Hanna's preference, sausage and veggies for the two adults. Pop all around, although he would have liked a beer. He was dragging some, but feeling more fatigue and disorientation than drowsiness. From experience, Matt knew that adjusting to the time change would take him days if not weeks. He was going to have trouble falling asleep tonight.

Once they were settled in a booth, he on the opposite side from Hanna and Linnea, he said, "So, Banana, what did you do today while your aunt Linnea worked?"

"I went to Grandma and Granddad's," she said in a soft voice.

He felt a spurt of anger, and his eyes met Linnea's. Why, in her message last night, hadn't she told him where Hanna would be? He could have gone to see her earlier today.

Her chin rose and she stared at him, making it obvious that withholding Hanna's whereabouts today had been deliberate.

"I've been looking forward all day to seeing you," he said to Hanna, while still watching her aunt.

Hanna drummed her heels and played with the straw in her drink. After a minute, Linnea said, "My mother is…not entirely rational right now."

He unclenched his teeth. "Exactly what does that mean?"

She slid a meaningful glance sideways at the six-year-old.

Matt leaned back in the booth. After a minute, he asked, "Did you do anything fun?"

Hanna shook her head hard and kept twirling the straw.

"She did help me walk the Millers' two Irish setters this morning," Linnea said lightly. "We'll go back tonight. I do petsitting," she added. "These two dogs love kids and are really excited when Hanna comes."

"Do you like dogs?" he asked her.

She nodded vigorously, still not looking up. Matt knew that she'd wanted a pet, but Tess and Finn hadn't let her have one because they were away from home so much.

"Does your aunt Linnea have a dog?" he asked.

She shook her head, her blond hair—damn near the color of Linnea's, he noticed for the first time—flying back and forth.

"I have a cat," Finn's sister told him. "A fat, elderly,

black cat named Spooky who particularly hates dogs. And cats. Um…and children."

A tiny giggle escaped Hanna.

"Except Hanna. Spooky makes an exception for Hanna."

"Because I'm quiet!" his niece burst out.

The cat, Linnea said, had just appeared on her doorstep some years back and bellowed to be let in. Her face relaxed as she talked, and he realized how much prettier she was when she felt confident or was happy. She had a quiet glow when she smiled at Hanna, who was listening even though she must have heard about Spooky's late-night arrival on Aunt Linnie's doorstep before.

"At my veterinarian's best guess," she said, "Spooky is fifteen or sixteen now and therefore entitled to be set in her ways."

"Is that your mother's excuse, too?" he murmured, then was sorry when her expression closed and that glow vanished. "Sorry," he tried to say, but she ignored him. Their number had been called, and she took Hanna with her to get the pizza and plates for all of them.

Eventually, after stealing a glance at Hanna, who had retreated behind her hair, Linnea did ask politely where he was staying, and whether his flight had gone smoothly, but all signs of any real personality were gone, thanks to his stupid dig. It wasn't that he regretted hurting her; she'd deliberately kept Hanna away from him today. But, like it or not, he needed her cooperation right now. Hoping to regain lost ground, he told her a little about the project he'd been working on in Kuwait City and a few impressions of the country. He'd e-mailed photos to Hanna, who had e-mailed back with a six-year-old's phonetic spelling to say that Mommy said the Kuwait

Towers looked like spaceships. Not rocket ships, she'd added. They looked like the spaceship in the movie *E.T.*

But the conversation was between the two adults. Hanna sometimes whispered a one- or two-word answer when he asked her a question. She stole looks at him, and otherwise hid behind her hair. She ate one piece of pizza, then shook her head when Linnea asked if she'd like more. He had no idea if that was a normal amount for a kid her age to eat.

By the time they left the pizza parlor, Matt was feeling edgy and unhappy to have to concede that maybe it was just as well that Hanna was able to stay with her aunt Linnea for a few days or a week. Despite their e-mails, she'd have been scared to death if she'd had to go with him right now. And, while he was being honest with himself, he also had to admit that he would have a hell of a lot to learn about parenting.

He offered to drive them to their dog-walking gig. Linnea politely declined. Apparently the dogs had to be taken out closer to bedtime. Nor did she invite him in when they got home.

He insisted on escorting them to the door. Hanna did say, "Goodbye, Uncle Matt," to his good-night, then turned a trusting face to her aunt. "Aunt Linnie, can I watch TV?"

Linnea looked briefly troubled but nodded. "Sure, honey. Let me talk to your uncle Matt for a minute and then I'll be in."

Both remained silent until they heard the TV come on. Linnea stayed on the doorstep facing him. He was aware of how slender she was, how he dwarfed her. He wondered if she felt as fragile to the touch as she looked, then cursed himself for even thinking about something like that.

When she spoke, it wasn't to share her worries about Hanna but instead to say, "You can't go to my parents' house."

The anger burned in his chest like an ulcer. "Why?"

"Mom's upset. You can understand that, can't you?"

"*She's* upset?" he said incredulously. "My sister is the one who is dead."

"She doesn't believe the charges. She thinks…" Her teeth worried her lip. "I don't know. That Tess fell, and this is all trumped up to get Finn in trouble. She thinks it must be political, either somebody in his firm who doesn't want him making partner, or because he was being talked about as a candidate for the house. She just…" Linnea struggled for words, then gave up. "I think it would be better if you'd stay away from her for now."

He swore, then reluctantly nodded. "All right. But I want to spend time with Hanna."

"I've promised her to Mom tomorrow, but if you want, the next day we can try to plan something."

"Try?" he echoed.

"You can take her for the day, if you want. I'll be home, so you can make the visit as short as you want or have her all day."

After a minute, he nodded. "All right. If you don't have to leave for work, shall we say…nine?"

They left it at that. He walked to his car feeling irritated and dissatisfied, but not sure if he was justified or was being churlish. He'd wanted Hanna to fly into his arms in delight, to chatter to him, to remember their good times together. He'd wanted to talk to her about her mother.

Instead, he'd been painfully aware that Hanna saw him as a stranger. So he'd spent his evening engaging in stilted conversation with Finn's sister, whom Hanna clearly did trust.

And, yeah, he was petty enough to resent that. He also had a suspicious enough nature to wonder if Linnea would use the advantage she'd gained by proximity to keep Hanna from turning to him.

It was a minute before he started his car. *One step at a time,* Matt told himself. *Find a house. Spend time with Hanna. Be patient.*

His jaw flexed and he put his car in gear.

Do not, for a minute, think about Finn Sorensen's sister as an ally. She's not one.

CHAPTER THREE

TODAY WAS HANNA'S FIRST solo outing with her uncle Matt, and it hadn't started auspiciously. She'd ducked her head when he said hello, and turned huge, pleading eyes on Linnea as he led her out the front door with his big hand on her shoulder.

Practically from the moment she had closed the front door behind them, Linnea had felt guilty. Why hadn't she said, "Stop. Hanna needs to get to know you again before you take her on your own."

Dumb question. She was so unaccustomed to being confrontational, it always took her half an hour to figure out what she should have done or said. Anyway—Hanna did need to spend time with him, if they were to build a relationship. And Linnea was so awfully uncomfortable with him, she didn't want to keep putting herself in the middle.

Now she had something else to regret. Why, oh why, had she felt compelled to answer the phone when she could see that it was her mother calling? And why had she chosen *now* to tell Mom that Tess's brother was in town, and she was allowing him to see Hanna?

"You had dinner with that awful man?" Mary Sorensen sounded aghast. "What were you thinking, Linnea? Or were you?"

Linnea gritted her teeth. How many times in her life had she heard that from her mother? *Don't you ever think?* Had she ever once said it to Finn?

"He's Hanna's uncle. He has a right—"

"He was always just shy of rude," her mother continued. "Poor Finn, having to put up with him! That was one of the things he and Tess disagreed about, you know. Finn didn't like Matt's influence on Hanna. So the least we can do now…"

Poor, misunderstood Finn, who couldn't possibly have argued violently enough with his wife for her to die? Outrage strengthened Linnea's determination.

"He has the right to see her," she repeated stubbornly.

The small, chilly silence was enough to make her brace herself. "Not," her mother snapped, "if Finn has anything to do with it. Didn't it occur to you to consult your brother before you made any decisions on your own? He is Hanna's father, after all. What's more, I feel quite sure he knows how to ensure that man has no contact whatsoever with our precious Hanna."

That man, said with such disdain, made it sound as if Matt was the accused criminal, not Finn. But why, Linnea thought in frustration, was she surprised? Her mother had always worn blinders where Finn was concerned.

"I don't think Finn is in a very good position right now to try to shut Tess's brother out of Hanna's life."

"As her father, he has every right—"

Linnea never interrupted her mother. Now she did, struggling to keep her voice level. "The police think he killed Tess. He's in trouble, Mom."

"Do you know what Finn told me today? They've decided Tess hit the coffee table too hard to have simply fallen. As if they can tell any such thing. They certainly haven't produced any kind of weapon. And even *they* don't deny that Finn called 911 the minute she fell. He was scared to death!"

That was it? The force of the blow to her head? So little to justify charging Finn with murder. And the police had arrested him on the spot, handcuffing him and hauling him away to jail like any common criminal. Linnea was shaking her head almost before her mother quit speaking. She didn't believe that was the only reason Finn had been arrested. She'd read enough mysteries to know that the police couldn't have determined how much force was applied simply by looking at Tess lying there on the floor. They would have waited for the pathologist's report to come to any such conclusion. Especially given who Finn was. They'd have been wary about charging a high-powered attorney with murder. No, there must have been something else. Something Finn wasn't telling Mom.

But arguing with her mother never got Linnea any-where, so she…didn't. In her rare moments of defiance, she quietly did what she wanted without telling her mother. This time, though, was different. For one thing, when Hanna was with her grandparents she would be likely to mention her uncle Matt. And for another, Linnea was determined to keep Hanna with her. Finn might be her father, but he wasn't a good one. If the courts deter-mined that he hadn't killed Tess, Linnea might not be able to do anything about him reclaiming his daughter. But if he really had killed Tess, he didn't deserve to have Hanna. She wouldn't be safe with him.

Linnea hadn't quite figured out how she would defy her brother if he showed up at the door to reclaim Hanna,

but somehow she would have to. One reason she was encouraging Matt, selfishly, was that he would back her.
He wouldn't want Hanna having any contact at all with
her father.

Linnea said, "Hanna is with Matt right now, Mom.
They went to the zoo."

Her mother's voice rose. "You let him take her, without
any supervision? What makes you think he'll bring her
back? What if he gets on a plane with her and takes her
to…to Egypt or Libya or wherever it is he lives these
days? We'll never see her again!"

Linnea rolled her eyes at the histrionics. "Mom, Hanna
doesn't have a passport. And Matt isn't going anywhere
until after Tess's funeral for sure, and probably not until
after the trial, if there is one. Anyway, he works for an
American company. He's only there temporarily. And
it's Kuwait, not Libya."

"What difference does it make? Linnea, I'm calling
Finn this minute. If you can't use any common sense,
perhaps Hanna would be better off with him, whether he's
preoccupied with this ridiculous case or not. Now, you
call me the minute Hanna's home again, and I'll—"

Heart pounding, Linnea hung up. On her mother. Oh,
Lord. She'd never done that before. Sometimes she…
well, tuned out. But Mom never knew she wasn't really
listening. This act would enrage her mother.

I don't care! she thought defiantly. If Mom was really
calling Finn, Linnea had to think what to do. She wanted
to believe she could stand up to her brother, but the quavering she felt inside made her horribly afraid she wouldn't
be able to when the moment came. And she hated the idea
of an ugly scene in front of Hanna, no matter the outcome.

But Hanna couldn't go home with Finn. It made Linnea shudder to imagine Hanna hiding up in her bedroom, afraid to see where her mother's body had lain, afraid to make her daddy mad, scared and lonely.

Linnea's parents weren't an alternative; Dad had battled multiple sclerosis for years, and stress made it worse. He was in remission right now, but still had up days and down days.

No. Linnea's fingernails bit into her palms. Somehow, even if she had to run away with Hanna, she'd keep her from Finn.

Hanna and her uncle had been gone for barely two hours. A new worry seized Linnea. What if Mom had called Finn, and he showed up just as Matt was returning with Hanna? Linnea had seen his cold rage. As volatile as Finn was, the idea of the two men confronting each other horrified her.

Her legs felt shaky when she went to the front window to look out, hoping—even though it was way too soon—that they would be back. The weather wasn't great for going to the zoo. If Hanna got cold, would Matt have made alternate plans?

Linnea couldn't make herself concentrate enough to read or settle to doing needlework or even stick to housecleaning. Her heart bumped every time she heard a car outside, and in the next thirty minutes she hurried to the front window half a dozen times. She always stood to one side of it and barely peeked around the edge of the drape. If Finn showed up, she didn't want him to see her. She wouldn't answer the door. He could knock all he wanted, but eventually he would go away.

If Finn did come, Linnea decided, she would call

Matt's cell phone and tell him not to bring Hanna home until she called again. She would head off a confrontation. He was reasonable enough to do as she asked, even if he was angry. At least, she thought he was.

An hour had passed before a car did pull up in front, and it was Matt's rental, not Finn's Lexus. Linnea hurried to open the front door, anxiously watching the street as Matt and Hanna got out. Hanna spotted her and raced up to the porch, flinging her arms around Linnea's legs.

"I missed you!" When she looked up, her face was pinched.

Linnea lifted her onto her hip and kissed the top of her head. "Didn't you have fun?"

Matt, arriving on the doorstep, looked grim. "No," he said. "I don't think she had fun."

"Why not?" she asked, then backed up. "Come in."

"Maybe I shouldn't," he said, handing over Hanna's pink parka.

"Please. I'd like to talk to you."

His mouth tightened, but after a moment he gave a curt nod and stepped inside. Linnea hurriedly closed and locked the door.

"Did you have lunch?"

He shook his head. "Hanna said she wasn't hungry."

Linnea looked down at her niece. "Not even a little bit? It's noon, and you hardly nibbled at breakfast. What if I make you a peanut butter and honey sandwich? Or... Oh! What about grilled cheese?"

The little girl snuffled and rubbed her face on Linnea's sweatshirt. "Okay," she whispered.

"I'll heat soup and make sandwiches," Linnea decided, leading the way to the kitchen.

He followed, to her relief. When she asked, he poured milk for Hanna and her and juice for himself while she dumped tomato soup in a pot and started slicing cheddar cheese. Hanna stuck close to her, a silent, ghostlike presence, while her uncle Matt sat at the kitchen table and watched her with a brooding gaze. The atmosphere reminded Linnea unpleasantly of home, when Finn would sulk about something and she tried to avoid drawing his attention and her mother insisted that obviously he'd been wronged and shouldn't she go into the school and talk to the principal? Dad, of course, slipped away to his den.

Naturally, Linnea felt compelled to chatter. "I think my favorite animals are the otters. Do you remember that time we saw one playing in the stream at the zoo?" she asked her niece, who didn't answer. To Matt, she said, "He kept sliding down, then going back up and doing it again. It was so cute. But I like the giraffes, too, and the lions. And, oh, when there's a baby gorilla!" Flipping the sandwiches, she stroked Hanna's hair with one hand. "Did you see the gorillas today?"

Hanna shook her head.

"We didn't get that far," Matt said. "She didn't even really look at the animals we did get to."

Oh, dear. "I'm sorry you didn't have fun," she said softly to her niece. "Oops! The soup is boiling."

She dished up three bowls and had Hanna carry saltine crackers to the table. Then she brought the grilled cheese sandwiches on plates, lifted Hanna into her seat and sat herself.

It felt…strange having a man here. Except for her dad, no man had ever eaten here in her kitchen with her. Tess dropped by casually once in a while, but never Finn.

Anyway, Linnea suspected her brother hardly ever ate lunch unless he was entertaining a client or talking on his cell phone or texting at the same time.

Matt seemed to fill the space in a way Linnea knew she didn't. It was partly physical; he was a large, solidly built man with broad shoulders. But it was also a matter of temperament. She could *feel* his tension, as if the very air crackled with it. Those gray eyes were both impassive and dark with what she felt sure was an incipient storm.

Of course, his tension wound Linnea tighter than a rubber band ready to snap, which, coupled with Hanna's withdrawal, didn't make this lunch an undiluted pleasure.

Hanna ate half a sandwich and a few spoonfuls of soup, then, to Linnea's relief, asked to be excused. "Can I watch TV?" she asked, after a wary glance at her uncle.

"Why don't you take a book and lie down instead?" Linnea suggested. "You look tired, kiddo."

She'd been letting Hanna watch entirely too much television. She always curled up at one end of the sofa, clutching a throw pillow as though her stomach hurt, and stared at the screen as if mesmerized. Mesmerized, or not seeing it at all, Linnea wasn't sure which. It had become Hanna's refuge, which didn't strike Linnea as entirely healthy.

She could tell now that her niece wanted to argue, but after a moment she gave a reluctant nod and trudged from the kitchen. Matt didn't say anything, but he watched her go with that same brooding expression. When Hanna didn't even look back, a muscle twitched in his cheek, and Linnea wondered if his feelings were hurt.

From her seat she could see the hall. She waited to say anything until Hanna went in her bedroom and shut the door. Then she looked at Matt.

"Was she just shy?"

"She wouldn't talk to me. Is that shy?"

"Well, of course it is," Linnea said in bewilderment. "What did you think?"

Very coolly, he said, "I wondered if someone had been talking to her about me. She almost acts as if she's afraid of me."

"Someone?" Then she got it, and her mouth dropped open. "You mean me? Why would you think...?"

"Perhaps your brother."

"I really doubt that Finn—" She couldn't tell him that she didn't think Finn actually talked to his daughter that often.

He raised an eyebrow, giving his face a saturnine cast that made her wonder if he'd read her mind. "Finn?"

"I doubt he gives that much thought to you."

"Then what's going on? Hanna and I have always been good friends."

"You haven't seen her in a year. That's forever for a child." She hesitated. "And things have been hard for her at home. I suspect Tess and Finn were fighting a lot. Hanna hasn't seemed very happy to me lately. She'd already...withdrawn. Become clingy when she was with me."

Matt frowned. "Tess hasn't said anything."

"Would she have?" Linnea weighed how much to say, then thought, *What does it matter now?* "Hanna wasn't *like* them," she explained. "She's quiet, and sensitive, and she shrivels when voices get raised. I'm not sure even Tess understood that she didn't react the way either of them would have to...anything."

His mouth flattened. "Then suddenly she's being told that her mom is dead."

"There were police in the house, and then I took her and she hasn't even talked to her dad since."

To his credit, he was listening. "Your parents?"

"They adore her."

He waited.

"Dad is always gentle with Hanna. But it wouldn't surprise me if Mom is saying more than she should to a child Hanna's age. She's pretty worked up on Finn's behalf. She and I—"

Gaze suddenly intense, he prodded her again. "You what?"

"We had an argument today. She's not happy that Hanna is spending time with you. Mom always defends Finn, you see. It won't surprise me if she calls to tell him."

"It doesn't sound like he gives a good goddamn."

"No, he does love Hanna. In his own way. And also—" She stopped, wondering why so many private thoughts were attempting to spill out today.

Matt's eyes narrowed. "She's his. That's what you're trying to say, isn't it?"

After a moment, she nodded.

He surged to his feet. His chair clattered back, rocked and almost fell over. "Not anymore, she isn't. I intend to get custody."

Her heart skipped a beat. "What?" she asked faintly.

"You heard me." His voice was as flinty as his gray eyes. "I've already retained an attorney. Finn murdered my sister. When he did that, he forfeited all rights to Hanna."

"Just because he's been charged—" Oh, how weak that sounded. And why was she defending the brother who had actively made her childhood miserable?

"Charged?" Matt snorted. "What's he claiming?

That she crawled under the coffee table and banged her head on it?"

"Under?" Her confusion must have been plain, because after a minute he straightened the chair and sat.

"You haven't heard the whole story?"

"No."

"Her skull was shattered. The hair and tissue weren't on the top edge of table, where they would have been if she'd fallen. They were on the lower edge." He slid a hand along the table in demonstration. "The bastard picked it up and slammed it into her head."

"Oh, God," Linnea whispered. "Mom doesn't know that."

His expression hardened. "Or does and won't admit it."

"He's her son…" No more convincing than her own defense of Finn. And the very words made her ache. *I'm her daughter, too. Why do I matter so much less?*

Matt rose to his feet again, looking down at her. "Frankly, I don't want Hanna to have any contact with your parents. That's one reason I don't want her staying with you."

"But—she's happy with me." Linnea stood, too, although being on her feet didn't help much with him towering over her.

His tone softened slightly as he made the grudging admission, "You seem like a nice woman. You're obviously well-intentioned, and Hanna is fond of you. But I can't imagine you defying either your parents or your brother. No." He shook his head. "I won't risk it. I'm asking for custody."

She felt sick as she stared at him, hating the way he'd dismissed her in a few words. *You're a weakling.* Maybe she was, but in defense of Hanna she'd do anything.

"She's scared of you."

"And whose fault is that?"

"Did you ever stop to think it might be yours?" she cried. "How is a child supposed to feel attachment to someone who's no more than an occasional visitor in her life?"

She thought her accusation had struck home from the way his eyes darkened. But then he shook her words— *her*—off with a flat, "We'll be changing that. I rented a house yesterday. I'm moving in this weekend. We'll start with a few overnights."

Linnea took a deep breath, clutched for all her courage and said, "No."

"What do you mean, *no?*"

"I mean, given your hostility to me and to her grandparents, to the family Hanna knows and loves, no. I don't have to let her go with you. I don't have to let her *see* you."

"You're threatening me?"

"I'm saying no. That's all." She swallowed. "Go to court. Until a judge orders me to let her see you again, I'm going to keep saying no."

He leaned forward, menace in every line of his body. "Why, you little…"

She was shaking, but stood her ground. "Please leave now."

"For God's sake…"

"Now. Don't make me call the police."

Along with the anger, his face held shock and disbelief. He swore, swung on his heel, and stalked out. An instant later, the front door opened and slammed shut.

Linnea's knees gave out and she collapsed in her chair at the kitchen table. "Oh, God," she whispered. "What have I done?"

But she knew: she'd whipped out a red cape and waved it in front of an angry, wounded bull. Encouraged him to attack. Not so smart, given that she had no sword.

Gazing at her hands, laid flat on the table and still visibly trembling, she thought, *He drove me to it.* It was almost as if he wanted to dislike her. Or as if she was nothing, merely an obstacle to what *he* wanted.

Linnea had discovered in the past week how very tired she was of being dismissed. She'd never been willing to fight back for her own sake, but for Hanna... Oh, that was different.

Still, she quailed at the idea of what he'd do now. She hoped and prayed that, in making an enemy, she hadn't been very foolish.

PACING HIS HOTEL ROOM, Matt muttered an obscenity. *Stupid,* he thought. He'd lost his temper. He never did that.

He'd needed Linnea's cooperation, and now he'd blown it.

How long would it take to force a family-court hearing? Days? Weeks? He could have been building a relationship with Hanna in the meantime. Instead, he would become an ogre in her mind. She'd probably heard the raised voices in the kitchen and quailed, re-membering Mommy and Daddy's fights and the terrible outcome of them.

God. He stopped, flattened his hands on the desk and bowed his head. He was breathing as if he'd come in from a run.

Had he misjudged Linnea entirely? Was Finn's quiet sister very capable of defending Hanna from anyone and anything? She'd become a lioness today. She hadn't relented at all, even though he'd been able to tell she was afraid of him.

And, damn, he hated knowing that. He could be a hard-ass at work, but women didn't quake at the sight of him. He couldn't remember ever feeling the blinding anger he had since the early-morning phone call that had him on the plane for the U.S. within hours.

Rocked by a tsunami of grief, he thought, *Tess*. For a moment, he saw her face. She was…what? Eighteen, twenty? In college, for sure. He couldn't remember what he'd said or done, but she was laughing at him. She was going through a stage with her hair short, spiked and dyed hot pink. He remembered thinking it suited her. She was five foot ten inches tall, slim but strong, a star basketball player in high school and college both. His baby sister, Tess, was also beautiful, with spectacular cheekbones, eyes a deep, navy blue, her mouth wide and sensuous and always flapping. As a kid, he swore she never shut up. The loss of their parents had tempered her, made her more thoughtful, given her a layer of sadness beneath the joie de vivre. He carried the memory of that laugh, of all the other laughs, of the way her eyes sparkled, the way she would fly into his arms and hug him as hard as he hugged her, even in front of her college friends. She was never too cool for her brother, Matt.

And now she was gone.

He was stunned to realize tears poured down his face and dripped onto his hands. He was paralyzed by this grief that ran like acid through his veins, damaging his heart as it went.

"Tess," he whispered. "Tess, no. No."

It had to be fifteen minutes before the tears spent themselves; the pain washed away and left him nearly numb. Matt staggered into the bathroom and turned on the taps, bending to splash first hot and then cold water over his face. He toweled his head dry, then went to the bed and sat on the edge of it, his elbows on his knees.

Now what? Would apologizing to Linnea get him anywhere?

He couldn't imagine. He'd been a son of a bitch; she'd threatened to call the police if he didn't leave that minute.

He hated remembering the expression on her face. Damn it, she'd been decent to him. More than decent. Encouraged him to spend time with Hanna, worked to include them both in conversation. Pretty clearly, that argument with her mother had been about him, and they wouldn't have fought at all if Linnea hadn't been defending him and his right to see Hanna.

And from the moment she'd opened her front door to him, he'd seen that she wasn't mousy as he'd always believed. Instead, she was…shy. Private. Gentle. Not a good fit in her family.

Maybe her gentle nature was exactly what Hanna needed right now, he thought, staring blankly at the far wall of the hotel room.

Maybe.

He wouldn't be opposed to her continuing to see her niece. Hanna did love her, and he even understood why. To his surprise, he'd liked Linnea. Even… No. He hadn't named whatever he'd felt as sexual attraction, and he wasn't going to. They had officially become enemies today. And even if they weren't… Good God. Imagine the complications.

No, pretty Linnea Sorensen wasn't speaking to him

anymore. She would be unlikely to even answer his calls should he try to apologize. He regretted coming on so strong today. She hadn't deserved it. But he had to concentrate on Hanna. On keeping her away from her bastard of a father.

He reached for his cell phone. The attorney would want to know that Hanna's aunt was now refusing him contact with his niece. This new circumstance was reason enough to push for a hearing as soon as possible.

He didn't know how he'd survive until then, unable to see his only family in the world, unable to talk to the one person who had seemed to understand what he felt.

Now his enemy.

My fault.

CHAPTER FOUR

INEVITABLY, LINNEA SAW Matthew at Tess's funeral.

The police had finally released her body. Matthew had made the arrangements, although he did call Linnea's mother several times to consult her. Instead of being grateful for his courtesy, she was furious that he'd had any voice at all in his sister's disposition.

He must have known Finn would attend the funeral, if only as a public-relations ploy. Linnea immediately felt bad, thinking that; neither Finn nor Tess had ever given any indication that their marriage was anything but happy, despite their heated arguments. Linnea had assumed that was their way of communicating. One she would hate, but that both of them seemed to find stimulating. Finn's grief had to be genuine.

The police detective attended both the church service and the graveside ceremony. He stayed at Matt's elbow through both, she noticed. Maybe she wasn't the only one afraid of a horrible confrontation. If fists flew at graveside, it might not look good for Finn. Or would he be seen as a victim?

Thank goodness, nothing happened. The two men stayed well away from each other, although several times she turned her head to see Matt staring with burning hatred at her brother. Once, Detective Delaney spoke in a low voice to him and he abruptly turned away.

She, of course, stood at her brother's side, holding Hanna's hand, their parents on his other side. This was the first time Hanna had seen her father since Tess's death. He made a show of keeping a hand on her shoulder throughout, the concerned father to any observers. Hanna moved robotically, as though she was present in body only, and not in spirit. She stared blankly at her mother's coffin. The service had been closed casket, for which Linnea was grateful in one way. But could a child Hanna's age believe her mother really was in that shiny box? And if she did believe it, would she picture her scrabbling to get out? The only death Hanna had ever seen was Confetti's, and whether she had the capacity to imagine her mother so still and stiff and cold, Linnea didn't know.

Matt had nodded at her and Hanna when he first saw them. Once the ceremonial clod of dirt had been flung atop the casket and the mourners started for their cars, she saw that he was walking as if to intercept her. Her pulse leaped with anxiety and possibly something else. Finn rejoined her and Hanna right then, and Matt stopped. She wondered what he would have said to her, or whether his thoughts were all for Hanna.

Finn walked her to her car, and there he did squat and wrap his arms around Hanna. They weren't in the camera's eye right now, and Linnea saw his face contort when his cheek was pressed to the top of his daughter's head. Oh, yes, he loved her. And he grieved, she thought, reassured.

When he stood, he hugged Linnea, too, and whispered, "Thanks."

For being here today to support him in the public eye? For taking care of Hanna? For remaining silent and obedient? She had no idea.

Unfortunately, he'd reverted to his usual arrogant self when he called three days after the funeral. In the worst of all possible timing, he'd received notice that Matt had filed a petition for custody.

"Who does that son of a bitch think he is, trying to take my daughter from me?" he snarled.

He had phoned after Linnea had already tucked Hanna into bed. The coward in her hadn't wanted to pick up the phone at all, but she did need to speak to him.

She let him rant for some time, her responses limited to, "Mmm-hmm. Yes, Mom told me." Eventually her brother worked his way around to the point of the call. "I'm *advised*—" His emphasis on the word made clear how ticked he was to be in the position of being forced to take legal counsel. "I'm *advised* that my contesting him would only give Laughlin a better chance of winning a temporary order. But when he seems to be doing battle with you, Hanna's beloved aunt Linnie, it's another story. Should be a cakewalk, getting him off our backs."

Linnea had to count to ten before she could reply, her voice shaking only the tiniest bit. "*Seems?* Finn, if the court awards custody to me, Hanna will stay here as promised."

There was a distinct pause. She could easily picture his eyes narrowing.

"Are you challenging me, sis? Hanna's *my* kid. Don't get ideas here. You'll get trampled."

She flushed hot, then shivered with the chill that followed. She was challenging her brother, but she didn't want him to know that. So she kept her voice mild. "You know Matt will be watching. He won't tolerate Hanna going with you if she's supposed to be with me."

His mood abruptly altered. "I don't have time for her right now anyway. She's okay there, right?" He didn't wait for an answer. "I'm paying for representation for you. Someone from Attley McKesson Cotter will be in touch with—"

"No," she said.

This silence was downright icy. So was her brother's voice when he said, "What the hell does that mean?"

"It means, I don't think it would look good if you were clearly behind my attempt to gain legal custody—"

"*Temporary* legal custody."

"Temporary legal custody," she corrected herself. "I've already got an attorney."

"Who?"

"Margaret Robinson. She specializes in family-and-child issues."

"I'll check her out." He fell silent, then muttered an obscenity. "All right," he conceded grudgingly. "That might be good thinking. A female attorney… Yeah. She could go over well."

Linnea gritted her teeth at his condescension. Why had Tess tolerated him?

"Don't screw up," he concluded. "Pretend you've got some spine, will you? No commissioner will see you as guardian material if you act like you're scared of your own goddamn shadow. You can pretend to be motherly, can't you? Determined to protect and adore your niece?"

Linnea was truly astonished at the firestorm of fury that ignited in her. She'd spent her life ducking and shriveling at Finn's scathing dismissals of her character. This time, she was mad.

"Don't worry," she told him. "I do adore Hanna, and I'll protect her." *From you,* she thought, proud of her calm voice.

"Is there going to be a trial?" she asked.

"Over this child custody thing? Of course not. You won't even be seeing a judge, a commissioner handles—"

"No, I meant you. Mom said you were arraigned."

"Hell, yes, there'll be a trial. What do you think, I'm going to take this lying down?"

"I'm just asking—"

"What do you imagine I'm going to do, cop a plea?" he snapped. "To a felony, that will get me disbarred? When they've got zero reason to think this was anything but an accident? Hell, no. We're going full-steam ahead." His voice changed. "You know how volatile Tess was. She was so mad, she kicked the coffee table over, then on her next pass tripped and fell right into it. I grabbed for her, but—"

She heard him swallow and wondered if that much, at least, was genuine. But as for the rest, Linnea knew perfectly well she was hearing his defense. He was probably practicing on her. She knew him. By the time he was on the witness stand, he'd be able to talk about Tess's last minutes with moisture glistening in his eyes, his resonant, musical voice hitching. He would sound heartbroken rather than perfunctory.

Suddenly repulsed, she said, "Hanna is asleep, in case you wanted to talk to her. I'm afraid I need to go. I think it would be better if you didn't contact her for now. Mom will keep you up-to-date."

She heard the TV in the background. He'd presumably just turned it on.

"Don't screw up," he repeated, and hung up on her.

Carefully, Linnea hit End and set down the phone. "Jerk!"

But her churning stomach told her he was worse than that. Far worse. He'd killed his wife, and he was now cold-bloodedly lying to protect himself.

She'd always believed he did love Hanna. Now she knew she had been wrong. It made her chest ache, thinking that. Hanna would know eventually, if she didn't already.

I can't fail her, Linnea thought, familiar self-doubt creeping from the shadows. *She doesn't have anyone else.*

Except, of course, for her uncle Matt, who was determined to take her away from everyone and everything she knew and loved.

MATT WAS SURPRISED AT HOW quickly a hearing on his custody petition had been set up. He'd been afraid he would have to wait for weeks. The circumstances had presumably had an influence, as perhaps had Finn's current notoriety.

Matt and his attorney had crafted the petition as carefully as they could. "Chances are, we won't have more than five minutes to argue your case," Shelton had explained. "So what's presented in writing to the commissioner has to be good."

Explaining why parental visitation should be limited or nonexistent was no challenge, under the circumstances. His attorney doubted Finn would be foolish enough to intrude himself in these proceedings. If he was found guilty of murder in the second degree, he would be going to prison, with a likely sentence of three to five years. If he was found innocent, he'd have a good chance of regaining custody. In the meantime, his hands looked damn dirty and he was better off relying on his sister to represent the Sorensen family.

Matt's belief that it was in Hanna's best interest to live with him rather than Linnea came down to her association with her brother and her closeness to the parents who were Finn's staunchest supporters and apologists. Matt thought he had a good case. He knew his attorney wasn't so sure.

But letting himself have doubts wasn't an option. Without Hanna, he'd have nobody. And Tess's child would be at the mercy of that son of a bitch Finn Sorensen and his family.

Not acceptable.

The hearing itself was scheduled for the week after he had filed the petition for nonparental custody. He and his attorney were already sitting in the waiting room when Matt saw Linnea walk in. His entire body went rigid. All he could think was how beautiful she was. How perfect, with her moonlight-pale hair drawn smoothly back in a chignon. Wearing a navy sheath dress and pearls in her ears, she was Princess Grace, he thought, lovely and untouchable.

He'd stared for a stunned thirty seconds before he realized her parents and another woman had arrived with her.

Shelton murmured, "Nod acknowledgment. Not a word."

God damn it. Gripping the arms of the chair, Matt met Linnea's gaze and nodded.

Cheeks flushed, she did the same. The entire group

settled in chairs as far away from him as they could get. From his peripheral vision, he saw the attorney speaking in a low voice to Linnea, the parents leaning forward to hear.

"You knew the grandparents would come," his own attorney said softly. "They're trying to present a united front."

"No *trying* about it," he ground out.

"But they're all tainted by association. That's our best argument."

Didn't "I love her" count? But Matt knew it didn't, if only because Linnea loved her niece, too.

She looked as uncomfortable as he felt. He studied the three of them surreptitiously, Linnea first. She sat stiffly, her back straight and not touching the chair, her hands gripping her purse on her lap. His eyes narrowed. Did it mean something that she'd had to walk past both of her parents so that she could sit beside her father and not her mother?

Finn had gotten his looks from his father. Paavo Sorensen was an older, stooped version of his son, his blond hair going to white, the effect of the tall body storklike rather than athletic. The resemblance would have bothered Matt had it been more than skin deep. Paavo lacked Finn's energy and intensity, perhaps in part because of the disease that he'd currently battled to a draw. He looked like the college professor he'd been—quiet, reserved, thoughtful. Maybe kind. Matt had never gotten to know him well enough to judge.

The mother, she was the source of Finn's sense of entitlement. Likely a beauty in her twenties, still slender and elegant with a close-cropped cap of blond hair, she had acquired wrinkles of dissatisfaction. Matt had never liked her, and, damn it, he'd tried—she was Hanna's grandmother! Her only grandmother. But her voice had a sharp edge too often, although never, that he'd heard, directed at Finn. Matt wondered if Linnea had noticed.

Stupid thought—she had to have learned her disappearing trick early. Because she hadn't measured up to her big brother? Or was there another reason?

Before the wait could become excruciating instead of just agonizing, they were all summoned into the conference room. He'd known the commissioner hearing his case was a man, which had given him some hope. At least he wouldn't be combating an automatic assumption that women were the preferred caregivers for a young girl. A recorder was present as well as a bailiff.

The commissioner was younger than he'd expected, no more than forty. Thin-faced, he wore horn-rimmed glasses. As they arranged themselves in seats, he studied them openly, one at a time.

Matt's attorney spoke first, followed by Matt, who emphasized his deep attachment to Hanna and his concern that Finn's sister would permit contact with Finn and that the entire family would cast the blame for any violence on Tess rather than her husband and killer. He talked about raising his sister after their parents' death and his deep desire to do the same for his niece. Sitting down, he felt drained.

Linnea's attorney rose in turn and gave a predictable spiel. Hanna was already staying with Linnea. Linnea had been present at her birth and at every important event of her life; Hanna loved her, felt safe in her home. The child's relationship with Mr. Laughlin was at best occasional, as he had been out of the country for the majority of her life. If the concern was Finn, in fact Ms. Sorensen was not allowing any contact with the child's father at present.

Linnea stood, cast a fleeting glance at him in which he read guilt and unhappiness, then lifted her chin and spoke in a voice that was only slightly tremulous.

"I love Hanna. She's spent an average of a night a week at my house for her entire life. She has her own bedroom in my house, keeps toys there, loves to go to the library with me and help me with my petsitting business. I do work, but her grandparents are happy to have her often, and otherwise a close neighbor who has a boy Hanna's age has been offering day care. At this point, I'm driving her to her existing school to give her stability, but would like to change her to a neighborhood elementary school after Christmas break. I believe with all my heart that Hanna belongs with me."

The commissioner contemplated them. "Have you two made any real attempt to work out a parenting plan for this child?"

They both spoke; stopped and exchanged glances. Matt said, "Initially Ms. Sorensen seemed willing to give me a chance to spend time with Hanna. However, when she learned that I meant to ask for custody, she refused me any contact with my niece."

His attorney nodded. "The core disagreement about Hanna's residential placement has put a roadblock in place we haven't been able to get around."

The commissioner's eyebrows rose. "Ms. Sorensen?"

Cheeks flushed, she said, "Mr. Laughlin expressed such anger at our family—Hanna's family, who she knows and loves—that I felt contact with him was to her detriment."

His head bent and the commissioner flipped through papers. "Were you asking for no contact with Mr. Laughlin?"

Matt froze.

Her gaze touched his, shied away. "Uh, no. I do believe Mr. Laughlin loves Hanna and…that she loves him."

"Should I give you physical custody, would you be able to cooperate with his visitation schedule?"

After a brief hesitation, she dipped her head. Beside Linnea, her mother glared at Matt.

"Very well." The commissioner looked at him. "Mr. Laughlin, I understand and sympathize with your anger at the child's father. I must remind you, however, that he has not been convicted in the death of Hanna's mother. He may, in fact, not end up being convicted. It is essential to her best interest that she not be prejudiced against her father. I'm concerned that you, as the deceased's only family, may have a difficult time suppressing that anger."

Matt opened his mouth and started to push to his feet.

The commissioner waved him back to his seat. "No, allow me to finish. I am making the ruling that Hanna Sorensen shall remain with her aunt, Linnea Sorensen, for other reasons, as well. She knows her aunt the best, is comfortable in her home, and therefore faces the least disruption. She can continue to have contact with her grandparents, as well—and supervised visitation with her father. Who, I again emphasize, has not been convicted. I'm going to order liberal visitation for you, Mr. Laughlin, to allow you to build a solid relationship with your niece. That is—" he tilted his head to look over his glasses "—assuming you intend to remain in this country and state?"

He unclenched his jaw. "I'll be here."

"Very well. Remember that this order is temporary. We can revisit it at any time, and certainly will following resolution of the charges filed against Hanna's father." He looked from Matt to Linnea and back again. "I'm going to give the two of you another opportunity to come up with a parenting plan, to include a visitation schedule, decision making and dispute resolution. Should you fail, I'll do it for you. Mr. Shelton, Ms. Robinson, I will ask that a plan be submitted to me within one week. Is that agreeable?"

Both nodded.

One last sharp look. "Good luck."

Feeling sick, Matt found himself on his feet, walking out, Shelton gripping his arm as if afraid he'd—what?—swing a punch? In the waiting room, Linnea and her parents stopped to face him.

Matt saw only the triumph on her mother's face.

"The nerve of you, trying to keep our grandchild from us."

"Mom!"

"Now, Mrs. Sorensen…" the attorney murmured.

The dam he'd put on his tongue crumbled. He looked her in the eye and said, "Your son killed my sister. He shattered her skull. You are apparently unwilling to acknowledge his fault or to protect Hanna from his next temper tantrum." Matt let his scathing gaze move from her to the father's face, and finally to Linnea, who appeared stricken. "Yeah, I think Hanna would be better off being raised the way my sister was rather than the way you raised your son." Feeling Shelton's fingers tightening on his arm, he said brusquely, "Linnea, I'll be in touch," then walked out.

THE NEXT MEETING TOOK PLACE in the office of Linnea's attorney, Margaret Robinson. Linnea made sure she arrived first, although she felt silly worrying about something so meaningless. This wasn't a battlefield, where holding the higher ground counted. Although remembering the way Matt had looked at her and her parents, she suspected that to him this *was* a battle in a war he was determined to win.

Margaret's law offices were on the ground floor of an old house a block off Broadway on Capitol Hill. She shared it with a partner, another woman whose specialty was landlord-and-tenant law. The floors were refinished hardwood, the ceilings ten feet high or more, the moldings a dark mahogany. Linnea would have loved to own a house like this, with a deep front porch and a bay window. The conference room, she decided, must have been a library, or perhaps the parlor.

She knew she was only trying to distract herself, but waiting was hard.

Voices, first the receptionist's then a man's, gave her warning. She set down her cup, lifted her head and did her absolute best to look serene.

She wished she thought she'd succeeded.

Matt came in first, his unreadable and rather grim gaze going right to her face. Linnea's pulse took wing in her throat.

His attorney, whose name she didn't remember, followed him. Margaret rose and welcomed them, offered coffee, which the attorney accepted and Matt refused. The receptionist, smiling, went away and quickly returned with another cup.

"Well, let's get down to business," Margaret said briskly, as soon as the other woman pulled the French doors closed behind her. "I'm assuming you've given some thought to a visitation schedule."

"Of course." The other attorney opened his briefcase and took out a file, then closed the briefcase and set it on the floor. "The commissioner did suggest *generous* visitation. His word, not mine."

"And very much open to interpretation," Margaret agreed, her tone bland.

He—Sheldon…no, Shelton, with a *t,* yes, that was it—inclined his head and spread papers out on the table in front of him. "We're currently asking for the equivalent of every other weekend as well as one evening per week. Mr. Laughlin would like to have Hanna for half of the approaching school breaks, with the holidays themselves to be negotiated."

Every other weekend? But Hanna didn't know him. She was so traumatized already. For him to insist on taking her for two days at a time—two *nights* at a time—to a strange house, where she'd have to sleep in a strange bedroom, was cruel. He was as bad as Finn, Linnea thought indignantly, staking his claim whether that was best for Hanna or not.

She knew emotions showed on her face too readily. She knew, too, that he was watching her.

"Don't look like that," he said abruptly. His attorney had started to say something else, but he stopped and everyone stared at Matt. "I'm not going to rip her out of your arms and drag her away screaming. Is that what you think?"

"Do you believe she'll go with you willingly?" Linnea couldn't tear her gaze from his eyes, so dark they were more charcoal than steel. "Like she did for the trip to the zoo?"

He almost hid his flinch, but not entirely. "I love Hanna."

"Do you?"

"She and I have been good friends. She loved staying home from day care and spending days with me."

"When she was three? Four?"

"And five. She hasn't forgotten. She reminds me of things we did together when she e-mails me. She's shy with me because we haven't seen each other in a while. That's all."

Linnea knew he was telling the truth. Before Tess's death, she'd seen Hanna light up for him, snuggle trustingly against his side. She'd heard her niece's giggle and looked outside to see them coming up the street from the school, two blocks away, pretending to steal a soccer ball from each other. Matt had been good to her.

"For one week a year," she whispered. Then said more loudly, "You were hardly ever here."

For an instant his eyes closed, veiling his response to her accusation. Then his lashes lifted to reveal a fierce stare. "She had parents. I have a job."

"What were you going to do if you got custody? Take her away to Kuwait? Or wherever you were going next?"

"You know I wouldn't have done that," he said quietly.

"How am I supposed to know?" Her voice wanted to tremble, but she forced herself to go on anyway. "Have we ever had a conversation before?"

She'd said that before. *I don't really know you.* He'd tried to claim the fault lay on both of their sides, and maybe there was some truth in it. He was the kind of man who intimidated her. If he had ever tried to talk to her, she'd have probably spooked like a skittish cat. But the truth was, he hadn't. She suspected he had hardly noticed she was there.

Linnea was a little shocked to realize how much she resented his indifference, even though she hadn't actually *wanted* him to talk to her. At least, she didn't think she had. But maybe… She was confusing herself, and none of that mattered anyway. Hanna mattered.

"You have no idea how much I regret that now," he said, gravel in his voice. As if, perhaps, he was ashamed of himself. He sighed. "Linnea, can we start again? We have to put a visitation schedule in writing. But I had no intention of jumping into it. I don't want to scare Hanna. I want to take it slowly. Maybe she'd enjoy a movie. Dinner at McDonald's. If you have a schoolyard nearby, she might like to kick the soccer ball. We used to do that."

Now she was the one who was ashamed. "I remember," she said, so low she wasn't sure anyone but Matt heard her.

He was still looking into her eyes, but his expression had changed. "Will you help me become friends with Hanna again?" he asked.

Linnea felt herself nodding. "I would have, you know."

"If I hadn't been such a jackass." One corner of his mouth lifted. "No, don't say anything. You don't have to."

"Then I won't."

His smile was full-blown now, if still wry. She felt odd, dizzy, as if she'd twirled several times and now nothing looked the same. Not that she hadn't seen him smile before, but for other people. Never for her. If he had…

I would have been even more frightened of him, she realized, still dazed. Because he smiled as if he meant it, with intimacy, warmth and surprising self-deprecation. His smile was utterly unlike her brother's far more charming one.

"What's this decision making we're supposed to discuss?" Matt asked, his gaze not leaving her face.

Margaret cleared her throat. "Ah, that's the kind of

decisions parents usually make together. What school a child will attend. What church, if any. Sunday school. To vaccinate or not. To skip a grade if it's called for, to seek tutoring if needed. Practical matters, personal values, the rules a child has to abide by."

He seemed to be waiting for her. After a minute, Linnea said, "Do you object to my moving her to a local school after the break?"

Matt shook his head. "That seems logical unless there's some compelling reason to keep her where she is."

"She hated her after-school care."

"The Rolls Royce of preschools?"

Linnea blinked. "Is that what Tess called it?"

"It's what I called it. Tess bragged about the Spanish lessons… Or was it French? I don't remember. The educational walks where the children were invited to notice architectural motifs. The plays they put on—"

"Hanna especially hated the plays. She was too shy to enjoy being in the spotlight. But of course she had to be included, so she always got stuck being the tree or something." Her tone of loathing was a dead giveaway. *She* had always been the tree in elementary school plays, too.

Matt was laughing, but gently, as if he sympathized. "When I got home from school, I liked to climb a tree. Or maybe lie on my stomach and read a comic book."

"It wasn't as if Tess and Finn had any choice but to put her in after-school care—"

"No. But she won't miss it."

Although they both knew she would miss her mother. Terribly, awfully and forever.

"Church is up to you," he said. "I tend to believe in vaccinations."

She nodded. "Me, too."

"What did we miss? Does she need tutoring?"

Linnea was smiling, just a little. "No. Her reading is way ahead of grade level. But not so far that anyone has suggested she skip ahead."

"Then…?" He looked at Margaret.

She suppressed a smile of her own. "I think we can agree that decision making will be by consensus."

"Dispute resolution?" his attorney said.

"Put down whatever is standard," Matt said. "If we have a problem, we can all meet again."

"Visitation schedule?"

"Let me see it," Linnea said. She turned the piece of paper he pushed across the table so she could read it. Really, she supposed it wasn't unreasonable. He wasn't asking for any more than a divorced father would presume was his right. Of course, he wasn't Hanna's father, but then she wasn't Hanna's mother, either. It felt funny, though, to realize they were standing in for those roles.

"This is fine," she said, "as long as you'll take it slowly. Not…push Hanna to do something she's not ready for."

"You have my word," he said quietly.

Meeting his eyes, Linnea took a deep breath and nodded. "Yes." The one word sounded so bald, she added, "Okay."

"Are we done?" Matt asked, turning a look of inquiry and possibly even impatience on both attorneys, his and hers.

They exchanged a glance. "Why don't I write it up?" Margaret said. "I'll fax it to you for comment."

"Works for me." Shelton spread his hands. "That was easy."

"For Hanna's sake, that's the way it needs to be," Matt said.

Overwhelmed by her jumble of emotions, Linnea picked out only the surprising bit of hope she'd found: perhaps they could at least pretend to be allies after all.

"For Hanna's sake," she echoed.

CHAPTER FIVE

FRIDAY NIGHT AFTER THEIR meeting at the attorney's office, Matt called and suggested that, if it didn't rain Sunday, he take Hanna to the nearest school to kick the soccer ball around.

"That sounds fine," Linnea said, "except that I didn't think to grab the ball the last time I was at Finn's house to get more of her clothes. I don't even know where they keep stuff like that. The garage, maybe?"

"I'll buy one," he said.

"That's probably a good idea. Would you like to stay for lunch?"

"Thank you."

Hanging up, he thought about how excruciatingly polite they had been to each other. God willing, they could keep it up.

He'd lost, and he was lucky Linnea was being as nice as she was about that visitation schedule—or, to put it another way, the measly amount of time he was to be allowed to spend with his niece. He was determined to be equally decent, but the truth was that his goals hadn't changed. He had every intention of raising Hanna. As far as he was concerned, the commissioner's ruling was a glitch, a temporary obstacle.

And even though he'd come to realize that he liked Linnea, he was going to use her to gain Hanna's confidence. He wondered if Linnea believed she'd won for good, or whether she guessed they'd end up opponents again.

Matt hadn't intended to get a job for now; he was on leave from Parker-Sinclair, hadn't even used up his long-accumulated vacation time. With that and his investments, he could certainly afford not to work for a good long while. But seeing Hanna one day this week, two another, left one hell of a lot of days in between. He'd go nuts, twiddling his thumbs. Truthfully, he was thinking of turning that leave into a resignation anyway. Even if— *when*—he was given custody, he wouldn't want to haul Hanna all around the world, Kuwait City this year, Buenos Aires the next, who knew where the one after that. The rootless lifestyle had suited him when he was on his own. He had coworkers who did bring their families along, and some of them seemed happy enough, considered it an adventure. But he believed kids should be rooted. And Hanna had always struck him in particular as a kid who needed to know where she belonged. She wasn't an adventurer.

Even he'd been growing tired of the frequent, drastic moves. He was thirty-three years old, and he'd never owned a house. Never planted a garden. His friendships had been transitory, close only until the next move sent him to a different part of the world.

If he got a job locally, bought a house, his chances of gaining that custody would improve. The commissioner had sounded doubtful when he'd asked if Matt would still be around in the near future. He wouldn't leave any room for doubt the next time he stood up to make his plea.

He'd have rather put off thinking about making his stay here in Seattle permanent until after Finn's trial, but he'd learned that was unrealistic.

"It could be a year away," Delaney had told him the last time they talked. "The prosecutor's office will keep you updated, but I gotta tell you, even if one side or the other isn't asking for delays, the wheels of justice move slowly. Why do you think police reports are so detailed? We need our memories nudged by the time we're called to the witness stand."

A *year?* Matt imagined all of their lives on hold. Not only Finn's—as far as Matt was concerned, that son of a bitch should be in prison while he prepared for trial—but everyone else involved was in a kind of limbo. Hanna most of all. Looming over any plans Linnea or Matt made for her was the possibility that Finn would somehow walk, and want his daughter back. Even a plea bargain could result in a very brief sentence—a year or two, say—and if the charges were reduced, Finn might have the possibility of regaining custody of Hanna. Matt was counting on Finn to refuse to accept any offers for a plea bargain. As long as the charge remained a felony, he'd never be able to practice law again, and then what would he do with his life? And, by God, the DA's office had better not reduce Tess's murder to a misdemeanor.

Matt swore aloud, his voice harsh in the quiet hotel room. He could live with having lost this opening battle to Linnea. But to ensure that Hanna never spent another night under her father's roof, he'd do whatever he had to.

He was careful to arrive at Linnea's place at ten on the nose. Yesterday he'd picked up a kid-size soccer ball and one of those nets to carry it in. He had it under his arm when he walked up to the door.

Linnea was friendly and chatty when she let him in. Hanna hovered ghostlike in the background again.

"Hey," he said. "You ready to go blast the ball into the goal?"

Linnea had to pry answers out of Hanna again. She didn't remember how to play. No, Mom hadn't put her in soccer.

"'Cause Mom had to work," she said, so softly he could hardly hear her.

"I've seen soccer leagues going on around here," Linnea said. "But they seem to end by November, with the weather getting so crummy. Maybe there are spring soccer leagues. We can find out. What do you think, Hanna?"

Hanna ducked her head and shuffled her feet.

"There's a school just three blocks that way," Linnea told him, pointing. "I don't think the soccer fields are being used on Sunday."

He kept his voice easy. "What do you think, Hanna Banana?"

She smiled a tiny bit at the nickname that used to make her giggle. Then she tugged at Linnea's hand, making her bend down so that she could whisper in her ear.

Linnea looked dismayed. "Oh, honey. I was going to get some housecleaning done and start lunch while you two had fun."

This time he wasn't surprised. He wasn't even disappointed. He liked the idea of Linnea coming with them. He wanted to see the brisk November air bring color to her cheeks. Maybe she'd laugh. He had never seen her give a real belly laugh.

He felt a little uneasy at how much he wanted her to

come, but encouraging her was the right thing for a lot of reasons.

"Why don't you join us?" he said. "I'll play goalie. You and Hanna can try to get one by me."

She searched his face. "Are you sure?"

He smiled. "I'm sure."

"Well, then…" She tugged her niece's ponytail. "You two will have to wait while I change shoes and grab a sweater."

While she was gone, Hanna stole peeks at him. "Is that my soccer ball?"

He shook his head. "Your aunt Linnie didn't know where you kept yours."

"Mommy said balls shouldn't be in the house," the little girl whispered. She was silent for a moment. "Aunt Linnie says you remember Mommy when she was my age."

Sudden pain compressed his chest and he had to swallow before he could speak. "Yeah. I do."

"Did *she* play soccer?"

He shook his head. "Your mom danced. She was really good. She did ballet and jazz and tap. When she was really little, she said she was going to be a ballet dancer when she grew up."

"How come she didn't?"

"She was too tall. In ballet, the men lift the women, so most of the women are tiny. She enjoyed playing basketball, too. That's a sport where being tall is good. And she loved art."

"I like to draw, too," Hanna told him shyly.

"I know. Just a couple of months ago, your mom sent me the sailboat you drew. I was really glad to have it." Tess had been proud of Hanna's talent, which he could see, as well. He had a steady hand and a good eye for perspective himself, but none of the creativity that had fired Tess's art. However young she was, Hanna, he thought, had an artist's eye. The sailboat hadn't been the usual static, one-dimensional kid's drawing. Rather, as an artist she had seen the boat head-on, the sails bulging with the wind, spray flung high by the prow, as if a storm made the seas high. The scene had almost seemed…ominous. Tess didn't seem to notice, or wonder if the sailboat had represented a force Hanna had seen bearing down on her. He couldn't swear it had represented any such thing, but the charcoal drawing had made him both proud and a little uneasy. It bothered him now to remember that in his hurry to pack he had left it on the refrigerator, where he'd hung it with a magnet. The rental agent had probably long since crumpled it up and thrown it away.

"Have you been drawing since you came to Aunt Linnie's?"

She shook her head.

Before he could ask why not, Linnea returned. "Ready?"

She'd changed from clogs to athletic shoes and now wore a heavy sweater over the jeans that clung to her long legs. Hair that had been carelessly bundled back was smoothly brushed into a ponytail that bobbed just like Hanna's.

"Sure we are," he said heartily, to hide his discomfiture. Damn it, being attracted to her was more than a little inconvenient.

He gave the ball in its net to Hanna, who began bouncing it off her toes as they started up the sidewalk. Walking a few steps behind, he found himself focusing on the sway of Linnea's hips and the shimmer of that pale blond ponytail.

Her neck was slender, the nape somehow vulnerable-looking as she bent her head to smile down at her niece.

To distract himself, he asked Linnea, "What about you? Did you play any sports?"

She glanced back at him. "I'm afraid I'm something of a klutz. I wasn't very good at most sports. Swimming is the exception. In fact, I'm going to get Hanna added to my membership at the health club so she can go with me."

"But I don't know how to swim!" Hanna said in alarm.

"You haven't had lessons?" For God's sake, what had Tess been thinking? Both of them had been like fish in the water by the time they were Hanna's age. Summer was for swim lessons. But he knew—she'd been too busy. Matt scowled. Why the hell hadn't the super preschool had the kids in swim lessons?

"Uh-uh." Hanna shook her head hard. "I don't like to put my face in."

"Well, we're going to have to take care of that," Linnea said firmly. "Everybody needs to know how to swim. Besides, it's fun. We'll want to go to the beach this summer. When I was your age, Mom took your dad and me to Green Lake a couple of times a week. She'd read at a picnic table and we'd swim."

She sounded sad, Matt couldn't help noticing. Because her family was irretrievably broken now, or because that memory wasn't as rosy as it sounded on the surface?

When they reached the school, they found some boys playing basketball on the paved area close to the building, but the fields were empty. Shouts of triumph and groans carried to the far soccer goal where Matt planted himself.

"A couple of girls," he jeered. "You don't have a chance."

Hanna and Linnea exchanged glances.

"It's pretty muddy there," Linnea observed. "If you go down, it won't be pretty."

He grinned, even though he'd had the same realization. The day was chilly, but not cold enough to make the mud crusty. Especially considering he wasn't wearing soccer cleats, slipping was a real possibility. "Good luck," he said.

Hanna dumped the ball out of the net on the sideline. The two of them whispered for a moment, then separated on the field and began passing the ball back and forth. He crouched, waiting as they neared. Linnea booted the ball, and he leaped and caught it.

"Slow motion," he mocked.

Already her cheeks were rosy, her eyes sparkling. For a klutz, she moved well. He hadn't thought to ask whether one of those sports she'd tried out along the way had been soccer.

They kept playing; he'd toss the ball, and one or the other would chase it down. They varied their techniques, sometimes playing the field farther apart from each other, sometimes clumping. Sometimes taking a kick from way out, sometimes racing for the corner of the goal. He made a production of waiting for them, enjoying the taunts and the faces he got in return. He had every intention of letting one of Hanna's kicks through, but not Linnea's. She was a big girl.

This time she rushed at him with the ball, making him commit and move to intercept her. At the last minute, a light tap with the side of her foot sent the ball to Hanna, who booted it straight in. They both laughed and met to do a high five.

Matt gave Hanna one, too, pleased to see how delighted with herself she looked. "You've got a bigger kick than you used to have, kiddo."

"I'm bigger!" she told him.

He kicked the ball out of the goal, and they started again.

Maybe it was inevitable. A couple of great stops—if he did say so himself—later Linnea shot the ball for the corner of the net. He had to let it go or dive for it. He dove.

He caught the ball, but paid the price of sliding head-long through the cold mud. Linnea gasped and she hurried to him with her hand out. "Are you okay?"

In the background, Hanna had a fit of giggles.

Making an inarticulate sound, he accepted Linnea's hand and heaved himself to his feet. He made himself let her hand go and refused to think about how good it had felt in his—how slender and yet surprisingly strong.

His eyes narrowed. "You know, I don't think I'm the only one who should get dirty."

Laughing, hands raised in alarm, Linnea began backing away. He turned and feinted at Hanna, who shrieked and ran. They ended up chasing each other around the field until, winded, he stopped and bent over, hands on his thighs. "I give up."

"Can *I* get muddy, Aunt Linnie?" Hanna asked. "I could be the goalie."

They played until all three of them were sweating and filthy. He hadn't had such a good time in years. Hadn't laughed like that in years, either, Matt realized as they started toward Linnea's house.

"You two have clean clothes to change into," he complained.

"Ugh." Linnea wrinkled her nose at him. "You don't?"

"Uh...I'm afraid not." He looked down at himself. She wasn't going to want him in the house. So much for lunch, damn it.

"I'll see what I can find," she said. "But Hanna and I get dibs on the shower first." Her face was still alight with laughter. "We'll leave you standing on the doorstep, like a soggy dog."

Hanna thought that was funny, too. She all but fell down, she laughed so hard.

At the house, Linnea let him in but insisted they all take off their shoes and socks right inside the door. She sent Hanna off to the bathroom, then directed him to a heat register.

"I think I can at least find a sweatshirt that will be big enough," she said, appraising him. "I may have you sit on a towel, though."

"Yeah, I'm pretty disgusting," he admitted. "Maybe that wasn't such a good idea."

"It was a fabulous idea," she said in a quiet voice, her gaze warm. "Hanna was happy. She hasn't been since…" She swallowed. "I'd better get her some clean clothes and take a quick shower myself before I start lunch."

"You need it." His voice came out huskier than usual and he touched a mud streak on her cheek. His fingertips tingled, and it was all he could do to withdraw his hand. It curled into a fist at his side.

She went very still at the fleeting, soft touch. Her eyes darkened as she stared at him. Then, without a word, she turned and hurried toward the rear of the house.

Damn it, damn it, damn it! What was he *thinking?*

He knew the answer: he wasn't thinking. Something about her drew him in a way he hadn't experienced in years, maybe never. Her air of fragility, coupled with a spine of steel. Her gentle voice when she spoke to Hanna, her honesty, the sadness that clung to her like a scent he couldn't quite identify. Yeah, all that, and her slender, graceful body, her generous breasts, the tiny tendrils of pale hair that curled against her nape. The whole package. He couldn't understand how he'd been so blind all these years.

Matt wished he was still blind. He and Linnea had been on opposite sides in the conference room last week, and they'd keep being on opposite sides unless he gave up his claim to Hanna.

And that was one thing he couldn't do.

Maybe, he thought, without a lot of hope, Hanna had relaxed with him enough today that he could start taking her on his own. He could say hi and goodbye to Linnea without making a fool of himself, couldn't he?

He grimaced. *Maybe.*

LINNEA REALLY WISHED she hadn't caught that glimpse of Matt Laughlin without a shirt.

Well, not entirely without one. She had produced a faded blue sweatshirt for him, which he was pulling over his head when she saw him.

The sweatshirt was one she wore sometimes when she was cleaning, the sleeves rolled way up, the hem reaching midthigh. She thought it must have been Finn's or her dad's. She couldn't even remember when she'd latched on to it. It was soft, and had a couple of spots she'd gotten bleach on, and the neck was fraying, but she loved it in the way of clothes you couldn't make yourself give up.

How could she ever put it on again without picturing Matt in it?

He hadn't shut the bathroom door. Linnea froze halfway down the hall, unable to remember why she was there and not in the kitchen where she belonged. His muddy shirt was on the floor at his feet. His arms were raised as he worked the sweatshirt over his head.

She stood frozen, staring. He had a powerful chest dusted with dark hair. Below… His stomach was lean, hard. A line of dark hair disappeared beneath the waist-band of jeans that hung low on his hips.

Her mouth went dry and her knees felt weak. She wanted to flatten her hands on that chest, even touch her lips to it.

Panic rose in her, but too late. He tugged the sweat-shirt down and saw her. The flicker of awareness in his eyes, the way they narrowed, set her heart to drumming.

"I—" Her voice came out high, unnatural. "Lunch is ready." *Oh, God—why did I come down the hall?*

"Should I bring a towel?"

That was it. *Thank you, thank you!* "I was going to grab an old one from the linen closet." She did, intensely grateful to be able to open the door and block the sight of him. Linnea snatched the first towel her hand touched, not caring if it was her best for guests or a scruffy old one she used to bathe Spooky. She was very, very careful not to look back when she closed the door and started toward the kitchen.

The meal was horribly awkward. Or maybe that was all in her head. She only knew that she tried not to look at Matt whenever she could avoid it. He must have seen the expression on her face. She hated to think what she'd given away.

And what was wrong with her? She'd never thought of him that way.

Except…Linnea had a niggling feeling that she had. Oh, she'd never acknowledged even to herself—most of all to herself—that she was attracted to him. He was too large, too blatantly male, too impatient. Too much like Finn and Tess: successful, ambitious, worldly in a way Linnea knew she wasn't. She had deliberately chosen a life that was small in scope. People like them looked down on someone like her. No one had ever made a secret of that.

Matt Laughlin hadn't been cruel about it, not like Finn was. But he hadn't been as kind as his sister, either. He'd simply ignored her.

He couldn't anymore, but she still didn't understand why now he looked at her with the same awareness she felt. Why he listened to her as if he really wanted to know her. Why, when he touched her cheek, he'd snatched his hand back as if he'd burned his fingertips on her, why she'd seen his hands fisted before she fled.

Why, oh why, couldn't he keep being cold, distant, disinterested in her? Hostile, even?

Her eyes closed in despair. No, for Hanna's sake Linnea couldn't want that. Today, for a precious hour, Hanna had forgotten that her mommy had died, that her daddy had inexplicably disappeared as completely, that her entire life had changed. She had laughed with open joy, run, flung herself into the mud, chattered.

For Hanna's sake, Linnea realized wretchedly, she had to keep seeing Matt. Had to keep welcoming him into her home, teasing him so that Hanna would giggle again. Had to encourage her niece, the person she loved most in the world, to trust him.

Had to take the chance that this would not end with her losing Hanna to him.

They had to have a relationship, and she couldn't bear it if he knew what longing had flooded her at the

sight of his bare chest. It was okay to have been
startled, even made a little shy. After all, she didn't
know him that well, and she hadn't expected to see
him undressing in her house. She'd simply have to
make sure that it never crossed his mind she'd felt
anything more than that.

Hanna did, thank goodness, chat somewhat more naturally with Matt over lunch, allowing Linnea's reserve to
pass unnoticed. She hoped. Darn it, if only he wasn't
such a large man. Or if only she had a bigger kitchen, or
a real dining room, so that the three of them weren't
cuddled up at a tiny table tucked against the wall so that
it had room for only three chairs around it and left all their
knees bumping beneath it.

He ate with relish, and even Hanna seemed to have
worked up an appetite. Matt talked about buying a car that
week, they laughed about an incident at the library when
a puppy in training to be a service dog had slipped his
leash and galloped and slid around bookshelves, determined to make friends with every single person in the
building. Hanna was particularly entranced with that story.

Matt was the one to finally say, "I suppose I should
take off." Linnea wondered if he knew how reluctant he
sounded. He stretched and winced. "I'm getting too old
to be diving for the ball."

She suspected he was in excellent physical condition
and well able to throw himself into any sport he chose.
She smiled, though, as he'd obviously intended her to do,
and said, "We had fun. Didn't we, Hanna?"

Her niece nodded vigorously. "Can I keep the ball?"

"Yep," he said. "It's for you. You want to play again
later this week?"

She nodded, but a little more hesitantly. Her gaze slid to Linnea. "Can Aunt Linnie play, too?"

"You bet." He lowered his voice to a rumble. "If she dares."

She laughed, some of her discomfiture fading. "You're the one with the aches and pains. Hanna and I are more than a match for you. Aren't we, kiddo?"

"Yeah!" her niece exclaimed.

He grinned at them both. "I went easy on you today. Just wait." He carried his dishes to the sink, then grimaced. "My jeans have dried. I can feel them crackling when I move."

"Why don't you take the towel?" Linnea suggested. "The rental company might not appreciate dried mud on the upholstery."

"I'll bring it back. And the sweatshirt, if that's okay."

When Hanna stood, he caught her into a quick hug against his side, releasing her before she could get shy. "See you, Banana."

"Bye." She turned a beseeching look on Linnea. "Can I watch *Bambi?*"

"Sure."

Hanna whirled away. Linnea watched her go, troubled enough to momentarily forget Matt was there.

"Why the unhappy look?" he asked quietly.

"What? Oh." She sighed. "It seems like she mostly wants to watch TV. And this is the third time she's watched *Bambi* this week alone."

He frowned. "I don't think I've ever seen it. Isn't it about cute animals?"

"Bambi's mom gets shot by hunters early on. It's my least favorite Disney movie because of that scene. It always made me cry. Hanna gets really quiet."

"You could say no."

"But maybe it's her way of…processing what happened to her mom. Is that necessarily unhealthy?"

His scowl deepened. "No. But I don't know. She should have counseling," he said brusquely.

Linnea hesitated. "Finn may not want to pay for it."

Anger flared in Matt's gray eyes, reminding her how cold they could be, but he bit back whatever he first wanted to say. After a discernible pause, he said, "If he won't, I will."

"Really? It can be awfully expensive. I wish I could help, but—"

"I have plenty of money put away. I'd have been happy to pay child support, but since your brother is presumably helping you with any extra costs—" He stopped. "He is, isn't he?"

She'd had to ask, which had embarrassed her and made her mad, but at least she could now say, "Yes, of course he is."

"All right. I don't know how you find the right person, but it seems to me Hanna ought to have someone neutral to talk to."

It hurt to think that Hanna didn't feel she could talk to her, but Linnea had to concede that he was right. Hanna wasn't doing much talking at all, which wasn't a good thing. She might not want to admit she was angry or scared or terribly sad. From a child's perspective, she might fear hurting Linnea's feelings.

"I'll call her pediatrician," she said. "I'll bet she can recommend someone." They'd reached the front door. "Are you still at the hotel?"

"No, I'm living at an extended-stay place. Sorry. I

meant to give you the contact info." He dug in a jeans pocket and produced a battered and muddy business card, which she took gingerly. "I backed out on the first rental," he told her, watching her face with an expression she read as wary. "I'm, uh, looking for one near here. I thought it might be best for Hanna if I was close. I hope that doesn't make you uncomfortable."

The idea of him living nearby, even mere blocks away, did unsettle her, maybe because of that unnerving aware-ness of him she couldn't seem to shake. But she pasted a smile on her face and said, "Of course not. That makes sense. Do you have furniture and stuff?" she asked.

"Some furniture, left from my parents'. I've had it all in storage. I don't remember what we kept. I might get lucky and find a furnished place. Otherwise…" He gave a careless shrug. "I'll start with the basics. A bed, a sofa, table and chairs."

"And pans and dishes and a can opener and silverware and—"

He held up his hand. "Stop. You're right. Good God, I don't even know where to start. You know, I haven't owned any of that stuff since college. We kept what we needed from home before we sold the house, so I've never actually bought any household goods."

"You're kidding," she said blankly.

He shook his head. "The places I've lived in since always came furnished and outfitted. I haven't even owned a car since I was in my early twenties."

"You sound as if you're really planning to stay."

He met her eyes, his own steady but…guarded. "I am."

Did that mean he was still going to try to take custody of Hanna from her? Linnea had let herself feel…safe, and now saw how foolish that had been. Even if he never challenged her for custody again, if he stayed in Seattle he would be over here constantly, not just in the next year, but for the next *twelve* years. She caught herself inching away, starting to push the door shut.

"Hold on," he said. "I left my shirt in the bathroom."

Linnea insisted on getting it while he waited. She brought it to him in a plastic bag. "If I'd had anything else for you to wear, I would have suggested running a load of laundry. I suppose you have to go to a laundromat."

"I read while I wait." There was a pause, him standing on her doorstep, her just inside with one hand on the door. "Thanks for today," he said finally. "Not only lunch, but—"

"This was the happiest I've seen Hanna since that night. This was a really good idea of yours."

"Maybe we can do it again next weekend."

"I don't see why not." She took a deep breath. "Would you like to come to dinner one night this week?"

His face relaxed. "Can I take the two of you out?"

"That would be fun," she decided.

They settled on Wednesday. He looked less…lonely as he left. Or maybe that had been in her imagination. Maybe he had a busy week planned. Somehow, though, she doubted it. She thought he was living for this time with Hanna.

And it simply wasn't in Linnea to deny it to him.

CHAPTER SIX

MATT FOUND A PARKING SPOT in front of Bed Bath & Beyond, a store whose door he'd never darkened. He hadn't been kidding when he'd told Linnea he had never had to shop for household stuff. Sure, he'd purchased coffeemakers; rentals never had decent ones. But can openers, pancake turners, towels... He wasn't picky about any of them.

Funny thing today, though, was that having Hanna and Linnea along meant he was enjoying the idea of shopping for all of the above. He had signed a rental agreement two days ago, and yesterday had moved into a house not much different from Linnea's, and less than a quarter of a mile from hers. Once Hanna changed schools over midwinter break, she would be able to walk to his house as well as Linnea's after school. He was determined to furnish the second bedroom so she felt it was hers.

Hanna had been excited about this expedition, Linnea less so but tempted, he thought.

"This would be a good chance for you to spend time with her alone," she had suggested.

"But neither of us have ever bought a toaster or sheets." He'd stopped. "The thread-count thing. What does it mean? Is it worth spending more for three hundred thread count instead of two hundred and fifty? I don't know. I'm hoping you do. Do I really need a doormat? Do I—"

She had laughed and sighed all at the same time. "Okay, okay. I'm convinced. You need my wisdom and guidance. Heaven knows what you and Hanna would pick out on your own."

"Pink. All pink, if it were up to Hanna."

Her voice brimmed with amusement. "Oh, come on. She'd throw in a little purple."

Two weeks into the parenting plan, and he was well satisfied with how it was going. All three of them had played soccer several times, after which it was assumed Matt would stay for lunch. Last Saturday they had gotten lucky with the weather, given that it was November, and had taken the ferry to Vashon Island. Hanna had insisted on staying outside the whole way over and back. She was positive she'd see an orca, but even though no pod had been obliging enough to be cruising that particular stretch of the sound, she seemed to enjoy herself.

One Sunday Matt had taken his niece to a movie on their own, after Linnea told him she had plans with a friend. Animated movies, he discovered, had changed a hell of a lot since he was a kid. This one was sharp and funny. He and Hanna shared a small bucket of popcorn, and she grabbed his hand happily on the way out to the car.

Halfway home, she did say, "I wish Aunt Linnie had come with us. She would have liked the movie, too."

Maybe his feelings should have been hurt, but the truth was he'd kept wishing Linnea was with them, too. He'd have liked to exchange a smile with her over Hanna's blond head, bump Linnea's hand with his when they reached for popcorn at the same time, hear her startled giggle.

He had to keep reminding himself that having Hanna get to be as comfortable with him as she was with Linnea was the point. Lusting after Linnea, savoring her laugh, imagining the taste of her lips was dangerous.

But damn, was it easy for him to be diverted from the main goal.

So here they were now, heading into a store where, Linnea had assured him, he could not only buy linens but also get a start on kitchen stuff.

"Why don't we start with the comforter and sheets for Hanna?" Linnea suggested on the way in. "In case…" She gave their niece a significant look.

A kid her age got bored. Matt guessed maybe a six-year-old would have a limited attention span.

"Good idea," he agreed.

Hanna turned out to be decisive, pouncing with delight at a pink—big surprise—comforter with fairy-tale castles, princesses with flowing blond hair and unicorns. It turned out to be a bed-in-a-bag, which meant matching sheets and pillowcases were included.

Linnea steered them next to choose mattress pads for both their beds, then on to the towel department. The house had two bathrooms, so he let Hanna choose pink and purple towels and bathmat for hers, while he went with forest green for his.

"Now my bedroom," he declared, turning Hanna to point her in the right direction.

"Why don't I go start looking at kitchen things?" Linnea suggested. "You can catch up with me there. Or us, if Hanna wants to come with me."

"Not a chance," he said, interested in the extra-casual tone of her voice, belied by the rosy cast to her cheeks.

She was embarrassed to help him pick out sheets. Maybe because she wouldn't be able to help picturing him between them. "Remember the mystery of thread count?"

Her eyes narrowed. "Come on. You've slept on sheets your entire adult life. You must have some idea what you like."

Yeah, he did. He liked the idea of her thinking about him in bed. He liked that so much, he was uncomfortably aroused here in the aisle of a linen store.

Matt had to clear his throat to be sure his voice wasn't hoarse. "I never looked at labels."

Her suspicious stare slid away from him, as if she'd seen something in his eyes that made her self-conscious. "Oh, fine," she muttered.

Even as he got her talking about how silky sheets should be and what was worth paying for, he wondered what in hell he was playing at.

We're spending time together for Hanna's sake, he reminded himself. *I'm using Linnea. I'm going to break her heart when I take Hanna away, remember?*

He wanted to be friends with Linnea. Just…not such good friends he felt guilty at stealing his niece from her.

Matt hoisted Hanna to his shoulders and laughed at her when she gripped his hair. Then he smiled at Linnea. "Let's start with flannel. What do you think, navy or green?"

She laughed at him. "I don't know. You could live wild and go for, say, brown. Or that dark purple." She read the label. "Eggplant."

"Purple," he said, in pretend disgust. "I don't think so."

"Uncle Matt!" Hanna drummed her heels on his chest. "Purple is pretty!"

He grinned up at her. "But I'm not."

"Oh, I don't know," Linnea said, after which her face flooded with color and she turned quickly away. "I'll go look at the regular sheets."

Desire tightened his body. "Forest green," he said, and tossed the set of flannel sheets in the cart before following Linnea.

"DID YOU BRUSH YOUR TEETH?" Linnea asked her niece, who rolled her eyes and said with exaggerated patience, "Yes, Aunt Linnie."

Matt hid his smile.

"You ready to be tucked in?"

The little girl nodded.

"How about if I let Uncle Matt do the honors?"

Hanna stole a look at him and shyly nodded again.

Linnea hugged her and gave her a kiss.

Matt felt ridiculously proud to be escorting a six-year-old down the hall. He'd been promoted. She trusted him. *Hot damn,* he thought in amusement mixed with pleasure.

Three weeks into the parenting plan, and he'd been promoted.

"Aunt Linnie always reads me another story once I'm in bed," Hanna told him.

"I'm up for that," he agreed, and let her choose a picture book.

He'd noticed before that she liked stories aimed at children considerably younger than her. When he'd asked, Linnea told him that since Tess's death Hanna had gone for some of the simplest, most comforting books, including classics for very young children like *Goodnight Moon.* Natural, he supposed. Didn't children typically regress with trauma? And also he guessed that she was clinging to the memory of her mother reading those stories to her.

Tonight she choose a longer one, about a warhorse named Clyde who was secretly terrified of everything and had to find his core of courage. The appeal to her wasn't subtle, he thought. She listened in rapt, wide-eyed silence, then slid down in her bed and let him pull the covers up, then kiss her forehead.

"Good night, Hanna Banana."

She chuckled sleepily. "Night, Uncle Matt." She stirred when he turned out the bedroom light. "Aunt Linnie leaves on the hall light. And she says it's okay if my door is open a little bit."

"Like this?" He adjusted the door to leave a six-inch crack.

"Uh-huh."

"Good night," he said again, and went to the kitchen.

Linnea stood at the stove. "Would you like tea or coffee?"

He'd been expecting her to be hovering to walk him to the front door. Surprised and pleased about this, too, he said agreeably, "Whatever you're having."

She nodded and poured boiling water into two mugs, then carried them to the table. "It's MarketSpice tea," she said. "I'm addicted."

Tess, too, had liked the tea made by the Seattle company. Matt recognized the rich fragrance.

"How's the week gone?" he asked, as she sat down.

This was Thursday night, and he hadn't seen her or Hanna since the Saturday shopping trip.

From the moment he stepped back into the kitchen, he noticed how much shyer she was than when Hanna was here. Linnea did relax sometimes, such as when they played their weekly game of soccer, but otherwise she was getting less comfortable with him, not more.

My fault.

Matt couldn't look at her anymore without being conscious of her quiet beauty, and all she had to do was smile or stretch or turn her head a certain way to give him a teeth-gritting jolt of pure lust. Obviously, he hadn't hidden his reaction as well as he'd intended to.

When she didn't immediately answer, he said, "You look tired."

Her eyes met his in surprise, and color touched her cheeks. "I am." She bit her lip. "Actually that's what I was hoping to talk to you about."

He waited, watching worries and hesitation cross her face so subtly he once wouldn't have been able to identify them. It bothered him that she had learned somewhere along the line to disguise her emotions so well.

He was fast becoming an expert on reading Linnea. How could he help it, he thought ruefully, paying as much attention as he had been?

Sounding determined, Linnea said, "To start with, Hanna doesn't want me to leave her at all. Just this last— I was going to say this week, but actually a couple of days the week before… But it's getting worse. I swear, every morning, I have to pry her fingers off me and practically push her in the classroom door. She doesn't cry, but she's so stiff—" Linnea broke off. "It's awful."

"Why now?"

"I don't know," she cried. "It's as if—"

"She's afraid you won't come back to get her."

She bent her head and her voice came out on a soft sigh. "Yes."

"Do you want me to drive her some days?"

He hadn't offered before; he'd been very careful thus far not to ask for more time with Hanna than the parenting plan prescribed. But it was ridiculous that Linnea, who was working more than full-time between her two jobs, should also be chauffeuring Hanna to school and home, when he had so much time on his hands he was desperate for occupation. He had started to do some serious job hunting, but hadn't seen what he wanted yet.

"Would you?" she said. "Maybe she won't cling to you the same way."

He knew what she meant, but felt a pang nonetheless. Hanna liked him, was coming to trust him, but she had latched on to Linnea with fierce and frightened love. The counselor Hanna was now seeing weekly said it was natural and unlikely to diminish until her permanent placement was established.

In other words, Matt thought grimly, until she knew whether she was going to be forced to live with her father.

"Sure," he said. "I'm looking for a job, but I'm not in any hurry. I can take her every morning if you want, or pick her up any day."

"I'm off Mondays. Could you do Tuesday and Thursday?"

When he agreed, relief suffused her face. "With traffic heavy, it can take nearly half an hour each way. I'm having to leave her early, which doesn't help. Mrs. Harris is fine with having Hanna sit and read until the other kids get there, but it must be boring for Hanna. She might be less clingy if other kids were arriving at the same time."

Matt made note of her doubtful tone.

She sighed again. "I can hardly wait until Christmas break. The only thing is I'm worried that she'll be scared of starting a new school. Maybe this isn't the best time. We could wait until summer—"

He was shaking his head before she finished. "It will be scary for her. Isn't it always for kids? But it's not as though she's happy about going to school now. I wonder..."

When he hesitated, Linnea finished, "Whether going back to part of her normal life isn't even more upsetting?"

"Maybe on some level she thinks she'll be going to her after-school care or that Tess will be picking her up."

"Or her dad," Linnea murmured.

Matt said nothing.

"I'm half-dreading Thanksgiving."

So was he, but for different reasons. "Because Finn will be there?" He was proud of his tone, a hell of a lot milder than he felt.

"I suppose." She took a sip of her tea, her blue eyes meeting his. "Finn came to see Hanna this week."

Matt's whole body went rigid. "Did he."

He knew Hanna was seeing her father when she went to her grandparents' house, but, unless Linnea was keeping it from him, this was the first time Finn had made the effort to visit here.

"I know you'd rather she didn't see him, but I was ordered to give him supervised visitation. I think it's been hard for Hanna to understand why she only sees her father at Grandma and Granddad's. Parents are supposed to be part of your everyday life. You know? She's talked to him on the phone, too, but it's not the same."

He nodded.

"The thing is, it didn't go very well. The visit, I mean."

Matt would love to hear that Hanna had completely rejected her father.

"She was shy, and that made him mad."

No wonder, he couldn't help thinking, that Linnea had purplish shadows beneath her eyes. She hadn't had a good week.

Very carefully, he asked, "Mad in what way?"

Linnea gave him a look. "Not what you're thinking. I've told you before, I don't think Finn has ever even thought about hitting Hanna. Why would he, when—" She screeched to a stop, all but burning rubber, her eyes widening.

"When he's so good at stripping a layer of skin off with his tongue?"

"He's my brother." She sounded miserable.

"We both know him. I wish I'd realized years ago that you didn't like him."

Her chin came up. "Why? Would you have deigned to speak to me?"

Okay. She knew how to hit him where it hurt.

"I jumped to conclusions. If I hadn't, we'd have gotten to know each other then. Maybe that would have made this—" he gestured to encompass her kitchen and their still-wary relationship "—easier."

"Maybe." She didn't sound so sure.

"Not that we could have anticipated a situation like this."

"No."

His eyes narrowed. She didn't sound entirely sure of that, either. Or was he imagining things? With rare exceptions, Linnea tended to be diffident when expressing her opinions, as though wanting to convey that she could be wrong.

Anger backed up in his throat, but he was careful not to let it show on his face. He took a sip of tea.

"This clinginess," he said. "Is that all—"

A scream tore through the small house.

Swearing, he leaped to his feet, the chair falling backward.

Rising more slowly, Linnea said, "She's having nightmares, too."

"God."

The cat came shooting out of Hanna's bedroom and vanished into Linnea's. The two adults hurried down the hall, wrenched by the gasping sobs. Matt crowded in behind Linnea, who immediately sank onto the edge of the bed and gathered Hanna into her arms.

"Pumpkin, it's all right. I'm here, honey," she murmured, in a voice as soft and loving as any he'd ever heard in his life. "I'm here."

Hanna cried more quietly against her aunt's breast. Matt stood, feeling both helpless and useless. What if he'd insisted on an overnight at his house and she'd had this kind of nightmare? He doubted that she would find in him the comfort she did in her aunt Linnie.

Linnea rocked her and cuddled and murmured until Hanna was ready to lie down. She let out a sad sniff, turned her head on the pillow and seemed to fall asleep in an instant.

Linnea gestured at him and they both slipped silently out of the bedroom and all but tiptoed down the hall to the kitchen.

"How often does she have these?" he asked.

She collapsed in her chair as if exhaustion had tackled her. "A couple of times a night."

Matt swore again as he righted his own chair and sat. "You can't go on this way."

Her spine stiffened. "Of course I can. Kids have nightmares. Parents—adults—comfort them. It's nowhere near as tiring as having a newborn."

He reached across the table and laid his hand over hers, feeling the quivering intensity in it. She gave a small jerk, as if he'd startled her.

"Of course you can." He made his voice a soothing rumble. "I didn't mean it. Just that I'm worried about you." In the face of her shocked stare, he added, "And Hanna. Have you talked to her counselor?"

Linnea's shoulders sagged, as if the momentary fight had left her. Her hand went slack, and after a moment he took his back.

She said, "Sonja was surprised Hanna hadn't started having nightmares sooner. Unfortunately, she either doesn't remember them or doesn't want to tell us what they're about. I've thought about letting her sleep with me in hopes she'd feel safer, but Sonja didn't recommend it."

Matt nodded, imagining the separation issues Hanna would have when Aunt Linnie wanted her to go back to sleeping in her own bed. She likely wasn't selfish enough to regret her lost privacy, despite being used to living alone.

Had a man ever spent the night in her bed? Matt had seen no sign of a boyfriend, but that didn't mean there wasn't one. The idea didn't sit well with him, he discovered, and knew damn well why.

He almost grunted. If nothing else, she'd be afraid he would take advantage of any indiscretion on her part to snatch custody from her.

No, that was a dumb thought. All he had to do was look

at Linnea to know she wasn't the kind of woman who would entertain a man in her bedroom while her six-year-old niece was down the hall. In fact, having caught a glimpse of Linnea's bedroom, he had trouble picturing a man in it at all. The antique bed was covered with a fluffy white spread and heaps of lace-edged and quilted pillows in palest pink and cream and white. What he'd seen was a virginal bower designed to make a man feel clumsy and crude. Or maybe designed with no idea that a man would ever stumble into it.

"You're quiet." Tiny puckers had formed on Linnea's forehead. "What are you thinking?"

Nothing he could tell her. "Worrying," he said.

After a minute she nodded. "Me, too."

"I wish there was something I could do."

Her eyes widened as she looked at him, and he'd have given one hell of a lot to tell what she was thinking. "If you weren't here…" she said softly.

Guilt roughened his words. "You wouldn't have had to fight me for custody and have one more stress." No, it was worse than that: she wouldn't have to live with knowing she was still going to have to fight him for Hanna.

"That's not what I was going to say. I'd have been alone. Instead, I know—" Her hesitation was microscopic, but noticeable. "I know I can depend on you."

She meant it well, but Matt took it like a blow. Sure, she could depend on him—two days a week, when he saw her and Hanna. The rest of the time, she was on her own even as she lived with the uncertainty of the future.

He wanted to be there for the nightmares. No, not just that. He wanted to be a part of Linnea's and Hanna's mornings and their evenings and everything in between.

Definitely there for the nights, Matt thought, wondering what the pretty, blonde woman still watching him would do if he kissed her.

Scream and scramble away, probably. Stare at him with dilated, frightened eyes. Lose what trust she had in him.

Concentrate on Hanna. This was a really lousy time to be thinking below the belt.

"You were right. I was wrong," he said abruptly. "She is better off with you." *For now.*

Now her gaze turned grateful, and he felt like crud. He would hurt even Linnea if that was the only way he could keep Hanna away from Finn.

"I'd better say good-night." He pushed to his feet again. He had to get out of here before he said or did something he'd regret.

"Yes." Linnea sprang up as if propelled. "Gosh, I didn't mean to keep you so late."

Either something in his expression had shaken her, or she'd been having dangerous thoughts of her own. Either way, she was suddenly eager for him to leave.

He went, pausing at the front door to say, "Call me if you need me." As he faced her, it was all he could do not to lift a hand to touch her cheek, brush strands of hair behind her ears.

She nodded. "Um...I meant to ask. What are you doing for Thanksgiving?"

Surprised, Matt said, "Probably nothing special." He sure as hell wouldn't join the Sorensens even if asked.

"Well, I wondered if you'd like to come here Friday. We'll have Thanksgiving Thursday at my parents', but—" Clearly she didn't want to say, *we won't enjoy it.* In a rush, she finished, "I could cook a turkey Friday and we'd have leftovers of our own and—" She swallowed. "We could celebrate. The three of us."

Oh, damn. He was rarely emotional enough to find himself without words. This time, it was a minute before he could clear his throat and manage to say, "I'd like that."

"Good." Her smile was both sweet and gentle, as if she knew she'd touched him. "Then I'll see you Friday. About noon?"

"Tuesday morning," he said hoarsely, "I'll take Hanna to school."

"Right. Tuesday morning. Eight-thirty?"

Out of long habit he was up by seven at the latest anyway. "Eight-thirty," he agreed.

"Okay. See you then." She shut the door, leaving him standing on her porch wanting back in.

Chronic state these days.

Making himself turn away and walk to his car at the curb, he thought it was past time he started building a life of his own, rather than hovering on the edges of hers.

CHAPTER SEVEN

LINNEA'S DEEP RELUCTANCE made her realize how much she'd come to hate all family holidays. They felt like command performances; she had never quite dared make other plans, with the exception of one Thanksgiving when she'd gone on a cruise with friends from the library. Her mother hadn't been happy.

Hanna withdrew noticeably during the drive to her grandparents', and, sneaking glances at her, Linnea couldn't helping remembering Finn's visit last week.

He'd been annoyed from the beginning at his daughter's shyness with him. He had—mostly—kept himself from saying anything too scathing to Hanna, but on the way out the door, he'd glowered at Linnea and said, "I can see this was a mistake. You're going to turn my daughter into a terrified mouse like you. For God's sake, at least she used to have some spirit."

That night Hanna had lain tense in bed, unable to sleep but also unwilling to articulate what she felt about her dad. When Linnea asked if she wanted to talk about the visit, she shook her head so hard her hair flew. Linnea felt very nearly violent toward her brother. She wished with all her heart that the commissioner had ruled against any visitation with Finn.

But then…what would happen if he was found innocent? He could reclaim his daughter, who would no longer know him at all.

If she ever had.

Oh, Linnea wished with all her heart that today was over and it was already tomorrow morning and the turkey was in the oven, starting to smell good, and she and Hanna were anticipating Matt's arrival.

But it wasn't tomorrow. And today was still to be endured.

Which was an awful attitude, she thought. She would *try*. Maybe Finn would be in a good mood, and he would tease his small daughter the way he used to and Hanna would giggle for him and they would feel like a family again.

No such luck. There were hugs all around when they arrived, and Linnea immediately began to help in the kitchen while Hanna sat on her granddad's lap. Finn had never been required to do women's chores; when they were growing up, their family had been completely traditional. Finn did carve the turkey, because Dad's hands were too shaky these days.

But the minute they sat to eat, Finn took over the conversation. Their mother agreed with everything he said.

He broke off once to ask Hanna if she missed her own house, a question that froze Linnea with her fork halfway to her mouth. Was he kidding? It gave her the creeps that *he* could continue to live there, in a home imbued with Tess, who had lovingly decorated it. How could he sit in the family room, where Tess had died, or stand in the kitchen where he'd be able to see the exact spot where she'd bled into the carpet?

Hanna gave her father a startled, scared look, then ducked her head and mumbled something unintelligible.

"For goodness' sake, speak up!" her grandmother snapped. "And look at you. You've hardly eaten a bite. Don't waste good food, Hanna. In this house, once you dish it up, you eat it."

Looking like she was going to choke on them, Hanna forked a couple of green beans into her mouth.

Finn was still watching her, his gaze brooding. "You'd think I was a stranger," he complained to all of them.

"It's been months, and she's hardly seen you," Linnea said, trying to keep her tone mild.

"I'm her father."

Hanna hunched her shoulders.

He swore. "I'm working on a defense so our lives can go back to normal. Isn't that what I should be doing?"

"Of course it is, Finn," their mother soothed. "This whole thing is absurd. Every day I wake up and wonder how this could be happening when Tess's accident was so obviously exactly that."

"Mom," Linnea said quietly, nodding toward Hanna. "Please."

"Well!" her mother said tartly. "What else should I talk about? Finn is right. Until this is over, all of us have to be focused on it."

"Hanna is six." Linnea glared impatiently at her mother and her brother. "It's the last thing she should be thinking about."

"Ah, I think I'll skip the pie for now," her father said, easing away from the table. He patted his stomach. "Maybe a little later."

Frustrated, Linnea watched him disappear toward

his study. Movements jerky, she stood and began clearing the table.

As if grateful for an excuse, Hanna joined her to help clean the kitchen. Linnea was wiping counters and Hanna was putting away pans she'd dried when Finn, still talking to their mother in the dining room, changed topics from what imbeciles the police were and said impatiently, "Having Hanna living at Linnea's isn't working. You and Dad can take her, can't you?"

Out of the corner of her eye, Linnea saw Hanna go still. Fury greater than she had ever felt rose in her. For her niece, she kept her voice calm. "Why don't you go get your coat, honey? We're going home."

Then she marched into the dining room and said, "You do know Hanna and I heard that? To suggest you'd take her away from me right now when she's already feeling terribly insecure is cruel. I am not a nanny you can dismiss. I'm her aunt. Hanna loves me. And right now, *I* have legal custody. Not you, not Mom and Dad."

Her brother's face reddened. "You think I couldn't take her away from you in a heartbeat if I put my mind to it? Don't mess with me, sis. Hanna is mine."

"We're going home," she said flatly, and walked out despite his rising voice behind her.

"Linnea, you come back here right this minute," her mother called.

Linnea was quaking inside as she hustled Hanna into the car and locked all the doors while she started the engine. She half expected the front door of her parents' house to fly open and Finn to charge out to prevent her from leaving. Even though he didn't come after them, she didn't quit trembling until they were blocks away.

"Your dad was venting," she said to Hanna. "He's scared with the trial, and I'm sure he misses you. He didn't mean what he said. I promise you'll stay with me. Okay?"

Eyes huge and dilated, Hanna studied her face for at least two blocks before she nodded. "I love you, Aunt Linnie."

Fury still burning in her chest, Linnea whispered, "I love you, too."

Quarreling with Finn had been a huge mistake, she was afraid. He would make a very bad enemy. But she had to somehow make him see that Hanna's needs should come ahead of his wounded ego. Surely, he loved his daughter at least that much.

Linnea prayed he wouldn't come over tomorrow to confront her. If Finn arrived angry on her doorstep while Matt was there…

She wouldn't answer the door. *I don't have to,* she thought, surprised at how defiant she had become. What was it Matt had said about how, in killing Tess, Finn had forfeited his rights to his daughter? She couldn't remember the exact words, but she felt the same. Finn didn't deserve Hanna.

For the very first time ever, Linnea let herself admit that he never *had* deserved her. As a little girl herself, Linnea had loved her brother. She still wanted to believe Finn hadn't meant to kill Tess. That the police misunderstood what happened or at least that Finn had picked up the coffee table and thrown it without actually intending to hit his wife. He always had thrown things and kicked furniture when he was mad.

But whether he'd committed second-degree murder or had merely been criminally careless in his hotheaded way and was now lying about it, he wasn't a nice man.

Linnea had been afraid of his razor-sharp tongue for most of her life. She hadn't figured out how she would fight her brother if he wasn't convicted, but she had made up her mind: Finn couldn't have Hanna back.

Ever.

MATT HAD SPENT THE WEEK anticipating Friday. Holidays meant something to him. His mother had loved traditions. Miniature pumpkins and gourds had spilled out of a cornucopia in the center of every Thanksgiving table when he was growing up. Certain foods were always served come Thanksgiving or Christmas Day. The outside lights had gone up on the eaves the day after Thanksgiving, regular as clockwork. Once when he was seven or eight, he had helped his dad put them up. And Mom was always firm about gifts: they could all open one on Christmas Eve, but the rest had to wait until Christmas morning. Beloved ornaments might get shabby, but they went on the tree anyway.

He thought about those ornaments, which had spent years in storage along with some of the furniture from his parents' house, Mom's best china, the log-cabin quilt Dad's grandmother had pieced by hand. Matt had told Tess to take anything she wanted once she had a home of her own, but after graduating from college she had shared various apartments with friends and never had room for much. Then once she married Finn… Nothing from their childhood seemed to fit into the home she and Finn had made. Their Christmas tree had a color scheme—silver and mauve one year, gold and red another.

Well, who was he to talk? At least Tess had made a home. Matt himself had gone from a Norman Rockwell childhood to a rootless adult career. There hadn't actually been a conscious choice—just one job leading to another, until it *was* his life. He had to guess that their parents wouldn't have been thrilled with the choices either of them had made.

Or, hell, maybe they would have understood. Tragedy had a way of severing past from future. He had raised his sister; there was never any question that he would do so. But since then he'd been careful to make no personal commitments to anybody but his sister and niece.

He didn't like the fact that it had taken Tess's death to motivate the change, but he found that he was happy about finally settling down. One of the best parts of renting a house had been closing out the storage unit and moving everything to his garage. Matt had been happy to see how much of the furniture from their family home he and Tess had kept. Two bed frames, a pair of dressers, the dining-room table and chairs, and an antique rocking chair Mom had used to rock him and Tess to sleep when they were babies went a long way to furnishing the small house.

Tradition.

Thanksgiving Day itself, he went for a run in Lincoln Park, then pretended he was content reading in front of a fire. He made burritos for dinner and tried not to think about last Thanksgiving, when he had flown to Seattle to be with Tess and Hanna. He hated the vivid memory of saying goodbye to both of them at the airport, or the way they'd lingered to make faces at him, laugh and wave until he disappeared through security. What if he had known then that his sister would be dead before a year had passed, that his niece would seem more like a ghost than a vibrant little girl when he next saw her?

Friday at noon on the nose he presented himself at Linnea's house. A joyous thunder of feet presaged Hanna flinging open the door. "Uncle Matt! You're here! Wait'll you smell the turkey. I'm *so-o* hungry, but Aunt Linnie says it won't be done for an hour and I can snack if I want but not too much or I won't be hungry anymore when we eat. But she's opening a can of olives 'cause I really like black olives. Do you like them?"

"Yeah, I do," he said, startled by the transformation from Tuesday's subdued child to today's ebullient one. He'd have guessed that she'd had a good Thanksgiving at her grandparents' house, except she seemed more manic than joyful. Maybe what she felt today was relief. "I like green ones, too."

"Eew," she declared, leading him to the kitchen where Linnea was peeling potatoes.

He took in Linnea's appearance swiftly. She'd dressed up for the day, wearing a short black skirt over black tights or leggings of some kind, and an apron over a pale blue sweater that looked like cashmere. The bow of the apron emphasized her slender waist and drew his eye to the perfect curves below it, outlined by that stretchy black fabric.

He had it bad, Matt thought, as he tore his gaze from her incredible legs and butt.

To please Hanna, he inhaled. "You're right. It does smell great. Now I'm hungry, too."

"Have a carrot stick," Linnea told him, laughing. Her eyes sparkled as if, like Hanna, she was in a fabulous mood. Maybe because of the hot oven, her color was high, but he thought she'd put on more makeup than usual, too. Because it was a holiday and she wanted to look pretty? Would she believe him if he told her she always did?

To distract himself he grabbed a handful of those black olives she'd put out in a cut glass dish, then said, "What can I do?"

"You're a guest. For goodness' sake, you don't have to do anything."

"No reason you have to do all the work." He took the potato peeler out of her hand and nudged her away with his shoulder. "This I can handle. You can do something else."

She tried to argue, but he started peeling and she gave up. Next thing he knew, she was making cranberry sauce from scratch, something his mother had done. Now his mouth was watering.

Hanna spread an ivory lace cloth on the small table, then set it with great care, repositioning the silverware several times. Matt watched her sidelong, and he and Linnea exchanged smiles when their glances intersected. When the turkey came out of the oven, he dug out the stuffing and carved while she made gravy and Hanna, standing on a step stool, mashed the potatoes.

"See?" he observed, after they'd sat and said a simple grace, then started passing serving dishes. "We can help, can't we, Banana?"

His niece's ponytail bounced emphatically. "Yes! I was good at mashing, wasn't I, Aunt Linnie?"

"Very good." Linnea leaned over to kiss her cheek. "And you're right. A group effort was more fun."

Looking at the food, then at the woman and child across the table, faces glowing, Matt was hit by the stunning realization that this might be the best Thanksgiving he'd had since his parents died. There had been good ones with Tess and then with Tess and Hanna, but those holidays had never been without complications or undercurrents. For the past eight years, on those occasions Matt had made it to the States, Finn had been there, too.

Today, grief should be a heavier weight than it was. He felt it—a shadow on his mood, a flicker of longing to hear his sister's laugh, to see her impudent grin. But he also had the startling realization that Linnea was becoming important to him. So important, he didn't like the idea of the day without her, or with her no more than a ghostly presence that barely registered on him, as had once been the case.

He and Hanna and Linnea... They felt like family. The kind he'd grown up with, and had, he realized, craved ever since.

So why, he asked himself, had he lived an essentially solitary life from the moment he'd fulfilled his obligation to Tess?

The answer to his question wasn't hard to find. He still remembered how he'd felt when the uniformed officer told him that both his parents were dead. He was a sophomore in college. *Home* was still his parents' house. He'd been a long way from being ready to let go. He hadn't only lost two of the three people he loved most in the world, he'd lost his foundation.

So, okay. He'd been running ever since from what he wanted most: a home, love, a true sense of security. He guessed he'd been too afraid that, if he tried for a real family, he'd end up devastated again.

But now... Stunned, Matt realized how much he wanted what was surely an illusion to be reality.

This was the family he wanted.

CAREFULLY CARRYING THE BOX of cupcakes she'd picked up at a bakery, Linnea walked down the broad hall at

Hanna's elementary school. She smiled at the bustle she saw through open classroom doors, not envying the teachers trying to contain their students' excitement. Today was the last day before Christmas break, and probably most of the classes were holding a party as Hanna's was.

She had already stopped at the office to sign in and get a badge. While she was there she scanned the list quickly to see if Matt had arrived yet. He might not come; he hadn't promised Hanna because he had a job interview today and didn't know how long it would last.

The night before last at dinner he'd told her and Hanna about the job, the first that had interested him since he'd begun looking.

"It's similar to what I was doing, although in this case the company primarily designs and builds manufacturing facilities. More modestly sized than most of what I was working on, but they've done some work on Northwest ports, too, including here in Seattle. I like having a completely different challenge each time, and this might offer that. We'll see."

He'd sounded nonchalant about the interview, but she knew how bored he'd become since his return.

Linnea wondered whether, if he started working, they'd see as much of him. She tried not to be dismayed at the idea. Thank goodness Hanna's holiday break had come, to be followed by her start at a new school. No more need for help chauffeuring.

Of course, he did a whole lot more than that. He was at her house at least briefly every day or two. The parenting plan had gone by the wayside in the nearly seven weeks since they had hammered it out with their attorneys. Those weeks had gone so fast, she thought in amazement, and yet…she could hardly remember a time when Matt didn't come to dinner at least one weeknight, and when he didn't spend a good part of every weekend with Hanna and often with Linnea, too.

Linnea hardly even knew how it had happened, him becoming such a part of the fabric of her life. The custody agreement had implied that he would have Hanna some of the time, her the rest of the time. At first, it had been natural that she was included when he came to see Hanna. Matt had said he could be patient, and he meant it. But the time had long since come when he could have picked her up for his weekends, when he and Linnea shouldn't be having to see each other more than to exchange hellos, goodbyes and information about the little girl they both loved.

Instead, they'd somehow fallen into routines. There was soccer, there were movies and walks on the beach at Lincoln Park. Linnea had enrolled Hanna in swim lessons at her health club, and one or the other of them and sometimes both took her and watched. Pizza out, dinners in.

He'd had them to dinner at his house, too. It was still sparsely furnished, but she liked knowing that much of what was in the house had been his parents' or, in the case of an armoire he had in the study and a marble-topped walnut commode that was in the living room, had been passed down from his grandparents.

Disconcertingly, this past month, since Thanksgiving, he had taken to touching her. Often. A light pressure on the small of her back to guide her, a hand on her shoulder, a brush of his shoulders. It was never in a way she could take offense at or even evade without letting him know how self-conscious he made her.

And she couldn't bear to do that. Some days he was all she could think about, which embarrassed her, given that she couldn't imagine he saw her in a romantic or even sexual way. If she was the kind of woman who attracted him, he'd have noticed her during those years when he was visiting Tess. He might not have liked being attracted to her then because she was Finn's sister, but he wouldn't have looked through her as if she were invisible, either.

It made her cringe to imagine him guessing how attracted she was to him. Most of the time now, they had such an easy relationship. What if she jeopardized that?

It was bad enough that they were already having to pretend the here and now was all that existed. To pretend not to be thinking about the what-ifs.

What if Finn gets off and tries to take Hanna back? What if he's convicted, and Matt contests again for custody? What if he wins? What if I win, once and for all?

They both knew one or the other of them would be devastated. So yes, their friendship now was nothing more than the hot-fudge covering the chill of ice cream hidden beneath, but she treasured it anyway.

A couple of women walking ahead of Linnea went into Hanna's classroom. Since they hadn't seen her trailing behind and had closed the door behind them, she was able to pause outside, pretending to admire the artwork hung on the wall. Students had glued cotton balls to construction-paper cutout Santas. Really, Linnea was collecting herself, preparing to hide this ridiculous awareness she felt for Matt before he, too, showed up and inevitably planted himself beside her. If she knew him, he'd be so close his arm would brush her shoulder. When he turned his head to smile at her, he'd be near enough to bend his head and kiss her if he chose.

Which, of course, he didn't. Why would she appeal to him, anyway? she wondered in deep depression. It wasn't that men didn't flirt with her sometimes; she knew she was pretty and her figure was adequate. But those men were most often the quiet, even shy ones, the ones vivid, exciting, beautiful women never noticed. For example, the guy who owned the pet-supply store where she bought Spooky's food got tongue-tied and blushed whenever she came in, although he hadn't worked up the nerve to start much of a conversation. And, while she felt shallow thinking it, the truth was that he was skinny and wore a scruffy goatee to hide what she thought was a weak chin.

Men like Matt Laughlin never saw her.

Well, he did now, of course. Once in a while she even imagined that his gaze lingered on her breasts or her mouth and that she saw his eyes darken, as if he liked what he saw. It was probably part of the playacting, given that he played the role of Hanna's father while she played Hanna's mother.

Linnea did not want to have a terrible crush on a man who wouldn't have noticed her in a million years were it not for *proximity*.

She'd been clutching at the hope that proximity was her problem, too. He'd turn almost any woman's head, after all, with his build and the intensity of his gray eyes. How could she help but feel a stirring of…whatever it was she did feel?

With a sigh she reached for the doorknob, but turned her head to glance down the hall. As she'd brooded, it had filled with parents heading for one classroom or another.

The majority were women, which meant that Matt was a head taller than the crowd as he strode toward her. What could she do but wait?

Usually she saw him in casual clothes—jeans, chinos and sweats. The only exceptions were the hearing before the commissioner and his sister's funeral, both occasions so daunting she hadn't really focused on his appearance. Today he wore a dark suit, crisp white shirt and deep red tie. His face was still tanned above that white shirt from the Kuwaiti sun, his dark hair a little longer than when he'd first arrived, as if he hadn't bothered to get it cut. He wasn't exactly handsome, not like a model, but he had a quality of raw masculinity that was more breathtaking.

And somehow she had failed to pull herself together in time.

"Hey," he said, his gaze zeroing in on her face.

She smiled, hoping he couldn't see her pulse pounding in her throat. "How did the interview go?"

"Well, I think—" he sounded satisfied "—I'll take it if they offer the job."

"Oh, good." Thank heavens two mothers she knew were coming down the hall behind him, and she was able to greet them, then open the classroom door.

Hanna beamed at them from her desk across the room. Mrs. Harris, a young woman only in her second year of teaching, greeted the newcomers and directed them to the long table where they could deposit their offerings for the party.

"Was I supposed to bring something?" Matt murmured in Linnea's ear.

"No, the cupcakes are Hanna's contribution. No double jeopardy."

He nodded. Then, as she'd predicted, placed a hand on her lower back to steer her to one side, by the windows. As if she couldn't figure out where to go without his help. Darn it, she should resent that masterful touch, but instead it made her knees go weak. That was particularly infuriating considering his touches were always so casual, as if he were unconscious of them. If his hand seemed to linger this time, his fingers to flex for an instant in something like a caress, she had to be imagining it.

She struck up a conversation with the woman beside her as other parents arrived. There were a couple of fathers, so Matt wasn't the only man present. Not, she suspected, that he would have minded one way or the other, and Hanna was wriggling with delight because they were there.

Had Finn ever come to one of her classroom events? Linnea tried to remember Hanna ever saying but couldn't. Most often, Mom and Dad had stood in for Tess and Finn both, because they could never get away from work.

Mrs. Harris spoke about the upcoming school break; her voice was soft but her control over twenty-seven students was impressive. She hoped they'd all have fun, and she added solemnly that Hanna Sorensen wouldn't be returning. She was changing schools, and wouldn't they all miss her?

Eyes widening, Hanna made herself smaller in her seat and shyly hung her head, but a couple of the kids said, "Yeah!" and others chimed in, then the teacher had a boy present her with a big, handmade card they had all decorated and signed. She blushed and mumbled, "Thank you." Linnea noticed how carefully she carried it when Mrs. Harris released the children to join their parents.

"Wasn't that nice," Linnea said, giving her a quick hug.

She nodded, a tiny dip of the chin that was almost birdlike.

"I like your teacher," Matt said. "I'll bet you're going to miss her."

A shadow crossed her face, and she nodded again.

"Just think, though, you'll be able to walk to school."

"Yeah," she agreed, brightening. She'd be attending the elementary school where they played soccer.

They all got food on the paper plates that were another family's contribution. Linnea chatted with the adults and children she knew best from field trips and the times she'd volunteered in the classroom. She tried to separate herself from Matt but failed—without being obvious about it, he stuck close to her. Once he even lifted a hand, took her chin in it and with his thumb whisked a crumb off her lip.

His eyes were heavy-lidded when he did that, and he didn't seem to be in any hurry to let her go. Only when Hanna bounced beside him and said, "Uncle Matt, how come you're dressed like that?" did he let his hand fall and turn to grin at his niece.

"Job interview. Remember?"

"Oh." Her forehead crinkled. "Do you hafta have a job?"

"Eventually. And I want one right here in Seattle, because of you, kiddo."

Linnea knew Hannah had listened to him talk about the interview, but she looked worried now. "Before, you were always somewhere else. So you could only e-mail. 'Cause of your job."

"That's true," he said patiently. "I liked traveling. When you had your mom—" his voice roughened for a moment

"—you didn't need me. But now you do. This new job might still mean a little bit of traveling, but only for a few days at a time. Mostly, I'll be right here in Seattle, working during the day while you're in school."

"Oh." Very quietly, her blue eyes solemnly fixed on his face, she said, "I missed you."

He mostly hid his reaction, bending to whisper, "I missed you, too, Banana," and kiss her cheek, but Linnea had seen his jaw muscles flex and the way he had to swallow before he could speak at all.

Both silent, they waited while the little girl collected all of her supplies and said goodbye to friends and her teacher. Then they walked out as a family, Matt carrying the paper bag full of crayons and pencils and scissors, Hanna with her pink book bag on her back, Linnea with the bakery box of leftover cupcakes. Hanna held Matt's hand on one side, Linnea's on the other. Linnea was oddly full of emotion, as if the occasion meant something to all of them and not just to Hanna, who wouldn't be back to this elementary school.

A skiff of snow had fallen the day before and remained because the temperature still hovered around freezing even now, in the midafternoon. The Olympic Mountains across Puget Sound were crystal-clear today, covered with snow. Linnea had parked close enough to the entrance she had chosen not to wear her coat. She shivered the moment they stepped outside.

"So, big plans this afternoon?" Matt asked.

"Get in the car and turn on the heater?"

He grinned. "After that?"

"Home, I suppose."

"Could I take you ladies out to dinner tonight?" He

waved at himself. "Since I'm all dressed up anyway. And Hanna looks especially nice today."

She'd insisted on wearing a dress even if it was cold outside. Her grandmother sewed and had made her this dress—deep purple velour with a high, gathered waist. The skirt was wide enough to swirl if she spun in a circle, which she liked.

Linnea smiled down at her and said, "I think Uncle Matt just insulted me."

"He only said—" Hanna got it. "'Cause he said *I* look nice, but he didn't say you do."

He pretended to look chastened and cleared his throat. "Actually, you look nice, too." His gaze moved slowly over her, making her toes curl. "But I had in mind a fancy restaurant."

"I can change before dinnertime. What do you say, Hanna? Does that sound like fun?"

"Uh-huh. I'd lots rather do that than go to Grandma and Granddad's."

Linnea didn't say anything about that very revealing statement, although she was conscious of the way Matt's gaze flicked from Hanna's face to hers, laser sharp.

But after agreeing he would pick them up at five-thirty and helping Hanna buckle in, Linnea did think about her parents during the drive home.

Since Thanksgiving, Hanna had only seen her grandparents once a week, on Monday evenings. Linnea's mother wanted her to apologize, and she had refused. When she did drop Hanna off for the visit, she and her mother were stiff with each other. The only time Linnea had stayed was when Finn was there, too. He, too, had been icy with her, but she was determined to be close in case Hanna needed her.

Thinking about how strained her relationship was with her parents made Linnea's chest burn, but she couldn't back down, even though the cowardly part of her wanted desperately to.

Lately she had felt this weird disconnect with who she'd been before Tess's death, as if she'd been away for ages and had changed while she was gone. Or had been asleep like Rip van Winkle, except she'd awakened to find that time had passed for her but not for the people around her, instead of the other way around.

Didn't she love her parents? That last visit she had slipped into her father's study to talk to him, and instead of finding comfort she'd gotten mad when he said awkwardly, "This has been stressful for your mother, Linnea. She's defending Finn the best she knows how."

"She always has," Linnea heard herself say coolly before she walked out. Anger boiled inside her. Hadn't he seen how Mom played favorites? Why hadn't he ever done anything about it?

He wouldn't, of course. He couldn't bear conflict of any kind. Her father was a nice man, gentle and kind, but he was no more capable of standing up to his wife than…than…

Than I've been, Linnea realized unhappily.

Either she had been born with his disposition or else she'd been shaped from such an early age she didn't even remember. Her role was to smooth everyone else's way, to be the good girl who never complained or demanded or expected her wishes to be paramount. Finn was the heir apparent, the prince; she was nobody very important in comparison.

But Hanna *was* important. She should be able to grow

up believing she could accomplish anything, *be* anything. Linnea was going to fight for that, even if it meant being estranged from her family.

At home, Hanna refused to take off her pretty dress even when she lay down for a short nap and, later, played games with her aunt. Tomorrow, Matt was taking Hanna, and the day after that was Christmas Eve, which they were going to spend with him. Christmas Day would be at Grandma and Granddad's, tension or no.

Not knowing how fancy a restaurant Matt had in mind, Linnea went all out. She wore a classic black silk dress that looked simple but clung in all the right places. She brushed her hair into a chignon, wore pearls in her ears and spike heels that weren't very comfortable but made her legs look long and sexy, if she did say so herself. She applied makeup with a reckless hand. When she was done, she expected to want to wash it all off, but instead she studied herself in surprise. In the mirror her eyes were huge and smoky, her lips a little sultry and her cheekbones had become…exotic.

Linnea gulped. Had she overdone? Panic gripped her as, stricken, she kept staring. Finn would tell her she looked like a clown. Her mother probably would, too. Then her dad would say, "Nonsense, you look pretty," but she'd know he was only trying to make her feel better.

Hand shaking, she reached for the remover, but something stopped her from taking off the lid. She hardly even knew what that something was except that lodged beneath her breastbone was a white-hot coal of resentment and defiance.

Tess had worn lots of makeup. She'd used dramatic swaths of eyeshadow and painted her lips an eye-catching scarlet. Linnea hadn't put on anything near that bright. She'd picked colors that suited her less-vivid coloring. She didn't look quite like herself, but was that so bad? Matt had no reason to know that she didn't usually—well, ever—go to quite such lengths.

The doorbell rang and she jumped.

Too late to change her mind.

CHAPTER EIGHT

HANNA THREW OPEN THE front door and let Matt lift her into a big hug. "Aunt Linnie brushed my hair so it would be especially pretty. Isn't it pretty, Uncle Matt?"

"*You're* pretty," he told her, struck again by how much she looked like her aunt. He couldn't see much of Tess in her, which he should regret but somehow didn't. "So," he said, "is Aunt Linnie dressing up for us?"

"Uh-*huh*." She gave a big nod.

He was still smiling when he heard the click of heels on the hardwood floor and looked up. As if he'd taken a fist in his gut, he expelled all the air in his lungs with an audible sound and barely avoided staggering back.

She was gorgeous. Stunning. Sexy, in a slip of a dress and heels that had to be four inches tall, her hair in a classic do, her eyes somehow mysterious and her lips curving and kissable.

He wanted to kiss her.

He intended to kiss her. Ever since he'd realized that he wanted the three of them to be a family, he had allowed himself to think about kissing her, and peeling her clothes from her slender, supple body. He hadn't acted on the desire because he'd been afraid she wasn't thinking about him that way at all. Since then, he'd been doing his damnedest to make her aware of him. By God, he'd been patient.

Watching her walk toward them, her hips swaying, her legs a mile long and perfect for wrapping around a man's waist, Matt knew his patience had run out.

Hanna tugged at his hand. "Isn't Aunt Linnie pretty, Uncle Matt?"

"Aunt Linnie is more than pretty." His voice was hoarse. "She's spectacular." Seeing those big eyes widen farther and the color heighten on her cheeks, he bent his head and said in a loud whisper, "And you, Hanna Banana, are going to be just as beautiful when you grow up."

"'Cause I look like her, don't I?" Her satisfaction was apparent. "Grandma showed me pictures. I look like Aunt Linnie when *she* was a little girl."

"Is that what Grandma said?" Linnea asked.

Matt's eyes narrowed at her surprise.

"Uh-huh. She has a whole album of pictures of you. Even your kindergarten picture. And your grade one. She says she made the dress you were wearing, like she did the one I wore on picture day."

"I'd forgotten that dress." Linnea sounded bemused. "I guess I'd forgotten she had an album dedicated to me."

"She showed me Daddy's, too." Hanna took her hand and lifted her face to Matt. "Do you have one with pictures of Mommy?"

"There is one. I thought your mom had it." But maybe not, he realized. He wasn't sure she'd ever really looked through the stuff they'd had in storage. "I'll tell you what," he said. "I may have it in a box. There's still a pile in the garage I haven't gone through. I'll find it."

"I want to see you when you were in first grade, too," she declared.

He groaned. "I was already the class nerd."

Hanna giggled and Linnea's lips quivered with a smile that was as merry.

"Ladies?" He opened the front door.

They both donned coats before letting him escort them out.

For once they left West Seattle. He took them to a restaurant he'd discovered on the shores of Lake Union not far from the Seattle Center and Space Needle. A call this afternoon had secured a table for them at the window, where they could see the cold blue water and boats moored at a marina north of the restaurant.

Talk about pictures inevitably led to stories about his and Linnea's childhoods. Both kept them light. He made fun of himself as a kid—serious, smart, taller than most of his classmates. Earnest, wanting to do the right thing, which sometimes made him a misfit. He was too gawky to be athletic until high school, when his social stature had risen with his prowess on the basketball court and football field.

He was stung by Linnea's expression of disbelief. Was she having trouble believing he'd been popular in high school, or that he'd ever been unpopular?

"Your mom," he told Hanna, "was the social butterfly. Did she ever tell you she was homecoming queen? That was after our parents died, but Dad always said he'd be beating boys off her with a stick. His favorite grumble was about the number of boys calling."

"How come I don't look like Mommy?"

"I guess you mostly got your looks from your dad's side. And it's lucky you don't quite look like him—" he ignored the flash of warning in Linnea's eyes "—because your aunt Linnie is lots prettier."

Hanna giggled. "That's 'cause he's a *boy!*"

"Right. And you're not."

Linnea in turn talked about growing up with her head in a book. "I did okay in math in school, but I never liked it. History was my major in college, but I liked English and creative writing, too, even if I can't write poetry to save my life. That's the only thing I ever cheated on in school."

Hanna's mouth fell open. "Aunt Linnie!"

Vastly amused at this tale of unexpected sin, Matt waited for her explanation.

She made a face at both of them. "I shouldn't admit that, should I? But I had this creative writing class when I was a junior in high school, and if I hadn't been able to turn in a decent poem I wouldn't have gotten an A in the class, and I deserved one!" Her cheeks were flushed with indignation. "So my best friend Jennifer wrote a poem for me. And I felt horribly guilty and had dreams where Mr. Marshall slapped it down on my desk with a big red F on it and told the whole class I was a liar and a cheat."

"That would be really scary," her niece whispered.

"It was. So scary I would never have had the nerve to do it again, but I didn't get caught. And, honestly, it was just an okay poem, not so brilliant it would have made him suspicious or he would have entered it in a contest to surprise me." She shuddered. "Wouldn't that have been horrible?"

Night fell as they ate. Strings of lights sparkled on the masts of sailing boats at the marina and bobbed on a few boats out on the lake.

Hanna had been suspicious of the offerings on the

menu, but she seemed to enjoy her spaghetti and dove into the caramel sundae her aunt reluctantly agreed that she could have. Matt didn't order dessert, knowing he'd be finishing the sundae.

Walking out after they were done, he felt again that swell of pride, contentment and something sharper edged he'd come to recognize. People smiled at the sight of Hanna in her cute dress and shiny patent leather shoes, then the smiles widened to encompass the beautiful woman they were bound to assume was Hanna's mother. And then he was wrapped in those approving smiles, too, because the three of them were so obviously a family.

But the knife's edge dug into his stomach every time he thought that because they weren't. He could lose them both; he and Linnea could lose Hanna.

Matt couldn't imagine his life without them.

The drive home was quieter. He sneaked glances in the rearview mirror and saw that Hanna rested her head sleepily against the car window and watched the passing scenery of a city at night. Linnea and he spoke occasionally, their voices soft.

"It's almost Christmas. If you don't want me to take her tomorrow…"

She shook her head. "I need the time to…you know."

Wrap, he presumed.

"And she's excited and has to be occupied. Do you have big plans?"

He shook his head. "A movie, I guess, although I like them better when you're along."

Her chuckle kicked his pulse up a notch. "So I can take her to the bathroom?"

Going along, he said, "It's embarrassing to have to ask a mother to take her. I figure she's too old for the men's room."

"She's probably old enough to go by herself as long as you're waiting outside."

"Probably, but I'd worry."

Linnea laughed again.

Hanna didn't fall asleep, and she revived some once they reached home. "Can I watch *The Little Mermaid?*" she asked.

The front door still stood open and he hadn't been invited in.

Linnea glanced at her watch and said, "Sure. Maybe I'll come and watch with you in a minute."

A minute didn't give him long. On the other hand, if Linnea had invited him in, he'd find himself watching Disney's spritely version of the more tragic Danish tale of the little mermaid before he knew it. Not exactly the end to this evening he'd had in mind.

Hanna disappeared into the living room. Matt smiled at Linnea. "You really are beautiful tonight."

Her shyness returned immediately. "Thank you."

"You always look surprised when someone compliments you. I can't believe you're not used to hearing them."

"I actually don't, not often." Her voice was very low, barely above a whisper. "Library patrons aren't likely to say, 'Can you help me find a book about writing résumés, and, by the way, you're beautiful.' And when I'm petsitting, the dogs lick me when I open cans of food, but they're not big on verbalizing their feelings."

She was trying to make a joke of it, although he heard embarrassment in the tremulous quality of her voice. As though most men were the idiots he'd been and hadn't had the sense to realize how exquisite she was.

He was a step lower than her, and with her four-inch heels their faces were about at a level.

Without letting himself have second thoughts, Matt wrapped a hand around the delicate nape of her neck, tilted his head and laid his mouth to hers.

THE FIRST TOUCH OF MATT'S lips was as soft as the brush of his thumb when he'd whisked the crumb from her mouth. So little to pierce her with a shaft of longing. Linnea simply stood, frozen, disbelieving…and wanting.

Matt's fingers tightened on her neck. He kissed her again, gently tugged on her lower lip. Heat pooled in her belly and made her sway toward him.

"That's it," he muttered, and urged her mouth open with his. Her head would have fallen back out of sheer weakness if his big hand hadn't moved up to cup it. Linnea reached out and flattened her hands on his chest, then gripped his suit jacket to hold on for dear life.

His breath was in her mouth; hers in his, warm and mingling. His tongue slid over hers. The sensation was indescribable.

It wasn't as if she hadn't been kissed before. Of course she had. She'd never felt all that much.

She hadn't been in the hands of an expert, she thought in shock as one of his arms wrapped around her and flattened her against him. No, not just flattened—*lifted* her, so that her toes barely touched the ground and her body all but cradled his erection.

Suddenly the kiss wasn't gentle at all. His tongue thrust, and hers answered in a duel that felt primitive and utterly essential. His heart slammed beneath her palm, and a groan worked its way from his chest to vibrate in his throat.

More shockingly *she* was making sounds, too. Whimpers, or moans, they had to tell him how needy she felt.

Linnea didn't care. She flung an arm around his neck and tried to squeeze closer yet, as if she could burrow inside him.

His next groan was raw, and his lips left hers. "I don't want to let go of you, but…"

She went completely still, humiliation spreading like fire over her skin. She was plastered to him. He'd kissed her, and she would have let him lift her skirt and have her right there, on the doorstep. Oh, God! With Hanna a room away.

Gasping with distress, she tore herself away. "Oh, Lord, I don't know what…"

Under the porchlight, she saw the flush on his cheekbones and the heat in his eyes. "It was good—that's what it was," he said roughly. "I've been wanting to kiss you since that first night when I took you and Hanna out for pizza and you were so prim and wary."

"I—" Linnea gulped. "Really?" Then she was mad at herself for sounding so pathetic.

"Oh, yeah." He reached up and ran his knuckles along the line of her jaw, a caress that nearly buckled her knees again. "I've been waiting for you to get on board."

She blinked. "On board?"

He hesitated and visibly regained his usual control. "Can we get together without Hanna and talk about this?"

This? What was this in his mind? Attraction? If so, he'd done a heck of a job of hiding it until now.

Yes, a small voice in her mind whispered, *but he kissed with conviction. And he was definitely aroused.*

She couldn't argue with that. And within earshot of a child wasn't the time to argue with him. But there was no way she could get away from Hanna tomorrow—they still had to finish Matt's gift tomorrow night.

"Yes," she said, with commendable cool, "but probably not until after Christmas."

He frowned, calculated, then scowled more deeply. "Damn it. Not tomorrow night?" He saw her expression. "Fine. The day after Christmas? Can you get a babysitter?"

"I'll figure something out," she told him. "We'll see you tomorrow at ten."

"Ten."

"Hanna? Lunch? Movie?"

He swore under his breath. "I haven't forgotten. Yeah. Okay."

Coward that she was, she had already retreated inside and was clutching the door. "Good night," she said, and shut it.

She half expected him to hammer on it but knew better. He'd been the one to end the kiss, after all, because despite the evidence of his arousal he'd also had the presence of mind to remember that their niece was only a room away. While she had quit thinking at all.

"Aunt Linnie?" Hanna's voice came from the living room. "This is my favorite song. Are you gonna come watch?"

"Yes," she called back. "Just let me change. These shoes are killing me."

Linnea stripped them off right there, in the small entryway. Even as she sighed in relief, a rare feeling of feminine triumph sang through her. Spike heels and makeup had accomplished something after all. She now knew what it felt like to be kissed by Matt Laughlin. And he was right. It was good. Very, very good.

She prayed the attraction on his part was real and not part of some scheme to manipulate her. Because tonight she'd given herself in a way that had let him know how utterly vulnerable she was to him.

With a moan, she rushed to the bedroom to tear off the dress and put on sweats, so she could feel like herself.

If only Christmas Eve wasn't the day after tomorrow, she thought miserably. How would she survive the holidays wondering what he wanted to say? What *he'd* felt.

What it all meant.

HE'D NEVER BEEN MORE nervous. Had he pushed too soon? What if he had damaged the fragile trust Linnea had come to feel for him? He wasn't the only one who'd pay, he knew; Hanna would, as well. She needed her uncle Matt and aunt Linnie to be the foundation she'd lost when her father killed her mother. Where was his self-control? Matt didn't like knowing that he'd rushed Linnea out of a desire to feel secure himself, to know she and Hanna were *his*.

When he picked up and dropped off Hanna the next day, Linnea's eyes never quite met his even though she sounded much the same as usual. Matt hated knowing he was responsible for making her shy again.

I should have waited, he thought. It hadn't even been quite three months since the shocking call from Detective Delaney had changed his life. Three months. And in that time he'd arrogantly told Linnea he was taking Hanna away from her because she wasn't capable of protecting the little girl they both loved. Really, it had only been in the past six weeks that they'd groped their way toward the delicate state of faith in each other they had found.

And he'd told himself he was being patient.

Somehow, Christmas Eve they were able to set aside what that kiss meant, even if he couldn't forget it for a second, even if his body ached the more for knowing what she tasted like, how she felt in his arms.

They had dinner, ham and sweet potatoes and homemade apple pie, then opened presents in Linnea's living room, where a fir tree had been wrapped in colored lights and hung with ornaments. A miscellany, he noted in satisfaction and no surprise, that included some Hanna must have made. Hanna and Linnea had even strung popcorn for the tree. Matt knew damn well his sister would never have allowed a string of popcorn on her Christmas tree, decorated for show more than sentiment.

Troubled by the implicit criticism, he dismissed the thought. Tess hadn't changed that much from the baby sister of his earliest memories. She'd become sophisticated; she and Finn entertained. That wasn't so bad.

But his mom would have loved this tree.

The thought gave him an odd bump of grief, because Mom and Dad had never known Hanna. Would never know Linnea.

They would have loved her, too.

"Uncle Matt! Uncle Matt!" Face shining with delight, his niece held up a package. "This one is for you. It's from me."

She had already opened half a dozen. He'd been afraid Linnea would disapprove of how much he'd bought, but so far her gentle smile hadn't wavered.

Hanna bounced at his feet and Linnea watched as he opened the package and found inside two quilted potholders. He recognized the log cabin pattern because it matched the old quilt he had displayed on the sofa in the living room, but these were stitched from calico fabrics in myriad shades of green.

"Aunt Linnie helped me," Hanna declared excitedly. "She showed me how to use the sewing machine."

"These are beautiful." He had a lump in his throat.

"We wanted to make ones like that quilt you said your grandma made. Only green, 'cause we know you like green."

He managed a laugh. Yeah, he did like green. He guessed they could tell, after shopping with him for towels and sheets.

"These are great. Thank you, Hanna." He grabbed her into a hug, then smiled over her head at Linnea. "And thank you, too." He could tell from the finely stitched edging and the loops at the corners of the potholders that she'd done most of the work. Hanna had likely sat on her lap in front of the machine and "helped" enough to let pride swell in her chest.

"You're very welcome," Linnea said serenely.

She'd bought him a book; not an intimate present, but well-chosen. Her exclamations of pleasure at the earrings he'd chosen for her sounded sincere.

Hanna accompanied him to the door rather than Linnea when it came time for him to leave. When she initiated another big hug, his sinuses burned and his chest hurt.

He loved this little girl, and he'd never been so scared of the future.

Christmas Day was a bitch; other people were alone, too, but nobody he knew was. He thought about calling Hanna and Linnea that evening, but didn't let himself.

He'd had his celebration with them, the most generous of the gifts they'd given him. He wasn't usually greedy.

Linnea called late in the evening and said, "Do you still want to get together tomorrow?"

"Yes."

"Okay. I've arranged for Hanna to go back to her grandparents for the day. She left some of her new toys there."

"Fine." They sounded as if they were setting up a business appointment. "What time?"

"Eleven?"

"Fine," he said again. "Did you two have a good Christmas?"

"Yes." She didn't sound as if she was being entirely honest, but continued, "Hanna wallowed in more presents than I can count, but thanked everyone nicely."

Everyone presumably included her dad. Matt didn't ask.

He couldn't think of a reason to prolong the call, and they said their good-nights.

To distract himself, he prowled the Internet, then tried to read. Neither activity succeeded in turning his mind from Linnea. He scarcely slept.

When he knocked on her door the next morning, she opened it almost immediately. She wore jeans and a turtleneck, and her hair was bundled back in a scrunchie that might have been Hanna's since it had—he thought—printed pink elephants on a midnight-blue background. She was back to not quite meeting his eyes.

"Coffee?" she asked, leading the way into the living room.

He studied the ponytail more closely. Yeah, definitely pink elephants. "No, thank you."

Spooky lay on the back of the sofa. She stared at Matt

for a long, thoughtful moment, then hopped down and strolled out of the living room. He recalled Linnea saying she didn't care for men. Or pretty much anyone at all.

Linnea sat at one end of the sofa, Matt at the other.

"What's this about, Matt? If it's just the fact that you were tempted to kiss me because we had a fun evening out..."

She was trying to let him down nicely, he realized with a spurt of annoyance.

"I told you the truth. I've been wanting to kiss you ever since I saw you that first time."

"Not the first time." Her eyes met his squarely now, and he was startled to see a flare of anger, or even hurt, in their blue depths. "We've known each other for eight years. You never seemed the tiniest bit interested in kissing me before."

"I didn't really look at you."

"I noticed."

His back teeth gritted, he said, "You seemed to do your very best to avoid me. Every time I entered a room, you left it."

Her cheeks pinkened. "I'm not very good at making polite conversation with someone who clearly dislikes me."

"I didn't dislike you—"

"You wanted to."

After a minute, he rubbed the back of his neck and said heavily, "Yeah. I did. And I'm sorrier than I can say for that."

She bit her lip and looked down at her hands, arranged on her lap. "I didn't think I'd like you, either. Except that you were good with Hanna. I'd see the way she lit up for you. So some part of me knew I was wrong to think you were a brusque, busy man with no...softer side."

"And now?" he asked quietly.

She met his eyes fleetingly. "You're very good for Hanna."

"What about you, Linnea? Am I good for you?" He intentionally echoed the words he'd used after their kiss.

"I've appreciated everything you—"

"That's not what I mean and you know it."

"What do you want me to say?" Color stained her cheeks now, and she sounded mad. "That I enjoyed kissing you? So what if I did? Are you suggesting we have an affair, sneaking around behind Hanna's back? Don't you think that would look really bad if Finn doesn't get convicted and one or the other of us ends up going to court trying to keep custody?"

He swallowed. "No. That isn't what I'm suggesting." Last night, he'd had himself talked out of doing this. Not yet, not so soon. But for a patient, even-tempered man, he had become extraordinarily impatient. Even, he thought in shock, desperate. His voice sounded odd when he said, "Linnea, I'm trying to ask you to marry me."

Her mouth opened, but nothing emerged. She simply gaped at him, stunned into silence.

"I know you probably haven't thought about me that way," he began stiffly.

"Marry?" she whispered.

"It makes sense for a lot of reasons." Damn it, he sounded as if he was arguing for a business proposition. He tried again. "We feel like a family. I...want to belong."

"You want to marry me so you can—" she hesitated "—see Hanna every day? That wouldn't really give you any more claim on her."

"No. I know it wouldn't. Hanna's only part of this. I want to marry you. No, damn it, not just to marry you. I want you. The other night, it was all I could do to take my hands off you."

She stared at him as if, God, he was trying to sell her a ride-on mower for her pocket-size lawn.

"Say something."

"Oh" was apparently the best she could manage.

He groaned, stood and moved to her end of the sofa. "Let me kiss you," he begged, sitting so close he could stroke her face, cup her jaw in his palm.

For a paralyzing moment she still stared, but finally she gave a tiny nod that wrenched another sound from him, relief and raw hunger. He bent his head and captured her mouth, his demanding. But, damn it, the angle was awkward and he wanted her closer yet.

Without taking his mouth from hers, he lifted her, drinking in her squeak of surprise, turned her and settled her on his lap facing him. Her knees straddled his hips. Now he could kiss her the way he wanted to, while his hands roved over her.

The scrunchie went first. He tossed it aside as he let his fingers sink into her hair, as silky and fine-textured as it looked. He thought of elusive winter sunlight. There was that whiff of vanilla again, a scent so redolent of home.

Then he stroked her neck, the delicate line of her collarbone. She had instinctively lifted her hands to brace herself against his chest, perhaps to hold him off, but if so she'd lost interest. Linnea was responding as deliciously as she had the first time he kissed her, her response shy but honest. If he tugged at her lip, she tugged at his; her tongue met his, stroked. Now her hands in turn began to move, squeezing, seeming to savor the involuntary reaction of his muscles to her touch.

He covered her generous breasts with his hands, rubbing gently. Her nipples were already hard against his palms. God. He had to see her.

Matt tore his mouth from hers and began working the turtleneck up.

"What are you—?" She started to scramble backward, but he wrapped his hands around her waist and held her in place.

"I want you," he repeated, his voice ragged. "Marry me, Linnea."

She had gone completely rigid in his grip, a wild creature terrified to be confined, her eyes so dilated they were unreadable. But she had to be tempted, too. She couldn't have kissed him the way she had, made those wanton sounds in the back of her throat, if desire wasn't raging through her the way it was through him. *Please let this not be some kind of experiment for her.*

He said the only other thing he could think of. "Please."

She closed her eyes, sank her teeth into her lower lip. Matt didn't move, waited.

"Yes," she finally whispered. "I want you, too."

That wasn't all he'd asked. "You'll marry me?"

Her eyes opened, panic darkening the slate blue to something deeper. "I don't know."

Ruthlessly, he said, "You know how happy Hanna will be."

"But my parents— Finn—"

"You'll let them stop you?"

"I can't think."

"What do you *feel?*" He let go of her waist to lift his hands to her breasts again, beneath her shirt. He rotated them gently, coaxingly.

Linnea's back arched and a moan escaped her lips.

"Say yes. Say you'll marry me."

She didn't protest when he yanked the turtleneck over her head and discarded it, then unhooked her bra even as his eyes feasted on the plump, perfect breasts he'd uncovered. She was as pretty and delicate here as everywhere else, her nipples pink and tight, her skin milk pale. He leaned forward and kissed first one breast, then the other. His tongue circled her nipples, and finally he sucked one into his mouth. Linnea gasped and stiffened again, her hips lifting, pushing against him, as if she couldn't help it.

Not until he had suckled both breasts did he lift his head again. "Do you like me?"

"Like you?" She looked dazed.

"Do you trust me?"

She blinked hard, as if struggling to clear her mind. "I— Yes."

"Aren't you happy when I'm here?" He stroked her breasts, swept his hands down to the waistband of her jeans.

"Yes, but—"

"But what?" He unbuttoned her jeans, slid down the zipper.

She stared down, seeming helpless to stop him, shivering in reaction.

"I don't know you," she cried. "Not really."

Talking was getting harder and harder. "We'll have years. A lifetime." His voice sounded as though his throat was lined with sand from a desert storm.

"But why?" She lifted her gaze to meet his. "Is it just Hanna?"

"No." He was telling her the truth, even though Hanna was part of it. Of course she was. They were a family. "I miss you when I'm not with you. You and I…fit. You feel it, too, don't you?"

She took a shaky breath. "Yes."

"Kiss me," he muttered. "Then say yes again."

"Yes," she said, even before their mouths met. "Yes."

A primitive sense of satisfaction roared through him, headier than a shot of straight whiskey. He shoved his hips up and gloried in the sensation of her riding him. Only the desperate need to divest them both of clothes enabled him to lift her off him for even a minute.

He'd been half afraid she would stand there like a china doll to let him strip off her jeans, but thank God she participated fully, fighting to pull his shirt over his head, reaching for the waistband of his jeans.

She was glorious, her slender waist curving into feminine hips. The curls at the juncture of her thighs were as moonlight pale as the silky, straight hair on her head. When he slid his fingers through those curls to her damp center, her hips bucked.

She stared at his nude body, but he didn't give her time to get alarmed. He'd been carrying a couple condoms since the day he had realized he wanted her, that they belonged together. He sheathed himself in one and entertained a brief fantasy of there being nothing between them, of them choosing to create life within her.

Soon, he thought, gritting his teeth against hunger stronger than anything he'd ever felt.

Then he sprawled back on the sofa and pulled her atop him. He touched her and kissed her and finally positioned her to sink onto him. She was a small woman, the fit snug. Shaken, he knew he was losing it. His big hands gripping her hips, he lifted her, pressed her down again, set an urgent, hard pace.

She squeezed him with her knees and matched his rhythm with hers. Too quickly, she convulsed, a keening cry of astonishment and wonder escaping her lips. It was sound as much as sensation that shoved him over the edge. The pleasure was almost unbearable, so far from anything he'd ever felt before.

Linnea slid bonelessly to lie atop him. He wrapped his arms around her, his heart pounding so hard he knew she could feel it against her breast.

With wrenching relief, he thought, *She's mine.*

CHAPTER NINE

LINNEA STOOD IN THE KITCHEN, looking at the sofa where they had made love. Her gaze lifted in shock to the big picture window above the sofa and she let out a cry.

"What's wrong?" Matt had come up silently behind her.

"The drapes are open. Anyone could have seen."

She'd stood, practically in front of the window, and let him take her shirt off and kiss her breasts. She had faced the window and the street and not given a single thought to who might be able to see in.

Matt gave a low chuckle. "Don't worry." He bent his head and nuzzled her neck. "The window's not at street level."

"No, but if Mrs. Henderson is home, she could have looked straight in."

He laughed again and turned her to face him for a kiss.

Her shock at her own immodesty didn't keep her from enjoying the feel of his lips. Truthfully, she couldn't remember ever being happier than she'd been today.

He had carried her into the bedroom and made love to her again. Eventually they showered together before getting dressed so that they could actually talk.

"Stop," she finally murmured against his mouth. "You said you were hungry."

"Did I?" He nipped her earlobe.

"Yes! And we should talk."

With obvious reluctance, he lifted his head. "Yeah. I suppose we need to."

While she made lunch, Linnea reveled in how amazing her body felt. A little sore, but also relaxed and sexy. Her utter lack of inhibitions astonished her. She'd had crushes a few times and even boyfriends, but she had never been able to get over feeling self-conscious. She'd pretended she wanted good-night kisses and even sex, but she hadn't really.

Until today.

Her hands went still and she stared straight ahead, glad Matt, currently getting drinks out of the refrigerator, couldn't see her face.

I'm in love with him, she thought in shock. No wonder she'd lived for the days he was coming over, for his smiles, his casual but proprietary touches. No wonder she'd said "yes" today even as she grappled with the knowledge of how her mother and Finn would react to the news.

I love him.

And he hadn't said a single word about love. He'd told her she was beautiful. He said they *fit* together. That he and she and Hanna together were a family.

Bereft of breath, she made herself stir the soup and turn off the burner.

He did want her. She couldn't doubt that, not after today. And wasn't that a miracle in itself?

He might come to love her. Mightn't he? He was a kind man, something she wouldn't have suspected back in the old days. He wouldn't hurt her if he could help it. She knew he felt intensely protective of Hanna. Once she was his wife, he'd feel the same about her. He took care of the people he cared for.

She poured the soup into bowls.

Fact: he wouldn't want to marry her if it weren't for Hanna.

He said he would, she argued with herself. *He knows that our marriage is no guarantee we'll be able to keep Hanna.*

Linnea took a deep breath and carried the bowls to the table, then went back for the bread to join the sandwich makings he'd already taken from the refrigerator.

His gaze was intent on her face when she sat. "What are you thinking?"

"I'm...dazed," she admitted.

He reached across the table and gripped her hand. "In a happy way, I hope."

"I think so." With surprise, she realized that despite all her doubts and fears she still felt as if her blood had turned to champagne, fizzing in her veins. This was her chance to grab at life, not let timidity rule her.

I've changed, she realized again, liking the knowledge. Ever since that night she'd gone to Finn's house to get Hanna, since she'd seen her brother handcuffed and furious, she had been undergoing a metamorphosis. She'd become fierce in Hanna's defense. Willing to defy Finn and her mother both, something she'd always shrunk from.

Matt was part of her change. She'd gained in strength even when she saw him as her enemy. He was good for her.

"What about you?" she asked. "I still can't believe you've been thinking all this time about something like this."

"Making love with you? Marrying you?"

She nodded.

His crooked smile lit a face that was nearly harsh when he was angry or brooding. "The marrying part is more recent. Once we started spending so much time together,

I started dreading the days I wouldn't see you. I wasn't too happy even when I had Hanna, not if I saw you only in passing."

So it isn't just Hanna, Linnea thought with relief. He did mean it.

"Did you look forward to seeing me?" he asked.

She wrinkled her nose. "You know I did."

His smile had become tender. "Will you marry me? Did you mean it?"

Linnea felt herself blushing. "You mean, was that what I was saying yes to?"

"Yeah."

She had the feeling he'd never let go of her hand if she didn't agree. He wasn't a man used to hearing no or willing to accept it. In fact, he definitely *had* been manipulating her today, using sex to persuade her to do what he wanted.

But…she wanted the same thing, even if it scared her, too.

So she smiled, too, and said tremulously, "Yes. I'll marry you."

"God." His fingers tightened. His smile had died, and something powerful burned in his eyes. "We have to get you an engagement ring. Let's go shopping this afternoon, before we pick up Hanna."

She wouldn't be able to hide it from her parents. "There's no hurry," she began weakly.

"I want my ring on your finger." He sounded completely inflexible, but also deeply satisfied.

Because everyone will know then, Linnea realized. He *wants* that.

Didn't any man who asked a woman to marry him?

Maybe, she thought, confused. But not necessarily for the same reasons.

Shaking off her trepidation, she decided she was being silly, her old cowardly self. She couldn't become engaged and *not* tell her parents. They wouldn't be happy—at least, her mother wouldn't—but so what? It was past time she did what *she* wanted with her life.

She would let Matt put a ring on her finger today, and she would glory in wearing it.

"Okay," she agreed simply, then said, "I can hardly wait to tell Hanna."

"We'll do that today, too." His voice held that same note of satisfaction. He finally let go of her hand and started spreading mayonnaise on a slice of bread. "This is a good time of year to buy a house, too. What say we start looking this weekend? Think about where you want to live. Do you intend to keep your job? I have plenty of money put away, you know. And the new job pays well. If you'd like to stay home, or try something else…"

He was going so fast. Too fast. But the possibilities were also alluring, part of this day that had made her Matt's lover and now his fiancée, that gave her a *right* to dream with him.

"I'd like to go to grad school," she said. "I can get my master's in library science. I'd love to manage my own branch library. Or maybe be a children's librarian."

"Then that's what you'll do," he said, with a matter-of-fact nod, as if she could accomplish anything in the world.

If she hadn't already been in love, she would have fallen right then and there.

We're getting married, she thought giddily and didn't taste a bite of her lunch.

CHAPTER TEN

LINNEA LOVED HER ENGAGEMENT ring, but it weighed heavy on her hand when she walked into her parents' house. Matt hadn't liked it when she asked him to wait in the car. He wanted to stand at her side when she told Mom and Dad she'd agreed to marry him, but she knew—just knew—how Mom would react, and he had reluctantly conceded.

Her dad and Hanna were in the dining room, both concentrating fiercely on a board game. The rattle of dice was followed by Hanna's giggle and the murmur of Dad's voice. They hadn't heard her come in, so she followed the whir of the sewing machine down the hall. Linnea stopped in the doorway of what had been Finn's bedroom, converted to a sewing and hobby room. "Mom."

Her mother gave her a rare smile, which made what Linnea had to say worse. "Isn't this pretty fabric? Hanna and I went shopping today and she picked this out. I'm going to make a pinafore to go over the dress.…" As if the diamond on Linnea's hand had flashed light, her eyes went to it, then rose slowly to meet her daughter's.

"Matt asked me to marry him, and I agreed."

Her mother seemed stunned. "Matt Laughlin."

"Yes." In the frozen silence, Linnea counted her heartbeats. "Will you congratulate me, Mom?"

Her mother's voice gained a razor's edge. "You know how Finn feels about him."

"Neither of them like each other, but that doesn't have anything to do with—"

"It's bad enough that you let Hanna see him, but now this? You'll marry a man who despises your family and wants nothing from you but to hurt us?"

That stung, because Linnea did know Matt wanted, first and foremost, to have his niece to raise. But he liked her, Linnea, and wanted her, too, and she wouldn't listen to this. She wouldn't.

"You don't know him at all," she said quietly. When her mother's mouth opened, she said, "No. I'm taking Hanna now. I would have liked it if you'd thought about my happiness, but I knew that wouldn't happen."

And she turned and walked down the hall.

"Linnea, you come right back here and listen to some sense."

Sense? she thought. *More like vitriol.*

In the dining room she kissed her father's cheek quickly and said, "Hanna, get your coat. Matt's waiting in the car."

Her niece exchanged a high five with her grandfather and raced for the coat closet. Linnea held out her hand for his father to see and whispered, "I'm going to marry Matt, Dad. Mom's mad. But shh. I haven't told Hanna yet."

Worry lines deepened on his face. "Are you sure this is right for you?" he asked.

There was either a great big hole in her chest or a rock that weighed two tons, she wasn't sure which. "I think so." Eyes stinging, she kissed him again, then took Hanna's hand and led her out to the car.

Matt was leaning against the fender, his gaze sharp on her even as he lifted Hanna for a hug and kiss.

He opened the door for Hanna, then closed it as she buckled in. "Didn't go so well?" he asked Linnea, in a quick voice.

She managed a smile for him. "No, but I didn't expect it to."

"Your mother is a—" He stopped himself, then shook his head. "Never mind."

Linnea looked at him. "A what?"

"A fool," he said with quick anger, before clamping his mouth shut again and circling the car to his side.

Once they were all in, he said, "Have you told Hannah?"

"Not without you."

"Why don't we go get an ice cream sundae?" he suggested.

"Yay!" Hanna declared from the backseat.

They had settled at a table in Dairy Queen with three sundaes when Linnea said, "Hanna, we have news for you." He reached out and took her hand. "Your uncle Matt asked me to marry him, and I said yes."

The explosion of joy on the child's face made up for all the hurt Linnea's mother had dealt.

"You'll live with us and everything?" she asked Matt, hope shimmering in her blue eyes. "Forever and ever?"

"Yeah." He sounded shaken. He reached out and gripped Linnea's hand, then hugged Hanna with his other arm. "Forever and ever."

He meant that. Linnea knew he did. If ever a man believed in commitment, Matt Laughlin did. When Tess and Finn had first started dating, she'd told Linnea about her parents dying when she was still in high school, and how her brother, although only twenty years old, had overcome all opposition and brought her to live with him, in a rental house close to the university campus.

"I don't think he had a beer or even dated until I graduated from high school," she had said with a soft laugh. "He was so determined to stand in for Mom and Dad, and that meant setting a good example. He gave the evil eye to every guy that dared to ask *me* out. Scared most of them off." She had sat silent for a moment, a faraway look in her eyes. "Matt came to every one of my basketball games, and he taught me to drive, and he helped me with college applications. He gave up a lot for me. He's a pretty amazing guy."

Linnea had tried to imagine Finn doing any of that for her and failed. He was sometimes carelessly kind to her, she'd thought then, or amused by her. He always assumed she'd give way so he could have what he wanted, whether it was the television when they were young or the family car after he wrecked his and Mom and Dad actually held firm for a memorable four months and refused to buy him another one. No, if their parents had tragically died when she was sixteen, he'd have told her going into a foster home was the best thing for her.

Looking at Matt and Hanna right now, love swelled in Linnea until she could hardly breath. When he said, "Forever and ever," it was a promise not only to Hanna but to Linnea.

I want that forever like I've never wanted anything else, she thought and pushed away the fear and disbelief.

HANNA HAD BROUGHT HER portable CD player and was singing along with the music from *Anastasia*. Matt was driving, of course, following the real estate agent's car.

They'd already looked at half a dozen houses, and Linnea's head throbbed.

"Why don't you put in your application to the university and see what happens?" Matt said.

She didn't want to talk about this right now. "The deadline was months ago."

He shrugged, as if that meant nothing. "They must get dropouts. If they put you on the waiting list, you'd have a good shot at starting grad school this fall instead of waiting another year. With your experience at the library, you're a top-notch candidate for them."

Linnea had never in her life envisioned herself as *top-notch*. She'd had good grades in college, but not a four-point-oh. And, yes, she'd worked for the Seattle Public Library for six years now, but only as a clerk, so that hardly counted. She thought—believed—that she would be accepted to the graduate program in librarianship if she applied in the normal way, but she wasn't anyone so special she could demand extraordinary treatment, not the way Matt thought she should. The way Finn undoubtedly would have done. *He* would have been sure deadlines were for other people, not him.

Matt was so much more forceful than she was that Linnea could understand the impatience she occasionally saw on his face. He was used to being decisive, cutting his losses when he had to, arguing bluntly for what he believed, ignoring opinions with which he disagreed.

They'd only been engaged two weeks, and already Linnea felt some days as if she was being swept along in a torrent. She didn't know why he was in such a hurry to buy a house, but when she suggested timidly that they wait until summer, he didn't even seem to hear her.

She had no idea what he'd told the agent they were looking for, but so far none of the houses she'd showed them were anything Linnea could imagine ever finding homey. What on earth had he said they wanted?

"Ah," he said with satisfaction, and she realized he was pulling to the curb in front of house number six—or was it seven?—and that he liked the looks of this one. "We're here," he said over his shoulder to Hanna, who shut off the music, thank heavens, craned her neck and scrambled to take off her seat belt.

Getting out herself, Linnea gazed at the beautiful Northwest-style home with shingled siding, a multipitched roof and a broad porch surrounded by beautifully designed gardens. "It's awfully big," she murmured doubtfully.

Matt barely gave her a glance. "Compared to your place, everything is." He joined the agent, an attractive woman who painted her nails and lips crimson and who had mostly ignored Linnea today.

Linnea had gotten so she really disliked people who looked right through her.

The agent talked about the home's features as they walked to the front door. Hanna pressed her face to the front window to peer in, then twirled on the porch while the agent fumbled for a minute with the keybox and unlocked the door.

Inside, the flooring was cherry with a rich, warm gleam. The four of them stepped into the enormous living room, designed for entertaining. A massive stone fireplace dominated one wall; the other was almost entirely glass, looking out over the roofs of other houses to Puget Sound and Vashon Island. They'd be able to watch the ferry make the crossing, the cargo ships and stately cruise ships arriving and departing. Linnea walked over to gaze out, Matt beside her.

"I could enjoy this view," he said.

"It's gorgeous," she agreed, then turned to face the room itself. "But, oh, gosh."

"Oh, gosh?" His tone was tinged with impatience. "I suppose you like having a living room I can cross in two strides, if I'm lucky enough not to trip over the coffee table?"

Her house *was* tiny. But there had to be something in between, didn't there? Linnea couldn't in a million years imagine herself curled in an armchair in this room reading a good book. It would be like lounging in a particularly elegant bus station that was bizarrely empty but for her.

From somewhere out of sight, Hanna begged, "Can I go upstairs and look at the bedrooms?"

By the time they followed her, she'd picked one out that was painted pink and had a wallpaper border with white, winged horses soaring over rosy pink clouds.

"This one's mine!" she cried giddily. She needed lunch and a nap, in Linnea's opinion. Her spinning had taken on a wild quality.

"Honey, I don't know if this house—"

"What's wrong with the house?" Matt frowned at Linnea.

"I— Nothing." Why couldn't she just say "I don't like it?" Instead, she heard herself placating. What else could she call it? "It's gorgeous," she admitted. "You know it is. I just can't imagine what we'd do with all this space."

"But did you see the playroom up here?" His big hand drew her down the hall, past open doors that led into four more bedrooms and three bathrooms.

There was at least one downstairs, too. *Why would any one family need four bathrooms?* she wondered semi-hysterically. *Or are there five?*

The playroom was carpeted in tan berber and had white painted built-in cabinets and shelves for toys and games. It, too, was beautiful. Perfect.

I don't belong here, Linnea thought helplessly.

Matt urged her to look at the master bedroom and the enormous bathroom with a whirlpool tub and separate shower that they would share if they bought this house. Enthusiasm hummed through him, and her anxiety climbed.

"Let's take another look downstairs," he said. Silently she followed him. Oh, Lord, she saw, there were two bathrooms down here; five total. Not to mention a media room and a study and a guest suite.

"I'm overwhelmed," she told him honestly, when the agent was out of earshot. "I can't imagine taking care of a house this size—"

"You don't have to." He smiled at her, his eyes warm. "We'll get a housecleaning service. You're going to be too busy with classes."

"That's a long time away—"

"With work, then." He flicked away her protest. "And look at Hanna. She loves the house."

Their niece was bumping down the stairs on her butt, singing out of tune, her cheeks flushed with excitement. "Can we go outside? I want a swing set." Having reached the bottom of the flight, she ran to Linnea and grabbed her hand. "Can I have a swing set?"

"I'm sure, whatever house we buy—"

Matt gave them both a big grin. "Let's go outside and figure out where we can put that swing set."

Linnea let them haul her along, even though her emotions roiled.

She had to say something. Now. Or Matt would be making an offer on the house before she knew it.

Stunned, she thought, *He didn't even ask if I liked it. He was irritated when I even* hinted *at a reservation.*

He'd be mad if she said, "No. This isn't the right house." Or even, "No, let me get used to being engaged. I'm not ready to buy a house, too."

Her stomach cramped. She didn't do well when people were mad. She'd stood up to Matt the once, because she'd had to for Hanna. But this time… She didn't even have a good reason, except that they didn't need a house this big. Need? She would hate living in one this big, just as she'd hated Finn and Tess's house. But it wasn't only that. She couldn't tell Matt why she wasn't ready to move at all, why she had this horrible, unsettling sense of having lost all control the minute she'd said, "Yes, I'll marry you."

So she looked at the back porch, the yard, the magnificent view, and told herself they would be talking later, when she'd had time to think through all these uncomfortable feelings so that she could make Matt understand.

"WHERE'S GRANDDAD?" Hanna asked, after hugging her grandmother, who had turned from the kitchen sink with arms opened wide.

"He's out in the backyard, pruning roses. I told him it's too early in the year, but you know him. He never listens. It's barely February. We're bound to get a hard freeze that will damage the roses." Linnea's mother shook her head. "Your grandfather," she told Hanna, "has let himself be seduced by sunshine."

Linnea laughed. Hanna's longing gaze was fixed on the French doors leading to the patio. She might not understand the word *seduced,* but she, too, wanted to be out in the sunshine.

"Can I go help?" she asked.

"I feel sure," her grandmother said indulgently, "that he would love to have help."

Hanna flashed her a grin and hurried to let herself outside.

Linnea's mother turned a far cooler look on her. "Will you stay for lunch today?"

Linnea braced herself and said as pleasantly as she could, "I'd love to, if we can talk about something besides Matt."

"You expect me not to care that you're making a foolish decision?" her mother demanded. "Not just foolish. You're hurting all of us. Finn is devastated."

Linnea swallowed. "I don't actually care what Finn thinks." It was a lie, of course; she'd spent too many years trying to earn her brother's approval or rare relaxed smile. "I don't want to upset you," she continued softly, "but I don't understand your objections. You've known Matt a long time. He quit a job he loved and took the new one so he'd be established in Seattle, he's wonderful with Hanna and—" *He loves me.* She wanted so much to say that, but that would be a lie, too.

Her mother's nostrils flared. "He's using you. I don't know what his objective is, but count on it, he thinks he's going to put something over on Finn. Or he has some elaborate scheme for revenge, or he might be trying to get an in with Hanna. But you know perfectly well he hasn't fallen madly in love with you."

Yes. She did. That didn't make her mother's words hurt any less.

Hiding her distress, she lifted her chin and said, "Because it's so unlikely anyone would fall madly in love with me?"

Her mother cast her an impatient glance. "You know that's not what I meant. Linnea, what's happened to you? Family used to mean something to you. You're pushing us away for his sake. Is that really what you want to do?"

"It's tearing me up inside. But Matt's not the one making me choose, Mom. You are." Linnea fought for her poise. "I'll be back for Hanna at five." And she turned and walked out of her parents' house.

Would it ever get better? Or should she quit trying to have her family and Matt, too?

Only twice since Christmas had she stayed for a meal. Both occasions had been miserable, with her mother working into the conversation, whatever the topic, jabs at Matt and at Linnea's betrayal of her brother's wishes.

If only she weren't having terrible doubts about agreeing to marry Matt. She should have gotten to know him better; waited to be sure she was strong enough to stand up to a man so accustomed to having his own way.

Two days after they had looked at the house, he'd called to tell her he had made an offer that had been accepted. He'd talked about closing and letting their respective landlords know they would be moving out. "I'll pick up some cardboard boxes for you to start packing," he'd said. "Lucky I never got around to going through the stuff from my parents'."

She had been nearly speechless. He didn't seem to notice.

She hadn't figured out yet whether she was more upset with him, or with herself.

He'd treated her once again as if she was nothing. Nobody who mattered. *But maybe,* Linnea couldn't help thinking, *I deserve it.* What had she expected, that he'd *beg* for her opinion? He'd dismissed her because she had…abdicated.

Linnea made a face. *Sulked* was probably a better word.

But the dreadful thing was, the house and the up-coming move had erased all the gains she'd made in self-confidence. And she kept finding herself remembering all the years when he had ignored her.

The first time she met him was crystal-clear. He'd flown home to Seattle for Christmas that year. The moment she walked into the condo Finn and Tess were then renting, she'd seen the two men bristling at each other, although she never knew why.

"Linnea," Tess had said, pride ringing in her voice, "come meet Matt."

"Matt, this is Linnea," Tess had said, and he'd turned quite deliberately away from Finn to look at her. His gaze had swept over her, just once, as if she wasn't worth a second glance. Then he'd been pleasant, because that was his way, but not really friendly. Not then, and not later.

It shouldn't still rankle. He'd said he was sorry, and she knew now how much he had already detested Finn. It was natural that he'd transferred some of those feelings to her.

The thing was, she realized today as she drove home from her mother's, it did still bother her. Not only that memory, but ones of his later visits to Tess, when he'd be laughing with his sister or Hanna and not even seem to notice Linnea was there, too.

Could his feelings really have changed that much?

No, she thought, but he had made a commitment to her, and that mattered to him.

He'd started his new job in mid-January, and had discovered to his pleasure that one of his coworkers was another engineer with whom he'd worked several years back in Argentina.

"We stayed in touch for a while," he had said, shrugging, "but it never lasts. That's one trouble with an itinerant lifestyle."

On one of the rare nights Hanna had spent with her grandparents, Linnea and Matt had had dinner with this Kevin Martin and his wife, Chloe. Chloe was pregnant with their first child, and Linnea had been shocked how jealous she was. Her devotion to Hanna was absolute, but she wanted more children.

Matt's children.

He hadn't commented on Chloe's pregnancy and neither did Linnea, but their lovemaking that night was especially intense and passionate. She hadn't asked Matt not to put on a condom—in fact, she'd recently started on birth control—but how tempted she'd been to whisper, "Why don't we start a baby?"

She suspected he would have agreed. Even been delighted. It was the cascade of doubts that stopped her, doubts that grew even though those first weeks as Matt's fiancée were glorious.

Last weekend she and Hanna had played tetherball at the school, and Linnea had thought in dismay, *That's me. I'm the ball.*

She still didn't entirely understand why she hadn't left home for college and never come back. She knew people who barely sent Christmas cards to their parents. Why wasn't she one of them?

Instead, she'd stayed tethered to family, as if she'd never believed she could live free of her mother's strictures. She'd *known* she couldn't measure up to Finn's accomplishments, so she hadn't tried.

That's me, she thought again, swinging around and around in a circle because there weren't any other choices. It was even more dizzying these days. After a few hours spent with Matt and Hanna, or an interlude in his arms, she would soar, certain that marrying him was the right thing to do, that she was happy even if her heart sometimes felt bruised. But when he was gone, she'd spin obsessively the other direction until she was wrapped so tight she could scarcely move. He would barely be out the door, and she'd feel a stab of pain at the knowledge that this was all pretence.

How much, she didn't know. He did want her; she had to believe that. But wanting alone didn't necessarily mean much. If he hadn't had a girlfriend or lover while he was in Kuwait, it might have been a long time for him. He'd come home to Seattle, realized he was stuck, and knew almost no one. Except, of course, that she was so conveniently there, standing between him and the niece he loved. Now he had Hanna partly because he also had her, Linnea.

She wanted to think he liked her and truly did enjoy her company, but she couldn't be sure about that, either. His experiences were so much wider than hers, his tales of his life abroad funny or breathtaking or horrific. She had never lived anywhere but Seattle. Her travels were all through the pages of books, her stories about demented dogs or peculiar library patrons. So she couldn't be sure that he wasn't sometimes bored with her and hiding it.

She supposed, in a nutshell, that was the problem. She wasn't anything special. Matt wanted to marry her because he loved Hanna, and Hanna loved her, and maybe it had all gotten tangled up in his mind with his sense of loss. She still remembered his words. *We feel like family.* He missed having a family. To him, that was good and ample reason for them to get married.

She didn't want to give him up because she had fallen madly in love with him and every moment they spent together was bittersweet bliss. But she also didn't know if she could bear to marry him knowing he *didn't* love her. Look what the knowledge had already done to her. Her hard-won confidence was in shreds.

What stung now would, she feared, become a sharper pain with time, especially if his kindness to her wore off. He'd try to veil his impatience and irritation. She knew he would, but she'd sense it anyway, and eventually they'd end up like her parents, with her slipping away from confrontation and him continually frustrated.

Or he would meet a woman he could love. Then what?

But I'd have months or years with him first. If one could wail inwardly, she did. *I don't want to go back to my life before Matt.*

Her cell phone rang as she pulled into her driveway.

"Hey," Matt said. "Are you at your parents'?"

"No, Mom and I started arguing, as always. I didn't even get a chance to say hi to Dad."

"I'm sorry."

Darn it, he had every reason to dislike her parents right now, but he never took advantage of the openings she gave him to tell her what he thought about them, or to try to influence her against them. It was one of the many reasons she loved him.

"Well, it wasn't anything new. How was racquetball?"

"I kicked Martin's butt." There was a smile in his voice. "Nothing new there, either."

Linnea had to laugh. On impulse she said, "Are you doing anything?"

"No, if you're free I thought we could get the agent to open the house for us so we could take another look. We can shop for furniture while we're waiting for closing."

Not anything she wanted to do right now. Instead, she said, "I was thinking maybe we could just take a walk. And, um, talk."

"Why not do both?" he suggested.

Would looking again be so bad? What if she discovered that she *could* live in it? Linnea knew quite well that her reaction to the house had a whole lot to do with her mood the day they'd seen it. If she loved it, she might feel silly about all this brooding.

And if you don't, a small voice in her head suggested, *well, maybe that's a sign.*

CHAPTER ELEVEN

LINNEA WAS STILL BATTLING panic when Matt picked her up. His kiss only quieted her doubts for a few minutes.

On the short drive to the house, he asked, "Did Hanna hear you and your mother arguing?"

Linnea shook her head. "Dad was pruning roses. Mom wouldn't have said anything if she'd been there."

That wasn't true, of course. Mom loved Hanna, but she didn't seem to have much discretion about what she said in front of her.

She'd said things in front of Linnea, too. Linnea all too vividly remembered a time when she was a junior in high school and she was reading a mailing from Whitman College, one of the West Coast's top liberal arts colleges. Finn had considered Whitman, she knew, but didn't like the setting in the middle of eastern Washington wheat fields and vineyards. He'd wanted bigger, urban, more prestigious and had ended up going to Stanford. Linnea liked the idea of a small college in a small town rather than a city. This one had a pretty campus, old brick buildings covered with ivy and mature leafy trees lining walks and open grassy areas.

Coming home from work, her mother glanced over her shoulder at the brochure, snorted and said to Linnea's father, who was puttering in the kitchen, "Paavo, please tell me you aren't encouraging Linnea to look at private colleges. For goodness' sakes, you know how out of her league she'd be." Linnea remembered bowing her head so that her hair would hide the hot shame on her cheeks. She'd quietly put the brochure in the recycling bin and applied only to the University of Washington and Western Washington U.

Now Matt seemed to accept her answer although she felt his gaze on her averted face. After a minute he started talking about an e-mail he'd gotten from a friend in Kuwait and didn't seem to notice how quiet she was.

The agent's car was already in front of the house they were buying. Matt parked behind it and got out. Linnea sat unmoving for a moment, staring at the house. She wanted so much for this crushing sense of fear to loosen, to know that she'd been wrong and Matt right.

He opened the passenger door and she had no choice but to get out and join him on the sidewalk.

She was aware of him watching her closely as they went up the front steps and into the house, where the agent met them. She was polite enough to smile and say, "I'll sit out on the porch while you two wander to your heart's content."

"Thank you," Linnea said. She walked slowly through the downstairs, aware of Matt behind her, his hands shoved into his pockets, his gaze frequently resting on her face.

Long before she got to the kitchen, she knew already that she didn't want to live here.

It doesn't have to be a sign, she pleaded with herself.

Running her fingers over the black granite surface of the vast kitchen island, she murmured, "You could conduct an autopsy here."

Even without meeting Matt's eyes, she knew they'd darkened. "Is it the granite you don't like? We can replace it."

"It's just so big," she said again, helplessly. "Every room."

"And that's bad because…?"

Linnea bit her lip. "It's not bad. Not for somebody who wants to entertain, or—" She couldn't think of another reason. Have five children? Roller-skate in the living room?

He muttered an imprecation under his breath. "But you don't want to have friends over, I take it."

Friends, yes. A hundred casual acquaintances, no. Then, feeling dense, she realized that Matt might feel he would have to entertain. Or he might really want to, after ten years living in transient housing.

Why, oh, why, hadn't they sat down in the first place and made a list of what they wanted and needed? They could have debated and argued then.

Because neither of them had suggested it, that was why. Maybe because both of them discounted the value of her opinions.

My fault, she mourned.

And it was. How was Matt supposed to know she was a fledgling at speaking up? So far, except for the one memorable confrontation with him, she'd reserved all her defiance for her mother.

And why was that?

Because I've stored up a lifetime of anger? She went very still. *Or because Mom is safe and Matt isn't?*

"Let's look at the rest," she said. He nodded, and together they went upstairs and walked through those rooms, too. The silence grew into a presence that walked between them, kept them from touching. It got harder and harder to imagine what on earth she'd say, so she said nothing. The few glances she stole at Matt told her nothing. His expression was closed in. Not angry, not anything. She had no idea what her face showed.

The tour finally concluded with him thanking the agent cordially then unlocking the car.

Not until they were both in, seat belts buckled, did he look at her with narrowed eyes and say, "You're in a mood today."

Maybe she was. The quarrel with her mother hadn't helped. "I'm sorry. I'm having a hard time picturing myself feeling at home here."

His jaw muscles tensed. "You wanted to buy a house."

"I think…it's too much change," she said awkwardly. "All at once."

"For Hanna? She was excited."

"She hasn't said anything about the house since." In fact, Linnea hadn't been able to draw her out about the move. "I wonder whether it reminds Hanna of hers." She stole a glance at Matt. "Finn and Tess's, I mean."

"I know what you mean." That note of irritation made his voice crisper. "Their place was god-awful. Pretentious."

Her lips formed the word *huge,* but she let it die unsaid. Her pulse was racing. She hated this tension between them, this sense she'd disappointed and annoyed him. The feeling was so terribly familiar.

He sat silent, as if waiting for her to comment. When she didn't, he started the car, glanced in the rearview mirror and pulled away from the curb. After several blocks, he asked, "Do you still want to talk?"

She shook her head. "I might lie down for a bit before I pick up Hanna." Her voice was a little higher than usual, breathless. Nothing he'd notice, she told herself, not the way he would have if she'd sounded sulky.

Matt's face had gone back to being impassive. "All right."

Fortunately the drive wasn't long enough for the silence to become as thick again. When he pulled up in front of her house, Linnea said hurriedly, "I'm sorry, I know I'm being—" she tried to smile "—difficult. I suppose I'm not very adaptable. I should have told you that earlier. Um…you don't need to walk me up."

He was out of the car and around to the sidewalk almost before she'd unbuckled herself and opened her door. "Of course I will," he said brusquely.

Heart still banging in her chest, she hurried to the porch and unlocked the door. She stepped inside and turned to face him.

"I wish you'd talk to me," he said.

Linnea opened her mouth and nothing came out.

He let out a hard breath that might have been angry or frustrated or… She didn't know. Then he crossed the threshold, too, and took her in his arms, pressing his cheek to the top of her head.

Her face briefly contorted and she pressed it to his chest, reassuringly solid.

Matt rocked on his feet, the subtlest of movements but comforting. "I've never done any of this before, Linnea," he murmured to her hair. "You have to help me."

Surprised, she pulled back a few inches, enough to tilt her head back and look at him. "Help you?" The words came out as a squeak.

He growled something under his breath and kissed

her. Her knees seemed to turn to water the moment his lips touched hers, and the next thing she knew, she was holding on and kissing him back. Her physical response to him was instinctive, helpless.

He wrenched his mouth away long enough to shoulder the front door shut and mutter, "If it wasn't for this…" before lifting her into his arms.

This? Linnea moaned, letting her head fall back to give him access to her throat. His teeth grazed it, and his tongue flicked out as if to taste her skin. Whatever he was doing sent heat flooding her senses.

Oh, she thought, in some distant part of her mind. *Yes. This.*

LYING IN HER BED, his arms around her, Matt stared at the ceiling.

For all that she was undeniably here, that she'd responded to his passion with her own, he wasn't quite sure who it was he held.

Lately he'd have sworn Linnea was disappearing right before his eyes. It was the strangest damn thing. The woman who'd stood up to him with quivering defiance when he informed her that he'd be taking Hanna away from her, the one who'd been stunningly generous in victory, had been replaced by a different Linnea, one Matt was dismayed to recognize from all those years of their nodding acquaintance under Tess's roof.

How the hell had he been so blind? he'd asked himself, more times than he wanted to count.

The answer, he was beginning to suspect, didn't have anything to do with his eyesight or his character. Yeah, a gorgeous, shy woman had been right in front of him, but she seemed to have an exceptional talent for making something near ghostly of herself.

She'd been doing it almost from the moment she'd agreed to marry him. She was still beautiful; Matt still wanted her with a breathtaking urgency. But he'd swear she had leached herself of color, cheeks and eyes both, as if moonlight but never sunlight touched her. She had somehow killed much of her vivacity. And she'd quit expressing her opinions. Damn near *any* opinions, from where they'd eat when they went out to the larger questions of what house to buy, when the wedding should be held, what their future would look like.

She wasn't like that with Hanna, of course, only him. So they still had good times, when the three of them were together, and she'd laugh and tease him and even flirt, a little. And when he could steal her away long enough to make love with her, the warmth would creep back into her cheeks, passion would heat her eyes to a brighter blue, and she would sigh and moan and cry out his name as if… Damn it, as if he was the only man in the world.

Then, afterward, she'd fall silent again, and withdraw into herself, leaving him with no idea what she was thinking.

If it weren't for the lovemaking, he'd be sure he was losing her. As it was…he didn't know. And he couldn't get her to open up and tell him what was wrong.

Was it her parents' and brother's opposition to their marriage? Even if her mother was a bitch, Finn an arrogant, self-centered, casually cruel son of a bitch, her father a nonentity, their anger and hurt still mattered to her. He admired her loyalty. They were her family, the only one she'd ever had, and some part of her still needed their approval. Matt did understand, even as he kept hoping the strength of the family he was making with Hanna and Linnea would become her bedrock instead.

So far, she was choosing him, but he had a feeling the necessity of making that choice over and over again was killing her. Maybe that agony alone was making her crawl inside herself and refuse to come out. He didn't know.

He needed to know, but Linnea wasn't telling him.

Matt had taken to goading her, trying to awaken a response. Any response.

Making her walk through the house again, despite her reluctance, had been part of his campaign to prod her into speaking out. Clearly, he was going to have to back out on the offer, even though it would mean losing the earnest money. What he needed to know was why she felt the way she did. Did she hate the house itself? The idea of committing to home ownership?

Or—and this was the possibility that made his throat close up—the idea of committing to him?

So, okay, maybe the house was bigger than they needed. But it had a hell of a view, and despite its size, the place was well laid out and finished with warm wood floors and moldings, wood-wrapped windows and custom cabinets. The front porch reminded him of the one that stretched across the front of the house where he'd grown up. His mom had loved to sit on that porch summer evenings. He'd never been a homeowner himself, and maybe he'd let his eyes get too big for his stomach, so to speak. He hoped he and Linnea would have kids of their own to join Hanna, which meant they'd want a place with at least four bedrooms plus an office for him, right?

Yeah, she *had* made a few quiet murmurs the day they had first looked at it implying she thought the house was too big. But he'd thought she had changed her mind as they continued looking. Hanna had been excited, he'd been excited, and Linnea… Hell, he thought now, recognizing that what he'd taken for awe and agreement had really been a retreat into silence.

At this point, he would have been relieved to see her get pissed off. Anything but this mouselike acquiescence coupled with obvious unhappiness.

Right now, she was pretending to be asleep. In case he was wrong and she actually had dropped off, Matt set the alarm so she wouldn't be late to get Hanna. *He* sure as hell couldn't pick her up at her grandparents' house. That would go over about as well as a brick through their front window.

He got dressed and left, feeling even more unsettled than he had been.

HE HAD DINNER WITH HER and Hanna on Wednesday night. Hanna chattered about the friend she'd made at school, another new girl. Polly took ice-skating lessons, and Hanna wanted to try skating, too.

He argued briefly in favor of hockey, a sport he had to explain to Hanna. "It's like soccer on ice. Except the players hit a puck with sticks, instead of kicking a ball."

"And get their front teeth knocked out," Linnea murmured.

"Mouth guards—"

"I want to jump. And twirl," Hanna said.

Hockey was clearly a no-go. Not that he'd been serious. Hanna might end up tall like her mother, but she was fine-boned and lacked the streak of competitiveness and even aggression that had made Tess a fine basketball player.

After dinner Hanna needed one of them to help her

practice addition with flash cards. Matt cleaned the kitchen while Linnea and she disappeared into the living room. By the time he was done and went to find them, Hanna was reading to her aunt Linnie. Clearly, he wasn't going to have a chance to talk alone with Linnea.

She did break off to walk him to the door, where he tilted her face up and said in frustration, "Damn it, I don't like going home. Why don't we get married? If you're waiting for your mother's approval, you're not going to get it."

She retreated without moving a muscle. "No. I know I'm not."

His jaw flexed. "Then what is it?"

"You're rushing me," she said with a spurt of defiance he hadn't heard in a long time.

Great timing, he realized. Hanna wasn't ten feet away, waiting for Linnea to sit back down with her.

"I want us all to be together."

Her voice softened. "I know."

Matt swore, kissed her again and left.

LINNEA LAY AWAKE A LONG TIME that night, mercilessly examining herself and hating what she saw.

She shouldn't have agreed to marry Matt. Not under the circumstances, with Finn's trial still to come, her custody of Hanna so uncertain, her break with her parents a knot of anxiety that never left her. Most of all, not when he didn't love her.

She couldn't escape the fear that her mother was right. This engagement, even the marriage, might be subterfuge on his part to get his way: custody of Hanna. Lose in court, win another way. She hated even suspecting such a thing, but she couldn't totally make herself believe he would truly want her otherwise. And maybe none of that was the real problem.

No, the real problem was *her.*

Practically from the moment she'd said yes, she'd reverted to habit. Her way of coping with the stronger, more aggressive personalities around her was to fade from their notice. Be biddable, pleasant and the closest thing to invisible she could achieve. Linnea remembered once, at about sixteen, looking at herself in the mirror and thinking that she could hardly even see herself.

Could Matt still see her?

But why had accepting his proposal sent her into flight? Linnea asked herself, bewildered. She wasn't afraid of him, even when she could see his barely suppressed frustration with her. Not the way she was of... Her eyes widened. *Finn. Not the way she was of Finn.* And, in a different way, of her mother.

Mom must have hated me, almost from birth, she thought numbly. It had started so early, she'd never known anything different.

Maybe what Finn had become wasn't any more his fault than what she'd become was hers. No, that wasn't right—they each bore responsibility, as everyone did, for their own choices. But they'd been shaped, even warped, from before their earliest memories. Finn to believe he was great and glorious and should, with a snap of his fingers, have everything he wanted, and her to believe she was a nonentity.

Linnea had trembled inside when she first defied Matt, but she had been fierce when she had to be. After all, she'd had the upper hand, in a way; he needed her. He had rights, yes, but modest ones, and she could give him more. More time with Hanna, more chance of winning Hanna's love and trust.

But when things got personal between them, it became different. She didn't have the upper hand anymore. He was masterful, demanding, determined, decisive. And, stupid her, she'd fallen in love with him and wanted to please him. The only way she knew *to* please was to defer, so she had.

Her eyes were dry now. Her lids felt gritty, as she gained this new, bleak understanding of herself.

Love would have made a difference, given her at least the power to hurt him. As it was she had no power at all and knew it. Her only offerings on the altar of marriage were her body and the child they both loved. But while Matt's smile could lift her to giddy heights, he could also cut her to the quick with one sharp-edged word or a frowning glance. He could hurt her easily, because she was vulnerable to him.

Linnea felt hollow. *I can't marry him.* Believing she could, that she'd be happy in the absence of love, had been a dream. What he wanted from her was truth, and whether she liked the house or not wasn't the truth that mattered. Her new knowledge that she couldn't bear the kind of marriage he'd offered, that was the truth she had to tell him.

She would hurt him, Linnea realized, even if not as much as if he had been in love with her. And she'd be hurting Hanna, too, something she'd sworn she would never do. But not even for Hanna would she go back to living this way, like a shadow, not a real person.

"Thank you for coming," Linnea said gravely. "This probably isn't convenient for you in the middle of the day, is it?"

Matt looked at her with raised eyebrows. "I take a lunch break."

"Yes, but—" She visibly choked off whatever she'd been about to say.

The day was warm enough she'd suggested they get fish and chips and take it across the street to Alki Beach. Both wore wool coats, but the weak sun did feel promisingly warm on Matt's face when they left the hole-in-the-wall restaurant in search of an empty bench.

They found one and laid out their lunch between them. Matt watched Linnea covertly. The sunshine found the richness of color in her pale hair, loose today—strands of gold and wheat amidst the silver blond. He hadn't been able to get a take yet on her mood and wasn't pushing it. She'd suggested this outing. He'd let her lead the conversation.

"Have you met Polly yet?" he asked. "Hanna's new friend?"

"Yes, she's really sweet. Petite—her mom's barely five feet, I think. Dad's with Boeing. They just moved here from Wichita."

As they ate, she talked about Hanna's new teacher, whom Linnea wasn't enthusiastic about. "I'm glad she'll only have her for half the year."

Matt wanted to believe she wasn't leading up to anything important, that lunch today had been an impulse on Linnea's part. He didn't believe it, which had the effect of stifling his appetite. Finally, he bundled what he hadn't eaten into the bag and said, "So what inspired this?"

Very slowly, she followed suit. "You were right that we haven't had many chances to talk. Just the two of us."

Matt made a noncommittal noise.

He saw her take a deep breath, as if to steel herself, then her eyes met his.

All in a rush, she said, "Matt, I'm so sorry, but I can't marry you."

He stared at her, her wide pleading eyes, and in disbelief replayed the exact words.

I can't marry you. Had she really said that?

He was vaguely aware that he hadn't moved. That the silence had grown uncomfortably long. He had thought he'd braced himself. He had guessed from some tone in her voice when she called that he wouldn't like what she had to say. But, damn it. He'd expected her to say, *I don't want to buy that house.* Or, *We can't have our wedding until after Finn's trial, it's not fair to Mom and Dad.* Or even, *I don't know how it happened, but I'm pregnant.*

No, that would have been good news.

"Why?" he asked, voice hoarse.

"I've realized," she said quietly, "that I don't like myself very much lately. You…overwhelm me." She raised a hand when he would have spoken. "It's not you. It's me. I'd end up letting you make all our decisions, and then I'd be miserable the way I've been about the house. I suppose there's a reason I haven't gotten married. It's…complicated, but I think I don't know how to balance with another person."

He reached across the crumpled remains of their food and gripped her hand. "Don't do this. I can listen better. We can work on it."

Very gently, she withdrew her hand, although he saw that it was shaking before she balled it into a fist and hid it in her coat pocket. "Not without love."

She didn't love him. Matt was stunned to realize

he'd believed she did, even though neither of them had said the words.

"I thought—" her voice shook now, too, and she had bowed her head "—that for Hanna, I could do this. We made her happy." When she looked up again, her eyes were filled with anguish. "But that's not enough reason, Matt, not for marriage. You must see that."

"I didn't ask you for Hanna's sake." *I didn't make love to you for Hanna's sake.*

God. Where was his pride?

"I know you thought we could be happy. But be honest. Have you been? What was it you said the other day? *If it wasn't for this...* The sex was the only part you, um, enjoyed. And maybe the fact that, when the three of us are together—"

She didn't finish. Didn't have to.

Desolation roared through him.

"It doesn't sound as if there's anything else to be said. What I think doesn't matter if you aren't happy, and obviously you aren't." He felt a muscle tic in his cheek. "What do you suggest we do now?"

"Well..." She peered uncertainly at him. "Go back to what we were doing before?"

"Pretend we can be friendly, for Hanna?"

"Can't we *be* friends?"

Right this minute, feeling as if he'd been gutted, he simply could not imagine it. But he nodded brusquely and said, "Shall we tell her together?"

Linnea's eyes widened and shied from his. "I'll do it. This is all my fault."

He shook his head in continued incredulity. "Are you done eating? Shall we go?"

She nodded and stood. Matt tossed their leftovers in the nearest garbage can and they walked back to the car in silence. During the drive, she said, her voice timid, "Would you like to take Hanna this weekend? I mean, for the whole weekend?"

His consolation prize. Thank God she hadn't suggested they go ahead and take Hanna sledding at Snoqualmie Pass this weekend together, the way they'd talked about. *Friends*.

"All right. I'll pick her up Saturday morning. Ten?"

"She'll be ready."

He pulled the car into the library parking lot. He didn't look at her, although in his peripheral vision he knew she was unbuckling her seat belt and opening the door. Then she paused, said in a broken voice, "I'm sorry, Matt," and jumped out. The door slammed, and she hurried toward the entrance, nearly breaking into a run before she reached the glass doors.

He let out a ragged, painful sound and gripped the steering wheel. The future suddenly looked so damn empty, he didn't want to put the car in gear, as if not moving at all would somehow save him.

TELLING HANNA WAS EVERY bit as terrible as Linnea had imagined it would be. To her dying day, she would remember the anguished look in Hanna's huge blue eyes and the way she'd whispered, "I thought we'd all be together." Or, maybe worse, when she said, "But Uncle Matt makes you laugh. And he holds your hand."

Yes, she'd thought. *Yes. But he doesn't want to hold my heart.*

Of course, she couldn't say that to a child, however inadequate it felt to offer the adult defense.

"I realized that we were getting married more because we love you than because we love each other. And that's not the right reason to promise to spend our lifetimes together."

Hanna had stormed to her bedroom sobbing. Linnea would have liked to do the same, but somehow held herself together, as she'd mostly managed to do since Matt dropped her off.

Now the moment she'd dreaded had come. Saturday morning, when she had to see him again for the first time.

This time would be the worst, she kept telling herself. Seeing him couldn't help but get easier as time passed. Wasn't that what people always said?

She let Hanna answer his knock on the door, but came out from the kitchen to be polite in response to his chilly civility. She wanted nothing more than for this handoff to go quickly, for him to leave, and he'd opened the door to do exactly that when she remembered their original plans for today.

"Wait. Matt, are you planning to take Hanna up to Snoqualmie?"

Hanna had been watching them already, her alarmed gaze moving between her aunt's and uncle's faces. Now she grabbed Linnea's hand. "But I want *you* to go!"

Matt winced. "We can have fun, Banana. Just the two of us."

"I want Aunt Linnie, too!" Hysteria edged her voice.

His eyes met Linnea's. He was trying for impassive, and failing. Hurt and anger darkened the gray to charcoal. *Your fault,* he was telling her.

She bent to brush her niece's hair from her face. "Honey, we can't always do things together. Even if…we had gotten married, there'd be days I had to work, or

Uncle Matt was away. Remember, he said he'd have to travel sometimes for his job."

"But now we'll *never* do anything together!" Her expression was heartrending, accusatory.

"We will." If she could bear it.

Hanna's grip hadn't lessened, and now her face was crumpling. "But you're not working today. Why not today?"

Grief and misery clogged her throat, but she managed to say, "I can't. I'm sorry, Hanna. Not today." *Please, please, let them go.* "I'll go get your quilted pants. You find your winter boots."

"Aunt Linnie!"

Matt, thank God, intervened and took Hanna's other hand. "Come on, Hanna Banana, let's find those boots. Are they in the closet?"

Freed, Linnea hurried to her niece's room. She fell to her knees and rifled frantically through the bottom dresser drawer, pulling out the pink quilted overalls, ignoring the other clothes now jumbled, some falling to the floor. She started toward the door, intent only on getting them out of here, then turned at the last second, some maternal instinct making her take long enough to retrieve a heavy pair of winter socks from the top drawer.

Matt had the pink boots in his hand and had bundled Hanna into her parka. In jeans and a navy parka, he dominated her small entry, his expression again—almost—stolid.

Hanna's stare, in contrast, was both woeful and stormy.

"I don't want to spend the night. Do I have to spend the night?"

Oh, God, Linnea thought. How did she say, *Thanks to me, that's the way it's gonna be?*

Voice thin, she compromised with, "This time, you do."

Hanna began to sob. Matt effortlessly scooped her up, gave Linnea a last look that was baffled, injured and angry, and left, managing to carry both child and her possessions.

Linnea watched until they reached the car and he deposited Hanna into her booster seat, buckled her in and went around to the driver's side without even glancing back.

Then Linnea locked the front door and, bent over in pain, made it to her bedroom.

She supposed that later, eventually, she'd call to give her mother the news. Somebody would be glad. Not happy—Linnea had come to realize that Mom never really was. This would be more in the nature of an acidly pleased "See, I was right and you were wrong" moment. Linnea didn't want to tell her, but how could she not without keeping Hanna from her grandparents?

Sometimes she thought that wouldn't be such a bad thing, but not right now. Hanna had lost so much. And Mom was better with her than she was with Linnea, perhaps because Hanna was Finn's child.

Knowing that hurt, too. Everything hurt these days: seeing herself so painfully true, thinking about her mother and aching to ask why, living with Hanna's new grief and—worst of all—imagining years of these child exchanges with Matt, loving him, watching him lose any interest in her.

When I could have had him.

Except, without love, she wouldn't ever really have, would she?

As if protecting herself from blows, she curled into a fetal position on her bed and cried until she ran out of tears.

CHAPTER TWELVE

MATT SAT IN HIS CAR OUTSIDE Linnea's house, fighting for the will to get out and walk up to her door. This was killing him.

He anticipated seeing Linnea, and he dreaded it. Every damn time, he'd think, maybe today her face would soften with a smile for him. Maybe the strain would evaporate, as if it had never been, and they'd find themselves talking easily. Maybe one of these times she'd suggest they go kick a soccer ball around and, in circling to the beginning, he would have another chance.

Uh-huh. Maybe that would make it worse. Because her easy friendship wasn't enough. Would never be enough.

He closed his eyes and rested his head against the seat. At least today he was invited in. Linnea was having a birthday party for Hanna, one of two; the other, of course, was at her grandparents' house, and he was emphatically not invited to that one. So today, for the next hour, say, he would have his chance to sneak under Linnea's guard.

A month had passed since she'd broken off their engagement. She had been, as always, generous when he asked for time with Hanna, who had spent three of the intervening four weekends with him. He'd taken her out for pizza two Wednesdays in a row. He'd even sat beside

Linnea in the school cafeteria transformed into an auditorium for the entire student body to demonstrate their musical skills for their proud parents. The youngest grades had sung, one class had played kazoos, the fifth-grade band played their cacophonous first concert for their parents. He and Linnea had managed to chat, civil adults that they were, and Hanna's joy afterward at finding them together had made him sick to his stomach.

He had moments when he thought he should contest custody now, not wait for Finn's trial. He couldn't walk away from Hanna, but they couldn't go on the way they were, either.

He couldn't.

But, of course, if Hanna lived with him, her aunt Linnea would have visitation rights, and he'd still have to see her. That, and live with having devastated her by snatching the one person he knew she loved.

The only positive news was that a date *had* been set for the trial, and a far sooner one than Matt had been led to expect. The son of a bitch would face a judge and jury only six months after killing Tess, rather than the year or more that seemed to be the norm. The unusual dispatch had been Finn's doing, not the prosecutor's; still arrogant, he assumed he'd walk out of that courtroom free and clear, having been judged innocent, and take up his life where he'd left off.

Without Tess, of course, but Matt couldn't imagine that his brother-in-law mourned Tess at all. Even in his own mind, Finn undoubtedly blamed the whole disaster on her. After all, nothing was ever *his* fault.

Matt intended to be present every goddamn day of that trial. He wanted the jury to see his rage. He was all

Tess had had, and except for taking care of Hanna, this was the last thing he could do for her. He'd accepted his job on the proviso that he be able to take a leave when the trial began.

Finally, with a groan, Matt made himself grab the wrapped gift he'd brought and get out. Earlier, Linnea had taken Hanna and the three friends she'd chosen to invite to see a movie. He was here for the cake and ice cream and presents.

He'd no sooner let the brass knocker fall on Linnea's front door than Hanna flung open the door. Wearing brand-new jeans embroidered with pink unicorns and a fluffy pink sweater over a white turtleneck, she was buzzing with birthday excitement. He didn't remember Tess ever being so girlie, but maybe he was forgetting.

"Uncle Matt!" Hanna accepted his hug, then tugged him into the living room where the other little girls were giggling and a heap of unopened presents sat on the coffee table.

Linnea stuck her head out of the kitchen. "Matt, thank goodness. Will you give me a hand?"

He couldn't seem to get over his reaction to her. Damn it, she was as sexy in chinos and a plain, aqua-blue turtleneck as she had been in a formfitting black cocktail dress and spike heels. Gritting his teeth, he ignored the surge of desire and followed her to the kitchen. At least she'd said *thank goodness* in connection with him.

Looking frazzled, she said, "Will you light the candles while I get the ice cream? If I carry the cake, will you take pictures? I want to be sure to get one of Hanna blowing out the candles."

"Matches?" he asked, studying the cake with white frosting and pink and purple confetti.

"I just got them out…" Distracted, she turned in a circle, then pounced when she spotted them on the counter. "The camera—"

"Is here on the table." He took the matches from her and lit the first one. "How was the movie?"

Carton of ice cream in hand, she grimaced. "Awful, actually, but they were happy." Her eyes met his. "Ready?"

Trying hard to be unthreatening, he smiled agreeably, even as he marveled that he could. "Ready."

The girls all squealed when Linnea appeared with the cake, the candles flickering as she walked. Matt snapped pictures, of her leading the birthday song as she set the cake on the coffee table, of Hanna's glowing face as she made a wish. He caught her huge puff and her triumph when she blew out all seven candles.

He continued to watch Linnea covertly as she sliced cake and added scoops of vanilla ice cream, as she teased the girls and deftly swept away the plates when they'd eaten as much as they could. Wrapping paper flew, and Hanna appeared delighted with her haul of Barbie dolls, a plastic horse statue with flowing pink—what else?—mane and tail, glittery fingernail polish and a jewelry-making kit. Linnea's smile for the girls was so natural, he ached for one aimed at him.

There would be more gifts from the grandparents and her father tomorrow, he knew. Lucky Linnea who got to do this twice. Or perhaps Grandma was baking the second cake. Matt wondered what Finn's mood was, with opening day of his trial only weeks away. Matt hoped like hell that doubt was beginning to eat at his gut, maybe spiced with fear. He hoped Finn had ugly nightmares.

Eventually the doorbell started ringing as parents

arrived to pick up their offspring. Linnea chattered and laughed with them, too, and with a mere touch on the shoulder had Hanna thanking her guests for coming and for the presents.

His welcome had run out, too, Matt realized. He wouldn't abuse it, not with Linnea's accusation that he *overwhelmed* her running in a nonstop loop in his memory. Hanna thanked him for his present and said wistfully that she wished he could come to Grandma and Grand-dad's tomorrow, too.

"How come you never do?" she asked, her forehead crinkling. "You used to always be there at Christmas, and Grandma and Granddad were, too."

He and Linnea exchanged a look. Hanna had never asked before, seeming to take for granted that the two sides of her family were isolated from one another.

"Ah…that was when your mom was alive. Having your mom and dad married made us all family." Out of the corner of his eye, he saw Linnea jerk. His voice rough-ened. "It's different now."

"Oh." Puzzlement still showed on her face. "But even if Mommy—" She caught herself. "You're still my uncle. Aren't you?"

"That's right." God. How did he say *I hate your father's guts? And don't think much of your grandpar-ents, either?*

Linnea said it before him, crouching to eye level. "Uncle Matt loved your mom. It's hard for him, while your dad is accused of being the one who hurt her."

"Oh." Hanna looked down. "I heard Grandma and Dad talking. They said that after the…the…"

"Trial?" Linnea prompted gently.

"Uh-huh. The trial. They said everyone will know it wasn't Daddy's fault. And that I could live with him again."

Rage ignited in his chest, a hell of a lot bigger flame than her birthday candles. He must have made an involuntary move, because Linnea flicked a warning glance at him.

"How do you feel about that?" she asked, in the same quiet, nonjudgmental voice.

Almost inaudibly, Hanna said, "I want to stay with you, Aunt Linnie. And Uncle Matt."

"I'm hoping you can, honey." Linnea kissed her cheek. "Now, say goodbye to Uncle Matt, then we'd better clean up the wrapping paper before Spooky decides to investigate and gets tangled in ribbon. Or samples the cake!"

A tiny giggle escaped Hanna. She hugged Matt, some tension still in her body, but her birthday ebullience returning, too.

"I love you," he said.

She hugged him again, harder, and whispered urgently, "I love you, too, Uncle Matt."

Letting her go was difficult. Here he was again, he thought bleakly, lurking around the edges of their lives.

Hanna headed to the living room. Linnea didn't immediately follow.

"Thank you," she said.

"For snapping a few pictures?"

"For not saying what you were thinking. You could taint Hanna's feelings about her grandparents—and her dad even more!—but you haven't."

"She's six years old." He remembered the candles. "Seven now. All of this is traumatic enough for her."

"Yes, but you have reason to be terribly angry." Her

eyes searched him, as if in perplexity. "It tells me you really do love her."

Abruptly pissed, he said, "You thought I didn't?"

"No." She made an abortive gesture. "No, I know you did. It's just... Most people I know wouldn't have let that stop them."

Her mother and brother, she meant. Her father...who knew? Linnea judged based on her family, logically enough. How, he wondered, not for the first time, had she ended up so different from any of them?

"I won't use her."

She gave him a funny, crooked smile, and he thought he saw a sheen of tears in her eyes. "I thought it wouldn't hurt, once, to say thank you."

"You shouldn't have to," he said, frowning. "You're so good with her. *For* her. It's because of you that she's emerging from her grief and confusion. I should be thanking you, not the other way around."

"She needs us both."

He spread his hands in agreement. If he'd opened his mouth, he would have said, *There's a way she could have us both—24/7*. She knew it, was backing away with some alarm, as if she hadn't anticipated this turn of the conversation.

"I'd better get to cleaning up."

He nodded and turned away.

She was closing the door behind him when she said, "Matt?"

He paused.

"You know Finn's trial starts on the twenty-seventh?"

"Yes."

"Will you be going?"

"Oh, yes," he said, letting some of his anger leak into his voice. "You?"

She didn't answer for a moment, then said, "I don't know. I'm sure Mom and Dad will be."

"I'll do my best to avoid them." He could promise that much.

Linnea only nodded, said goodbye and shut the door.

He'd give a great deal to know whether her feelings about the upcoming trial were mixed at all. Did Linnea love her brother? Maybe foolishly, he'd assumed not. She'd said enough things to make him sure she didn't *like* Finn. But love was way more complicated. They'd grown up together, presumably played together, squabbled together, like any other siblings. Yeah, he realized, not happy with his own conclusion, she almost had to be confused, her determination to protect Hanna at odds with instinctive loyalty to family.

He hoped she had someone she could talk to. He wished that someone was him. Not that he could be neutral. But for her sake, like Hanna's, he'd have done his damnedest to give her what she needed.

Matt was slammed by an unpleasant thought. Had he tried, when they were engaged? Or had he been focused entirely on what *he* needed?

He didn't like the answer.

LINNEA ATTENDED THE opening day of her brother's trial, sitting beside her parents behind Finn and his phalanx of attorneys. Matt arrived as she was sitting down. He gave her, then her parents, an ironic tip of his head before he sat behind the prosecutor, who turned around to speak to him.

Cheeks burning, Linnea stared straight ahead. She

hated being here, dressed up as though this were a job interview, but really so she could play her part in saying to the jury, *See what a lovely family Finn has? How absurd to say he could be a murderer.*

Finn had greeted them all with big smiles and hugs. Linnea stood stiff in his embrace. Her stomach churned, and she had a dizzying moment of…something rather like film being double exposed. Her big brother, patiently talking her down from a tree she'd climbed only to impress him with her daring. What an odd image to come to her now—his face tilted up, what seemed terrifyingly far below her—his voice steady and calm.

"Lower your left foot to the next branch, Linnie. Yes, like that, but a little to the right. It's a good, solid… Yes! Okay, now your left hand. See that smaller branch, right by your shoulder?"

He hadn't once demonstrated any exasperation with her. She thought he'd been genuinely scared that she'd fall. But somehow he had made her think she could do it. If she could get up, she could get down, and she had. He hadn't even told Mom later.

But the other Finn, the handsome man sitting in front of her, was something else. He murmured to his defense attorney, anger in every rigid line of his body, his tone impatient because he must *hate* having to depend on someone else, someone he'd believe wasn't his equal in ability. No one ever was. She saw the notes in front of him, saw his quick, irritated shake of the head deny some possible strategy because it wasn't *his*.

She didn't like being around that Finn, the controlling, manipulative man her big brother had become. She'd been on the receiving end of his temper enough times to believe he could have killed Tess. Linnea quailed, but Tess had always gone toe-to-toe with him, earning his respect but also enraging him. Oh, yes, if she said the wrong thing, he could have picked up that heavy coffee table and swung it at her. Not intending to kill her, no, Linnea didn't believe that, but not considering any consequences, either. His entire life, Finn had slithered free of any unfortunate aftereffects of his own behavior.

Partly, she remembered, because he was such a good liar. He could radiate outraged sincerity.

And she was tacitly supporting him by sitting here.

Listening to the prosecutor's opening statement was excruciating. It painted Finn as a serial abuser, claiming he'd sent Tess to the hospital before. Fury flashed on his face, and he wrote something for his attorney in slashing script so fierce, it must have penetrated to imprint the entire tablet of paper below the sheet he wrote on.

The prosecutor walked the jury through the awful fight that had led Finn to smash his wife's skull, then described him in the aftermath—collected enough to place the coffee table upright and aligned so that it would look as if Tess had fallen into it, before he called 911.

The defense attorney stood in turn and described Tess as volatile, impulsive, often clumsy. Was it true that she'd broken her arm and collarbone both in the past couple of years? he asked.

"Sure, but there's never been any suggestion that her husband caused her injuries. This was a successful, strong-minded woman, yet not once did she so much as hint to doctors, friends or family that Finn had raised a hand to her."

No, he told the jury, the prosecution was trying to

support their flimsy case with unprovable insinuations. Finn and Tess had exchanged words. Finn, in his anger, had kicked the coffee table over. In a rage, his wife had flung herself at him but tripped on the rug and gone headfirst into the overturned coffee table. Distraught, Finn had knelt at her side and pushed the table away to minister to her.

"Yes," the attorney said, prowling in front of the jury box, "Mr. Sorenson thinks he picked up the table and righted it while he waited for the police. It was…instinctive. One of those things you do while your mind is engaged in horror. He honestly doesn't remember what he did during the ten minutes between his call and the first unit arriving."

Linnea listened carefully. At the end, she thought, *It sounds so plausible.* And—with a chill under her breastbone—*I don't believe it. Any of it.*

It seemed hard, suddenly, to breathe. Court was being recessed until morning, but she couldn't stand to sit here for another minute. She had the sudden, awful realization that the press would likely be waiting to interview them outside the courthouse. It was Finn they wanted, but they'd expect quotes from his family members, too. What would she *say?*

Finn was turning to speak to them again, and on the other side of the courtroom she saw Matt standing and shrugging on his overcoat. To her mother, Linnea said, "I can't stay, Mom. I have to get Hanna." She fled before other spectators had a chance to crowd the aisle.

She heard her name being called behind her, but she kept going, her steps faster and faster. Down the hall, out of the courthouse, to the parking garage where she was nearly running. Inside her car, she locked the doors and sat gasping, not even understanding why she was so upset, only knowing she couldn't come again, listen to the evidence being carefully laid out to prove her brother guilty, not only of rage so terrible he could kill, but also of cold-bloodedly lying ever since with no apparent cost to him.

She remembered Tess's broken collarbone. A skiing accident, she'd claimed. And the wrist—she'd slipped on ice and banged it against the porch step's railing. Both explanations had been made in Finn's hearing. If he was the one to have hurt her, would she really have lied to protect him? Would she have forgiven him, not once, but twice? Or had he raised a hand to her other times, too?

Tess, Linnea thought, would have struck back. Then what? Did those fights end in black silences or laughter at their idiocy or even passion?

Huddled there in her car, she thought, *We'll never know. Not truly. Finn is incapable of honesty, not when it would show him in an unfavorable light.*

A hand rapped on her side window, and her heart jolted as if electrified. She reached frantically for the gear shift even as she turned her head to see who wanted to talk to her.

It was her dad's face she saw. He was stooped to peer worriedly in at her.

Shakily, she wondered what she'd expected. The entire press corps, who of course would have streamed in pursuit of her, because she was such an important player in this trial? The ogre of underground Seattle? Her parents had followed her into the parking garage earlier and parked right beside her small car.

She rolled down her window. "Dad."

"Are you all right? The way you ran out of there…"

Her mother appeared at his shoulder. "It didn't look

good, Linnea. Surely five more minutes wouldn't have mattered to Hanna's sitter."

A snapshot from the funeral flashed before her mind's eye: Matt, watching his sister's coffin being lowered into the ground, his face contorting. Finn's expression one of deep sadness, unchanged from the moment she'd first seen him in the church. He might have practiced it in a mirror, or—fine actor that he had always been—perhaps he hadn't needed to do that. How odd, that she was so certain he was thinking about the TV cameras trained on him and not Tess's burial at all.

"I'm not coming again," she said.

Her father's face creased in perplexity and increased worry.

"Of course you are," her mother snapped. "You know how important appearances are. We have to be seen supporting your brother."

Linnea shook her head and kept shaking it. "I won't. I think…I think he did kill Tess. I won't say that to anybody but you, but I also won't play a part in convincing the jury that he's a wonderful family man who couldn't possibly have done something like that."

For once, she'd shocked her mother, who gasped, "What a terrible thing to say."

Linnea looked straight at her mother. "I was scared of Finn. Did you know that? He didn't hit me, but he said cruel, hateful things all the time."

Somehow her father had faded back. He was unlocking their car doors, pretending, probably, that this wasn't happening.

The lines in her mother's face, Linnea realized, were becoming permanent. Furrows in her forehead, carved from unhappiness and irritation. Her nostrils flared. "That's absurd. This is the influence of that man, isn't it? Oh, Linnea. Why can't you see—?"

"I do see," she said flatly. The truth was determined to spill out as if she had suddenly exceeded her capacity for hiding it. "He could never do wrong in your eyes, and I could never do right. Every time I tried to talk to you about him, you'd twist whatever I said until I was at fault." Her mother tried to interrupt; Linnea talked over her. "After a while, I started believing I was. I believed I wasn't entitled to an opinion, that I wasn't very smart or pretty or capable. But you know what, Mom?"

Her mother's mouth worked like a puffer fish's.

"Lately, I've realized that I might be as smart as Finn. And I *am* pretty and capable, too. Why did you try so hard to make me think I wasn't?"

"Did it ever occur to you that I was being realistic?" Mom's voice was as sharp as glass, shattered into shards. "That I was protecting you by not letting you get your hopes up too much?"

Linnea felt…nothing. The numbness would wear off, but she was grateful for it.

She only shook her head. "What you did to Finn isn't any better, Mom. He needed to be told no, to be punished when he lied, to learn humility and empathy and regret. He never had the chance."

They stared at each other. Her mother's face was frozen, like a death mask, shock congealed.

Linnea's numbness cracked, and horror suffused her. She was being hateful. So what if Mom did look back and realize how unequally she'd treated her children? What purpose was served now by her feeling even partially responsible for the crime Finn had committed?

I should have let it go, Linnea thought in anguish.

She opened her mouth, but her mother recovered her voice first.

With dignity, she said, "I hope by tomorrow you regret saying such hateful things and are ready to apologize."

She turned away, opened her car door and got in, staring straight ahead as if Linnea wasn't there. Paavo looked over the roof of the car at Linnea and said in a soft voice, "We'll understand if you don't want to come tomorrow, Linnie. Finn will, too. Today was hard."

A small sob escaped her. Had he *listened* to her? Had he ever, really?

"Dad…" She shook her head. "Never mind." With a push of the button, her window glided closed. Still dry-eyed, Linnea put her car in gear, looked both ways and backed out.

She started home on autopilot, remembering every word she'd said, every word her mother said. One minute she thought, *I was childish and petty.* The next instant, she knew she'd needed her mother to hear how hurt she was, if only this once. Whether their relationship could be repaired, she had no idea. Linnea wasn't sure she cared.

Somehow, tears never came. Instead of going straight home, she picked Hanna up and they went out for hamburgers and french fries. Afterward, she listened to Hanna read then read in turn to her. Before bedtime, she laid out their clothes for the morning. She'd asked for the whole week off, but she would call the library in the morning and see if she could go in after all.

Not until she had turned out the lights and gone to bed,

Spooky a comforting, warm lump against her side, did Linnea identify an odd sensation she'd been aware of all evening. It was more an absence of something than an addition, as if a weight had been lifted from her. Her heart ached, yes; she was conscious of lingering regret every time she pictured that frozen, somehow ugly, expression on her mother's face. But she also felt...

"Free," she whispered in the dark, her hand going to stroke Spooky's head when it lifted at the sound of her voice.

She didn't care what Finn thought, when she didn't go to sit in that courtroom. She didn't care how angry her mother was.

Linnea thought, *If I get permanent custody of Hanna, I can move away if I want. I can live on my savings and go to grad school without any help from anyone. I can...stretch.*

It was odd to realize this was exactly what Matt had wanted for her. Only, he was used to making things happen, and it wasn't in him to be patient, so he'd tried to propel her forward using his momentum and not her own.

Had he seen how she'd stifled herself? she wondered. Had he tried to nudge her forward because his ego demanded that his wife be someone more than a meek library clerk and dogwalker? Or because he wanted for her what she wanted?

Another answer she'd never learn. Another twist of pain, stronger than regret, to join the knot in her chest.

Linnea stared into the darkness with dry, burning eyes and wished... The puff of air that escaped her lips was almost a laugh. She wished for so much, but perhaps most of all that Matt Laughlin loved *her.*

CHAPTER THIRTEEN

MATT STRETCHED OUT HIS LEGS under the table at the pizza parlor and reached for a second piece of pizza. A family a couple of booths away was laughing, and some young teens in the arcade area hooted. Hanna, he couldn't help noticing, hadn't eaten half her first slice, and since those few bites had done nothing but fiddle with it, mangling the crust.

"Aren't you hungry?" he asked.

She didn't lift her head. "Daddy called this morning."

Obviously startled, Linnea said, "When? Oh, was I in the shower?"

She nodded. "Uh-huh."

They were two weeks into the trial, and Matt had felt soul-sick when he walked out of the courthouse today. The prosecution had wrapped up their case last week; since then the defense had dragged in expert witness after expert witness to puncture holes in the central arguments, saying that neither the force of the blow nor the angle of the wound to Tess's head could be explained by her falling. She had to have been standing, not prone, when the table struck her head, and it had to be propelled by greater force than a fall could account for.

Tonight was Matt's usual evening to take Hanna out.

When he called earlier, he'd gotten Linnea. He'd asked, rather abruptly, "Would you join us tonight, Linnea? Just for pizza?"

Somewhat to his surprise and very much to his relief, she'd agreed. He was in a lousy mood. Spending time with her as well as his niece was making a difference.

But this…

"What did your dad say?" Matt asked.

Hanna drew her head in, turtlelike, and kept twisting and tearing at the narrow slice of pizza. Her hair veiled her face. "He sounded funny." She paused. "Like…he was sad."

When she didn't go on, Linnea cleared her throat. "What was he sad about?"

"He said he missed Mommy. And me. He asked if I was happy with you." She stole a look at her aunt Linnie. "When I said I was, and I like school 'n' stuff, he said good, only his voice was all choked, like…"

"Oh, pumpkin." Linnea smoothed her hair back, then drew her into an embrace.

"I think he was crying." Hanna's face crumpled. "Why was Daddy crying?"

Because the son of a bitch knew he was going to prison, Matt thought. Because—maybe—it had finally hit him that his ugly temper tantrum had cost him everything. Maybe he'd even realized that his smart, gentle, sweet daughter was the most precious thing he'd lost.

"I think," Linnea murmured, "he really does miss you."

"He said—" Hanna's eyes were wide and scared. "He said he was sorry, and he loved me. And then he hung up."

Did Finn have a conscience after all? Matt didn't know if he believed it. But it was important that Hanna did.

"You know about the trial," he said.

The little girl nodded. Linnea eyed him askance but didn't signal him to stop.

"Your grandma and granddad have been going every day. So have I. I loved your mom. I'm…bearing witness."

Of course he had to pause to explain what he meant and wasn't sure Hanna understood. But finally he continued, "In another few days, the lawyers will be done presenting their cases." He asked a few questions, and found that Linnea had told Hanna the parts performed by the prosecution and the defense as well as the judge and jury. So he said, "The jury will go off to a room by themselves and talk about everything they heard over these weeks. And they'll decide whether they believe your dad killed your mom or whether it was an accident. I imagine your dad is pretty scared right about now."

Face stricken, Hanna nodded.

"If they decide he's guilty, he'll go to prison. He'll lose his job because attorneys can't have committed a crime themselves. And he knows that, by the time he gets out of prison, you'll have grown up quite a bit and may want to stay with your aunt Linnie or me and not go back to live with him."

She took all that in, her eyes shadowed. At last she said, "If he's sorry, does that mean…?"

"He did kill your mother?" Matt kept his voice steady, quiet. "I don't know. He may just be sorry all of this happened and that you got hurt."

She nodded and bowed her head again. After a minute she pushed her plate away. "I don't want any more."

"Okay." Linnea kissed the top of her head. "I'm done, too. Matt?"

They got a box for the leftovers and he drove them

home. When he pulled up to the curb, Linnea asked, "Would you like to come in?"

Very aware of Hanna in the backseat, Matt said casually, "Sure. Will you read to me, Hanna?"

"Uh-huh."

Linnea smiled at him, causing a bump in his chest. "Have you heard her read these past few weeks? If not, you're going to be impressed."

He cranked the wheels to make sure the car didn't roll backward, then accompanied the two inside. Hanna dug a book out of her school bag, and they settled on the sofa while Linnea went to put the pizza in the refrigerator.

He knew that Hanna was reading exceptionally well, at least a grade ahead of most of her classmates, according to Linnea. As she got into the story, she gradually relaxed and her voice gained animation. When she finished a chapter, she looked up at him. "This is a good book, isn't it, Uncle Matt? I wish *I* had a pony, like Jessica does." In the chapter book, Jessica had been surprised by her parents on her birthday morning with her very own pony. "Only I want mine to be white."

"I'll bet a white one would be hard to keep clean. Horses like to roll in the dirt or on grass, you know."

"Have you ever had a horse, Uncle Matt?"

"No, but I had a friend who did," he told her. "His name was Gabe Mackey. His dad was a horse trainer, and I rode with Gabe sometimes. It was fun."

She gazed at him speculatively. "Does he still have a horse?"

"You know, I have no idea. Gabe's family moved when we were in seventh or eighth grade. His dad wanted a bigger farm with an indoor arena for riding and more pasture and stalls. Gabe and I wrote each other a few times, but I guess he made new friends and we lost touch."

Hanna mulled that over. "*I* made a new friend, too."

"I know." He grinned at her. "And I'll bet you'll make more."

"Uh-huh. I like this girl named Calliope, too. She's in Mrs. Rodriguez's class, but sometimes she plays with Polly and me. She's real good at four square."

Matt saw Linnea leaning against the doorframe listening. She wandered in and joined them, encouraging Hanna to continue chattering until the disturbing phone call from her father was no longer in the forefront of her thoughts. She went off cheerfully to brush her teeth, and neither Matt nor she mentioned Finn when he read her a picture book and kissed her good-night. He left her bedroom door open the requisite six inches and the hall light on, and returned to the kitchen where he found Linnea lifting a steaming teakettle from the stove.

"I was making a cup of tea. Would you like one?"

"Yes, thanks." Wondering what was up, he watched her put a tea bag in a second mug and pour. "You haven't mentioned Hanna's nightmares lately. If she had one at my house last weekend, she didn't wake me."

"No, she's only had a couple this week. I think they're fading." Linnea handed him the mug and said, "Why don't we go in the living room."

He followed her, hungrily taking in the sway of her hips in jeans and the vulnerable, smooth nape of her neck beneath the bundle of silky fine hair. When she turned to settle herself at one end of the couch, her gaze turned startled then shy, making him grit his teeth. Damn it, he had to hide what he was thinking better than he'd apparently been doing if he wanted to regain any of her lost trust.

He chose the easy chair rather than the other end of the couch, not wanting to alarm her. "I wonder why she didn't tell you earlier today about Finn's call," he said.

Linnea made a face. "Probably because I hustled her out the door. We were running late this morning."

"Ah."

She took a sip of tea and seemed to gather herself before meeting his eyes. "Is the trial really almost over?"

"Maybe a few more days, tops."

"Oh." Her forehead creased. "Um…how do you think it's going?"

"I think he's going to be found guilty. Not just because that's the result I want," Matt said, seeing her expression. "I spend a lot of time watching the jurors. Trying to tell how they react to testimony. There are a couple who seem to like Finn. I'm not sure about them. The rest of them don't." He eyed her. "You've stayed away since that first day."

"Yes." Her mouth twisted. "I felt too conflicted. Of course, Mom's mad that I'm not supporting Finn by being there every day. We're not speaking."

"I'm sorry," he said quietly.

Her chin came up. "I'm not." She blinked. "That's an awful thing to say, but I mean it. Isn't it strange, that it took something like this to make me see—"

Careful to keep his tone undemanding, Matt asked, "See what?"

"How differently Mom treated Finn and me. I don't know why. I'm not sure she knows. But it hurt. I told her that, which upset her, but I think I needed to say it, if only once."

Matt wished he'd been a fly on the wall. No, damn it. What he wished was that he'd been at her side, silently lending his strength, there to listen to her afterward. Yeah, and while he was throwing pennies in the fountain, he'd also wish that he'd troubled to see what was under his nose all those years when he'd dismissed her as inconsequential.

"That took guts," he said. "Good for you."

"I told her she had some responsibility for the kind of man Finn turned into, too. I don't think Mom had a clue what I was talking about, and I regretted saying that." She looked troubled. "I mean, what good does it do now?"

"It might make her think a little more carefully about what she says to Hanna," he pointed out. "And you'll presumably have kids someday. What if she treats them unequally?"

"I wouldn't let them see her," Linnea said fiercely. "She's— I don't know what's wrong with her. But I've discovered I'm really angry."

His protective instincts were firing on all cylinders. If she thought she was angry, it was nothing to what he felt. The depth of his fury took him by surprise.

He had the sense to hide it, though. The fact that she was talking to him at all was an unexpected gift. His feelings would scare her off.

As mildly as possible, he asked, "You didn't realize before that you were angry?"

Linnea shook her head. "Isn't that strange? But, you know, it really does hurt, to wonder if your own mother loves you. And I'd spent so many years believing her when she implied I wasn't smart enough to do whatever, or pretty enough to think some boy I had a crush on would ever ask me out. She really had me convinced Finn was smarter and better at everything and more worthy."

Matt hoped like hell the mug was sturdy, because he was gripping it so hard his knuckles must be white. After a careful moment, he set it down on the coffee table. "You make me want to punch someone on your behalf."

Her eyes widened in startlement. "Really?"

"Really." His voice was low, but even he heard how lethal it was. He cleared his throat. "You must have hated your brother's guts."

She stared at him. "It's funny, but no. I didn't. I spent years wishing I could impress him. Finn was nice to me sometimes, you see. I lived for the moments when it was us against Mom. Thinking back, I suspect when we were young he was a typical big brother." She wrinkled her nose. "Obnoxious. Weren't you, sometimes?"

He had a few memories of tormenting Tess until she started yelling for Mom or Dad. "Oh, yeah," he admitted.

Linnea nodded. "But by the time he was eleven or twelve, he'd changed. When he teased, he could be mean." Her eyes closed for a moment. "Really mean." Those words were a mere breath; he barely caught them. "By the time Finn was a teenager, he looked down on me, too. Like…I was an embarrassment to him. And when he did notice me, he was unkind."

Matt had overheard the bastard say cruel enough things to Tess, and he knew Finn had been one hell of a lot more than unkind to his little sister. His ego hadn't allowed her to shine, too. Or maybe he'd bought into his mother's warped view of her children. If Linnea had become convinced she had little value in her family, it was logical that her brother believed it, too.

Very softly, she said, "I lived with this sense of shame."

In a strangled voice, Matt said, *"God."* Maybe this wasn't smart, maybe she'd recoil from him, but he couldn't sit here, pretending to be dispassionate when she all but bled in front of him. Moving swiftly, he circled the coffee table and sat on the middle cushion of the sofa.

When he wrapped Linnea in his arms, she momentarily went rigid. Then, with a sigh that felt like a knife to his gut, she leaned into him, her face against his shoulder. He laid his cheek on the top of her head and said roughly, "I don't know how you survived. You're an amazing woman, Linnea Sorensen."

She shook her head, as if a compliment triggered an automatic response, and started to pull back. "Oh, no. Not me. I wish I was."

He released her, because he thought she needed to assert her hard-won sense of self. But this was one argument he wasn't letting her win.

"Maybe you can't see it, but I can. The way you fought for Hanna impressed the hell out of me. With the comfort and love and strength you've given her, she's a lucky kid."

She gazed at him with an expression of wary hope that was painful to see. She wanted to believe him. She wanted it so much, but had no practice in thinking highly of herself.

"What about your father?" Matt asked roughly. "Why didn't he intervene?"

"He did sometimes. He'd quietly encourage me to try things Mom said I couldn't do. But Dad—" She hesitated, and Matt could see that she didn't like to criticize her father. "Arguments upset him. He mostly lets Mom have her way. I guess I'm more like him."

With quiet force, Matt said, "But you would never

have let your own child be demeaned to the point where she couldn't believe in herself."

She flinched. After a long moment, she said softly, "No."

He wanted, as he'd never wanted anything before, to make her life different. Easier. Happier. To give her the praise and encouragement she'd lacked, to go on bended knee and offer his faith in all she could be as if it were the Hope diamond.

He sat, stunned, watching her averted face—so damned sad.

I love her.

That shouldn't be such a shock; he'd asked her to marry him, for God's sake. But he hadn't thought then that he wanted her as his wife because he loved her desperately, passionately. He was ashamed to realize that he'd proposed because he found her desirable, because he enjoyed her company, because she and Hanna together had made him feel complete.

In other words, his motives had been utterly selfish.

Oh, he'd been in love with her, even then. He simply hadn't known it. And as she withdrew, in the weeks after he'd put a ring on her finger, he hadn't tried to figure out what their relationship lacked, what he should be giving and wasn't. He'd succumbed to panic as he saw his idyllic future threatened, but he hadn't stopped to understand that she was hurting.

His chest felt as if it was being crushed. Would it have made a difference, he wondered, if he'd ever once said those three, small words?

I love you.

But she'd implied that she didn't love him.

Yeah. Maybe.

Or—was it possible?—that what she'd been doing was voicing a plea? Begging him to tell her how he felt? Here she was, a woman who'd never been sure even her own mother and father believed in her and truly loved her. And him, he'd bulldozed her into agreeing to marry him by saying, *We feel like a family.*

Really wrenches the heart, doesn't it? he mocked himself. He suspected she'd said yes only because he wouldn't accept no. He'd pushed and pushed until she agreed. Then, when she wasn't eager to choose a ring, he'd discounted her motivations. Had to be because she didn't want to tell her mother she was marrying him. No chance the reluctance had stemmed from her uncertainty about whether she wanted to go through with it at all.

Rubbing his chest with one hand, he faced the fact that he was an idiot. He'd gotten his just deserts.

Matt suddenly became aware that her head had turned and she was gazing back at him, a couple of tiny furrows between her eyebrows.

The aggressive part of him that wouldn't accept a no was prodding, *Say "I love you." Give her the magic words. Then everything will be fine.*

But he didn't know that she'd believe him. Why would she? What had he ever sacrificed for her? He'd asked for everything from her. No, not asked—demanded. Even the house, which he'd thought of as the ultimate gift, wasn't one she'd ever wanted.

Even the damn house had been for him.

He had to think about this. Wait, until the uncertainty of her brother's trial was over. If Finn triumphed, there might be nothing Matt and Linnea could do to keep him from reclaiming his child. Would she refuse to see him at all then?

If Finn lost…

Matt's throat closed. If Finn went to prison, there would be another hearing to decide Hanna's future.

The only true gift he could give Linnea was the child she loved. The most meaningful way he could demonstrate his faith in her was to stand up in court and say, "Hanna is better off with her aunt."

Bleakly, he faced that future. He wouldn't be able to do for Hanna what he had for Tess. He'd never be the most important person in her life.

He'd still be part of it; Linnea wouldn't deny him that much. But Hanna would never live with him. He'd be the equivalent of a divorced father permitted only small slices of his child's time.

Sitting barely a foot from Linnea on the sofa, Hanna down the hall, Matt had never felt lonelier in his life.

He blundered to his feet and said in a thick voice, "I'd better get going. Uh…thanks for coming to dinner. I've missed talking to you." Talking to her? No, missed *her.*

Eyes widening, she rose, too. "I'm sorry. Here I was dumping all my woes on you."

He turned on her almost savagely and said, "Don't do that. I want to hear anything you have to tell me. I'm honored that you trusted me with your story. And ashamed. God, I'm ashamed, that I never wondered before."

"No." She looked astonished, dismayed. "Why would you be? I never gave you any reason to think—"

"Yeah." His throat was still constricted, his voice not his own. "You did. I just didn't let myself see what was right in front of me. I'm sorry, Linnea."

"I don't understand," she whispered.

He shook his head, turned and headed for the front door. He opened it, paused and said good-night.

Her good-night sounded so confused and unhappy he thought, *I've made things worse again.*

But he had to keep walking. By the time he reached his car, her door was closed and he saw no shadow of movement behind the front window.

Hell.

He braced his hands against the roof of his car, bowed his head and fought for control.

Love hurt like a son of a bitch.

THE PARKING GARAGE WAS very nearly full today. Linnea felt lucky to find a spot in a far corner, a good distance from the elevator. She'd have farther to run if she fled the courthouse today.

Well, then, don't flee.

She knew she could stand up to her mother, and there was nothing harder than that. If the press waylaid her, she was perfectly capable of saying "No comment" and repeating it until they gave up.

After locking her car, she walked at a steady pace to the elevator, which she shared with two men in expensive suits who ignored her. They did stand back so that she could exit first, the younger one smiling at her with a glint of appreciation in his eyes.

She blinked, and smiled uncertainly back.

Maybe they hadn't ignored her. Maybe they were being polite, so she didn't feel threatened by two strange men. Maybe, Linnea thought, she wasn't as invisible to other people as she often believed herself to be.

The very idea caused an odd shift, as if the earth had moved subtly beneath her feet.

Feeling unsettled, she joined the traffic into the court-house and through the metal detectors.

She was here because her father had called the evening before, his voice heavy.

"It's almost over, Linnie. The closing arguments were this morning."

"So soon." Matt had told her how near the trial was to ending, but she supposed she hadn't quite believed it. They had all been in this state of suspension for so long now.

"The judge gave the jury their instructions after lunch and sent them out, but they hadn't reached a verdict by five. Erlanger sent everyone home. The jury is to start up again at nine in the morning."

"How do you feel about it, Dad?" she asked.

He was silent for a long time. "I don't know," he finally admitted. "I want to believe. Your mother is so sure, but... Kershner tells Finn it's a good sign the jury didn't come right back."

Deciphering this fragmentary speech, she understood that her mother, of course, was absolutely convinced Finn was innocent and that any moderately intelligently human being would agree. Ergo, the jury would return a verdict of innocent. Her father, though, was less certain. And, although her brother's attorney was pretending confidence for Finn's sake, he might in fact be bracing for a loss.

"Do you just go sit there tomorrow, waiting all day?"

"Your mother thinks we should. I'll bring a book."

She'd thanked her father for letting her know, and hung up the phone pensively.

This morning, Linnea had sent Hanna off to school,

called the library to let them know she wouldn't be in and driven downtown to join her parents in their wait. She might have mixed feelings about Finn's fate, she and her mother might be estranged, but this was still her family.

Her parents were already there when she entered the courtroom, seated as they'd been that first day in the front row on the defense side.

When she sat beside her father, he smiled at her with approval and welcome. Her mother's face softened for an instant, then tightened into a scowl.

"Why would you bother to come now?" she snapped.

"Because you're my family." She hesitated. "I love you, Mom."

Her mother sniffed. "Well, it's about time you came to your senses."

Linnea's sigh was inaudible, but her father gave her arm a quick, sympathetic squeeze.

"How are you, Dad?" she asked him quietly. "This has to have been hard on you."

Stress seemed to play a part in exacerbating the symptoms of his multiple sclerosis. How sad, she thought, that he lived with someone who practically embodied stress. His fear of the ravages of the disease, she'd always known, was a significant reason he hadn't battled on her behalf.

"I'm holding up," he murmured. "I'll be glad when today is over."

Linnea looked around at the nearly deserted courtroom. "Where is everyone?"

"Apparently, the jury signals when they've reached a verdict. Gives the attorneys something like an hour to appear. That way, they're not sitting around twiddling their thumbs for what might be days."

Like we're doing, Linnea couldn't help thinking. But it didn't matter; she was here for her parents' sake. Especially Dad's. She could wait.

Yes, but where was Matt? she wondered. At home, waiting alone for the phone call? She shuddered to imagine his emotions right now.

She and her parents had all brought books and read, with only occasional, desultory conversation, until lunchtime, when they went out together. Predictably, over sub sandwiches Linnea's mother could talk about nothing but the trial—Finn's irritation at what he saw as missteps his attorney had taken, the foolish testimony of some of the expert witnesses, the absurdity of the whole proceeding. Imbued with nervous energy, she ate only a few bites. Watching her, Linnea thought, *She's terrified.*

And why not? Finn was Mom's life. She might love her husband, and to some extent Linnea and Hanna, but what she felt for Finn was different. It was as though she could hardly believe she had borne and raised a personage so glorious. Sometimes she seemed in awe of him. Even, maybe, a little afraid of him, or else why did she always rush to agree with him, or to soothe his irritation or to head criticism off at the pass?

Was it at all possible that Mom sometimes, secretly, feared that she'd created a monster and was desperate that no one else ever see what he was? Linnea shook her head. She felt so strange today, as if her vision had acquired an odd clarity, as if she herself was at once removed and able to be dispassionate.

They walked to the courthouse, took their same seats and opened their books. But they hadn't been reading long when there was a stir outside, and other people began to arrive. Linnea saw her mother go rigid. Dad grasped her hand and held it, then gave Linnea's a squeeze, too.

The prosecution team arrived and settled at their table, then the defense. Finn, with them, stopped to hug Mom and Dad over the waist-high railing. He hesitated, then held out his arms to Linnea. Neither the jury nor judge had reappeared. Finn's face was somber, and he looked older than he had the last time she saw him. He was scared, too, she realized. After only the briefest of pauses, she hugged him and felt his arms close tightly around her.

"Thanks for coming," he murmured, before releasing her. For an instant, their eyes met and she thought she saw a younger Finn, the big brother she'd once adored.

The judge entered the courtroom and took his place. Was Matt going to miss the verdict? Where on earth was he?

She turned in her seat and saw him walk in the door. Wearing a dark suit, white shirt and tie, with his air of contained energy and impatience, he could have been another attorney. When he spotted her, his stride checked and his eyebrows lifted in surprise. She gave a jerky nod and he inclined his dark head. He came even with her and stopped. Did he intend to say something?

To her shock, he entered their row and took the seat beside her rather than his accustomed spot behind the prosecutor. What was he *doing*?

But she knew. Up until this minute, Matt had insisted the jury see him every day right behind the prosecutor, the face of their consciences. How was it he had put it, talking to Hanna? *Bearing witness.* Yes, that was what he'd done. Now, the jury had already reached a verdict and he could do nothing more for his sister. Even though, in outrage and loyalty, he wanted to hear "Guilty as charged," he'd chosen to sit beside Linnea to say *I'm here when you need me.*

Unbearably moved, she looked at him. He smiled, a rueful, twisted smile in which she saw irony and pain and—oh, God, was it possible?—love.

For Hanna. It had to be for Hanna. He'd said himself they felt like family, but it wasn't just a feeling. They *were* family. *That's what he's acknowledging,* she thought now, the quagmire of emotions inside her tangling into a mass that pressed against her rib cage, constricted her lungs, *hurt.*

And, oh, what must Finn be feeling?

Matt took Linnea's hand and laid it on his thigh, still encased in his warm grip. Clearly, he had no intention of letting go. His muscles tensed, and she followed his gaze to see the jury filing in, their expressions solemn. None of them seemed to want to look at Finn.

The judge asked the foreman to stand and whether they had reached a verdict.

"Yes, Your Honor."

"And that verdict is?"

The courtroom was utterly silent. Nobody breathed.

The foreman looked directly at Finn. "Guilty as charged."

Linnea's mother let out a terrible cry. Finn's shoulders sagged, and he abruptly bent his head. Seated at the back, members of the press hurried out of the courtroom to file reports for the morning papers.

Even sound seemed hollow and distant to Linnea now. The judge set a date for sentencing. Finn's attorney started talking about appeals. Linnea's father held his wife in a protective embrace.

Matt said, very formally, "I'm sorry for your family."

Numb, she nodded. "Thank you."

His gaze stayed on her face for a moment, his gray eyes intense. Then he gave a clipped nod, stood and walked away.

As Linnea steered her grieving mother and her weary, stooped father out of the courtroom, she caught a last glimpse of Matt shaking the prosecutor's hand. Inside, he must be rejoicing.

And me? What do I feel?

Linnea didn't know, only that nothing would ever be the same for any of them.

CHAPTER FOURTEEN

HANNA TOOK THE NEWS of her father's conviction quietly. Too quietly.

Linnea explained that they didn't yet know how long Finn's sentence would be.

"He's selling the house," she said. "He has to pay all the lawyers who defended him. And…it would sit empty anyway, which isn't good."

Hanna looked up at her. "If Daddy is going to jail, do I get to stay with you?"

Linnea gave her a swift hug. "You bet. Or…" Would Matt contest for custody now? On a cramp of alarm, she thought, *Of course he will.* He wanted to raise his niece the way he had her mother. What was more, he'd have a better case now that Hanna knew and loved him. He had a good job right here in Seattle, he could afford to give Hanna anything she needed, and a judge might well believe she'd be safer and better off with Tess's brother than with Finn's sister. Finn's family wouldn't look very good right now. Trying to keep distress from her voice, she said, "Or maybe Uncle Matt."

Part of her wanted Hanna to clutch her desperately and cry, "You! I want you, Aunt Linnie!" But she didn't. She only nodded and asked whether she could watch TV. Linnea, drained, agreed. Later, she'd have to drag Hanna along to take care of the Dorman's elderly cocker spaniel, but maybe by then a walk would be good for both of them.

Hanna seemed much as usual in the morning, if still rather quiet and introspective. Linnea dropped her at school and went in to work herself. She was startled, at noon, to be told she had a visitor. She came out to find her father waiting at the reference desk.

"Dad!"

"Linnie." He gave her one of his grave, gentle smiles. "I'm hoping you can have lunch with me."

"Of course I can. Let me tell Susan where I'm going."

He let her pick the restaurant, and she chose a nearby small café. Not until they were seated and had ordered did she ask, "Where's Mom?"

"She's not herself today. She planned to lie down."

Her energetic mother rarely napped, but the trial would have exhausted her and now, with its devastating conclusion, she must be crushed.

Either that, Linnea thought ruefully, or she hadn't wanted to see her daughter.

"Do you know how Finn is doing?"

"He seems resigned." Her father frowned, as if puzzled. "I think his own culpability, whatever that may be, has finally caught up with him."

Linnea nodded. She'd guessed the same after his odd phone call to Hanna. She noticed that her father was careful not to say how much culpability he thought Finn actually bore. It would be awful, as a parent, to believe your child could commit a brutal crime.

"I asked you to lunch," Paavo said, "because I need to tell you how deeply I regret not taking your part more with your mother."

Alarmed, she laid her hand over his. "Dad, you don't need to do this."

"Yes, I do. What you said to your mother that day in the parking garage laid bare all my faults. No," he said, stopping her from interrupting, "I know you were talking to her, not to me. But I can't deny that I saw what was happening and did nothing."

Stricken, Linnea stared at him. "I always knew I could count on you. Sometimes I wished…" Her throat seemed to close and she said in a hurry, "But I'm fine. You can see I'm fine."

He shook his head. "No, you're not. You should have a successful career, be married, maybe have started a family. You deserved everything and more that your brother got."

Linnea sat still for a moment. She looked at him with a lifetime's heartbreak and bewilderment she could no longer contain. In a small, bleak voice, she asked, "Does Mom hate me?"

His eyes were full of grief. "No! Of course not. Never doubt your mother loves you." He'd aged, too, she saw with that new clarity. His thick hair had thinned, his complexion had acquired a gray tint and bags sagged beneath his eyes. "It's more complicated than that, Linnie."

"Then what?" she asked. No, begged.

"You never met your grandparents."

She shook her head. She did know her uncle, although not well because he lived in Houston and Mom and he had never been close.

"I had the sense that Robert was her parents' favorite. Your mom desperately wanted a son first. She wouldn't even talk about the possibility of having a girl, not with that first pregnancy. It was as if she *had* to have a boy to prove her own worth in a way I didn't understand. I don't know." He shook his head sorrowfully. "I'm afraid our family ended up mirroring your mother's. You stood in for her. I think, Linnie, without knowing what she was doing, she turned on you everything she felt for herself. Maybe she couldn't bear to give you what she hadn't been given herself. I don't know," he said again. "She was different when we met. It wasn't until Finn was born that she changed. He triggered something in her. I could never make her see—" He stopped and looked at her with bitter honesty. "But I didn't try as hard as I should have. I was proud of Finn, too. He was a beautiful baby. All parents brag, don't they? But I loved you as much when you were born, Linnie, you must believe that. I thought your mother did, too, until…there were small things. Somehow, I never let myself see how bad it was. It was easier to leave the raising of you kids to her."

The waitress brought their food, although neither of them reached for silverware or napkin.

"I never blamed you." She hated seeing her beloved father torn by guilt, and yet… It helped, somehow, to know it wasn't all in her mind. To learn that her mother had been damaged long before her second-born child came along. Linnea could have been brilliant and beautiful, and it wouldn't have mattered because she was a girl. Or maybe because she was second, and Finn had already claimed everything Mom had to give.

Was it true that her mother had been venting self-loathing, perhaps truly without understanding what she was doing to her daughter?

"You should blame me," her father said. "Just…know

that I do love you. And that your mother does, too. What you said to her hit hard, you know. I don't believe she *can* let herself accept her fault. That kind of self-knowledge might be past bearing. But…since you confronted her, she's talked to me, some, about her parents and how she felt about her brother. She's caught a glimpse of patterns. If you'll give her a chance, Linnie, she may be able to change."

Could she give her mother another chance? Resentment and hurt seemed to provide the fuel she needed to break free. Was she supposed to feel sorry for Mom?

"I worry about how she treats Hanna," Linnea said. "I know Mom loves her, but she's awfully critical, sometimes. And if she starts associating Hanna with me rather than Finn, it might get worse."

"I know she can be sharp. But she'll be terribly hurt if you cut her off. Right now, she needs you and Hanna both."

After a moment, Linnea nodded. "I'll think about it. That's all I can promise."

"I can't ask for more than that," he said quietly. "Now, why don't we eat."

They did, although neither had much appetite. Partway through her sandwich, she asked, "Why does Mom dislike Matt so much?"

"Perhaps because he saw right through Finn. Your mother's never liked him, you know."

"I had that impression."

"Tess used to talk about him. He sounds like a good man, Linnie. Are you sure you made the right decision?"

For the first time in this harrowing conversation, tears burned in Linnea's eyes. "No. I love him, Dad."

"Then why…?" Worry creased his thin face. "Did you let your mother's disapproval influence you?"

Had she? Linnea couldn't be sure. Her panic had awakened almost from the moment she agreed to marry Matt. She thought now it had been made up of a whole stew of ingredients. If her greatest fear had been that he didn't love her, why hadn't she asked how he did feel about her?

"I think mostly I was afraid he wanted me only because I won custody of Hanna over him."

"Are you saying that he thought marrying you was another way of winning?" Her father sounded perturbed.

"That sounds so competitive. I don't think it was that, exactly." Her brow creased. "I needed to know that he loved me. Not because I was Hanna's aunt and I had custody of her. Just me," she finished sadly.

"Are you sure he doesn't?"

Thinking of Matt choosing to sit beside her for the verdict, holding her hand in that warm, reassuring clasp, of the way he'd said, "I'm sorry," Linnea shook her head and whispered, "No."

Dad surprised her, this man who'd never been very good at expressing emotion himself. He gave her the gentlest smile. "If he does love you, I'm guessing Matt will find a way to let you know."

Linnea carried that thought with her long after her father had dropped her off at the library and she had returned to checking in books.

Matt hadn't been happy when she told him she wouldn't marry him. She'd assumed some of it might be punctured ego. Was it possible she'd wounded him more than she had believed?

Yes, but if he loved her, why hadn't he ever said so? Especially when she told him she couldn't marry him without love.

She froze, hearing herself. That sounded an awful lot like she was telling him *she* didn't love *him*. Was that what he'd heard?

She closed her eyes and moaned.

"Are you okay?" she heard someone ask her.

Linnea flushed and turned to see that Susan, the branch librarian, had paused at her side with an armful of books.

"I'm fine," she said quickly. "I just thought of something dumb I did." She waved the librarian on. "One of those epiphanies."

Susan laughed. "Boy, do I know what that's like." She went on into her office.

Linnea looked down at the half-full book-drop cart she'd been emptying and thought, *It's a little late for an epiphany.* What was done was done.

Recognizing one of her mother's favorite aphorisms, she wrinkled her nose in distaste. But in this case Mom was right. Or maybe Dad was the one who was right. Matt was an assertive man who wouldn't give up so easily, not if he really loved her. She thought he would find a way to let her know.

And if he didn't... Well, she'd have her answer, wouldn't she?

LINNEA WAS STUNNED AT how quickly the hearing to decide Hanna's placement was scheduled. They were all to appear before the commissioner again only two weeks after the end of Finn's trial.

A few days before, Matt asked her and Hanna out to dinner again. This time they went to a small Mexican restaurant, where Hanna was content with a cheese quesadilla.

She was to attend the hearing tomorrow at the commissioner's request. He wanted to speak to her first, privately.

"Can't you come in with me, Aunt Linnie?" Hanna asked anxiously. "Or you, Uncle Matt?"

They both shook their heads. Matt said, "I think the commissioner wants to find out who you'd like best to live with. He's afraid that if I'm with you, you won't want to hurt my feelings and say Aunt Linnie, or the other way around if she's with you."

"Oh." She pondered that. "So I get to choose?"

"Well… He's going to consider other factors, too. Like, if you said you wanted to live with your friend Polly's family, he'd probably say no."

Hanna gave a small giggle. "I wouldn't say *that!*"

Matt was the one to steer the conversation another direction, which relieved Linnea. She thought he'd managed to reassure Hanna, though, for which she was grateful. He seemed to have a gift for talking to her at a level she'd understand, and his strength and certainty were contagious. Linnea felt some days as if she could just soak in confidence from him, as if he shared it freely.

So why hadn't that worked while they were engaged?

She didn't expect to see him again until they met before the commissioner. Those last few days felt strange to Linnea, as if she were hovering above watching herself walk through her life as if nothing had changed and nothing would change.

The night before the hearing, she took Hanna to her last swim lesson in this session. No surprise, once past her fear of dunking Hanna had taken like a fish to water. Tonight, she was finishing the advanced beginner class. This summer, she'd be in intermediate.

Linnea settled on the bleachers beside the pool, not bothering to take out her book. Tonight, she'd watch the whole lesson. A few other parents sat scattered over the bleachers, some in pairs, some reading, one mother knitting, a strand of red yarn emerging from the tote at her side to be seized by the clacking needles. Watching Hanna grab another little girl's hand before both jumped into the water with a splash, Linnea didn't pay attention to the man who emerged from the men's dressing room. Not until he was nearly to her and the bleachers were quivering as he climbed did she see that it was Matt.

He'd obviously come from work, and still wore dress pants and a white shirt unbuttoned at the neck, although he'd jettisoned the tie and suit jacket.

"Matt," she said in astonishment. "I didn't expect you."

He sat beside her. "I wanted to see Hanna's last lesson. Plus…I was hoping to talk to you."

Something tightened inside her. He wanted to talk to her about tomorrow. Warn her that he was going to fight tooth and nail for custody?

He seemed reluctant to begin though. Elbows braced on his thighs, he looked toward the pool rather than her, but in a way that made her wonder if he even saw Hanna. After a moment he sighed. "I won't be asking for custody tomorrow."

She gaped at him, replaying his words to be sure she'd heard him right. "But you wanted her so much."

He straightened and turned his head to look at her. "She needs you." There was a long pause. His expression was strained. "Even if I thought I could win, I won't hurt you, Linnea. I can live with the current visitation."

Shell-shocked, she whispered, "I don't understand."

A flare of some emotion darkened his eyes, and his voice came out sandpaper rough. "I love Hanna, but…" For a moment he looked at her, a moment during which her heart seemed to stop beating. Then he gave his head a shake, said, "I've changed my mind about staying. Don't tell Hanna I came," and stood and descended the bleachers.

He didn't look back, just walked into the dressing room and disappeared. Linnea sat completely still, oblivious to the smell of chlorine, the whistles blown by instructors and the splashes and high voices of the kids. All she could do was absorb his words and the expression on his face.

I love Hanna, but…

But what? Was there even the smallest chance he'd started to say, "I love Hanna, but I love you more?"

Breathless with hope, she wondered whether she had the courage to find out.

So MUCH ABOUT TODAY ECHOED his arrival for the previous hearing, and yet Matt was conscious of how much had changed.

Having gotten here first, he was sitting beside his attorney in the waiting room when the Sorensens arrived in a group. Hanna's grandparents chose seats across from him again, although this time Paavo bent his head in greeting, which Matt returned with a nod. Linnea and Hanna, hand in hand, came to him to say hello while her attorney, Margaret Robinson, chatted with Shelton.

Linnea was beautiful today in a flowery skirt and white sweater, her hair loose. Only the pearls in her ears were the same. Her smile was soft and her entire look was somehow open, as if she were relaxed in a way he didn't remember ever seeing her.

"You ready for this, kiddo?" he asked Hanna.

The seven-year-old nodded solemnly. "I practiced what I'm going to say."

He grinned at her. "Good for you." Inside, he ached. What if she would have chosen him?

But he knew she wouldn't. He had begun to believe she loved him, but her aunt Linnie had always been her stability, perhaps the person in all the world who made her feel safest even before her mom's death. No matter how much she had loved her daughter, Tess, ambitious, creative and restless, hadn't been as accessible as Linnea, Matt suspected. The realization didn't sting the way it once would have. No, Hanna would choose Linnea, and that was right for her.

The commissioner himself came out to get Hanna. He greeted the two attorneys, Matt and the Sorensens, then asked Hanna if she was willing to join him for a talk before the proceedings.

Matt smiled at the way she stood, nodded and said, "Uncle Matt said probably you wanted to ask me who *I* want to live with. So I thought and thought."

Behind his horn-rimmed glasses, the commissioner's eyes crinkled even as his mouth stayed grave. "Good for you."

Back straight, Hanna took his hand and marched into the conference room beside him.

Matt looked over to see Linnea's misty smile as she gazed after her niece. She murmured, "I would have been so shy at her age. Did you see how brave she was?"

"I saw."

Paavo smiled, too. "She's quite a girl, our grand-daughter."

Linnea's mother said nothing, but she seemed different today, too, he thought. Less starchy, her anger transformed into a kind of bewilderment he understood.

When, not five minutes later, the bailiff poked his head out to ask them all to come in, she faltered as she stood. It was her husband who steadied her and kept a firm hand under her elbow as they went ahead of Matt and his attorney into the room.

Hanna was waiting there, sitting partway down the table, her feet wrapped around the legs of the chair. Linnea went straight to her. Matt started to, as well, then halted. It was her right, not his. After a moment, he made himself turn away, circle the table and sit beside Shelton opposite the Sorensens.

At the head of the table, the commissioner had an odd expression on his face. He cleared his throat. "Perhaps I should start by telling you that the young Ms. Sorensen has a very firm opinion."

Matt braced himself.

"She refused to decide whether she'd prefer to live with her aunt or her uncle." He gazed at both of them in turn. "Hanna," he continued, "chooses *both* of you. And that creates a dilemma for me."

Matt heard the words, but it was Linnea he was watching. She stifled a cry, and looked at him with wide, shocked eyes.

Shelton rose to speak, but Matt didn't hear a word he said and he suspected Linnea didn't, either. He couldn't tear his gaze from her. Color had risen in her cheeks as they stared at each other.

He saw her take a deep, shuddering breath, then she pushed back her chair and rose to her feet.

Shelton stopped midsentence and everyone around the table turned their heads in surprise.

Still, her eyes hadn't once left Matt's. "You asked me to marry you," she said tremulously, "and I thought it was mostly for Hanna's sake."

He found he was on his feet, too, without remembering the act of rising.

"But I never did ask you why you wanted to marry me. So now I will."

He was no more conscious of their stunned audience than she was. Voice guttural, he said, "Because I love you and want to spend the rest of my life with you."

He felt as if she was looking deeper inside him than anyone ever had before. When she finally turned away to the commissioner, Matt had to brace his hands on the table to prevent himself from staggering.

Still standing straight and strong, Linnea said, "Then that's my choice." She touched her niece's shoulder and turned a tender smile on her uplifted face. "To give Hanna hers."

God. The relief and pure need that flooded him would have dropped him to his knees if the table hadn't held him upright.

It seemed suddenly as if everyone was speaking. Matt and Linnea had gone back to gazing deeply into each other's eyes. Ebullience rose in his chest and spilled out in a broad grin that probably looked stupid. Her face was pink, but a smile had begun to curve her mouth, too. Hanna was grinning as foolishly as he was. Matt didn't know what Linnea's parents thought. Right now, he didn't give a damn.

She loved him. She *had* to love him, to have defied her own nature and done this so publicly. He was the luckiest man on earth. He wanted to kiss her. No, damn it, he wanted to hear the words from her, too.

The commissioner banged a gavel. Expression flummoxed but his eyes betraying amusement, too, he said, "I think we should delay this hearing to give Mr. Laughlin and Ms. Sorensen time to be sure they're making this life-altering decision for the right reasons."

Shelton cleared his throat and stood beside Matt. "As I started to say earlier, Mr. Laughlin wishes to withdraw his petition for custody of Hanna Sorensen. He has come to the conclusion that his niece, Hanna, is best off living with her aunt, Ms. Sorensen. I don't believe there's any reason for a resumption of the hearing."

"Is that correct, Mr. Laughlin?"

Matt pulled himself together. "Yes, sir. I'm happy with the current visitation schedule, even should Linnea, ah, decide not to accept my proposal after all."

The commissioner smiled. "Very well. In the absence of objections—" he glanced at Shelton and Margaret Robinson, who both spread their hands in identical gestures of acceptance and bemusement "—then I award custody to Linnea Sorensen, with the issue to be revisited after Hanna's father serves his sentence." He raised his eyebrows at Hanna. "Is that satisfactory, Hanna?"

She beamed at him. "Uh-*huh*."

Matt heard everybody laughing. He was barely keeping himself anchored in place, when all he wanted was to take Linnea in his arms.

"I believe this is the happiest ending to any hearing over which I've ever presided," the commissioner said, after which he inclined his head. "Good day, folks."

Matt bumped into chairs and the corner of the table in

his haste to circle it. Linnea must have moved as fast; she
met him at the foot. He snatched her into his arms and
held her close, reveling in the way her arms encircled him
in turn and held him as tightly.

"Losing you…" he said in a choked voice. "It's been
hell. Don't do that to me again."

"No." Her head shook hard against his shoulder.
"No, never."

He pulled back a few inches, enough to see her face.
"Do you love me?"

Her eyes flashed indignation. "Of course I do! Do you
think I could have done that if I didn't?"

"No. But when you said you couldn't marry me
without love…"

"I thought you didn't love me. You never said, you know."

"Yeah," he admitted. "I was idiot enough not to have
recognized what I felt."

"We were convenient."

He grimaced. "Yeah. And, damn, but I wanted you."

"I noticed," she said primly. Almost primly. The color
of her eyes had deepened, and her cheeks gained new roses.

Matt's head bent. He had to kiss her…

A cleared throat was an unwelcome reminder that they
weren't alone.

Linnea started guiltily. "Dad!"

Paavo smiled at them. "Didn't I tell you?" he said to
his daughter.

Still encircled by one of Matt's arms, she rose on tiptoe
to kiss her father on the cheek. "You were right, Daddy."

"Congratulations," her father said, holding out his hand.

Matt and he shook with a solemnity that made Matt
realize he was agreeing to a pact.

Don't hurt my daughter ever again.

I swear I won't.

He saw Linnea looking around, and realized it was for her mother, who was nowhere to be seen. She must have hurried out the minute the hearing ended.

Paavo's expression was sad as he saw his daughter's grief. "She'll come around, Linnie. Don't worry. I promise she'll be at your wedding."

Linnea tried to smile. "As long as you are."

"You know I will be. Your Matt is a good man. And, you," he said to Matt, "are very lucky." He smiled down at Hanna, who wormed into their small circle. "Isn't he, Hanna?"

"Aunt Linnie's really pretty," Hanna declared.

"Yeah, she is," Matt agreed, enjoying Linnea's embarrassment—and the glow she couldn't hide.

"Hanna has agreed to come home with her grandma and me," Paavo said, his hand still on his granddaughter's shoulder. "If that's all right with you. We thought you might like some time alone."

Hanna nodded, watching the two adults she adored with the delight of a child opening the most coveted Christmas present ever.

Matt decided that he liked his father-in-law-to-be. Apparently he'd misjudged Paavo all these years.

"We have things to say to each other," he agreed.

"You don't mind?" Linnea asked her niece.

"Uh-uh. Granddad said he'll play games with me. And he said I could spend the night."

The man rose another notch in Matt's estimation.

Linnea hugged her dad again and managed a muffled thank-you. Then both she and Matt swept Hanna Banana up in big hugs and promised to pick her up for school in the morning.

Hanna and her grandfather went ahead. Matt took Linnea's hand and smiled at her. "Ready to go home?"

THEY'D ARRIVED IN SEPARATE cars, of course, but Matt gave Linnea one quick, hungry kiss and promised to follow her home.

Every time she looked in the rearview mirror during the drive, his car was right behind her. She felt more as if she was floating than anything as mundane as sitting behind the steering wheel. Honestly, she was in such a daze, she probably shouldn't have been driving.

She couldn't believe she'd done something so...so *brazen,* as to stand up right there in a legal hearing and ask a man if he loved her.

But he did. He did! Her blood seemed to fizz with happiness and disbelief. Having her mother refuse to share her happiness was a sad note, but she felt closer to her father than she had in years, since she was a young child and he and she would sneak out for ice cream and agree not to tell Mom about it.

When Linnea pulled into her driveway, Matt parked at the curb. Long strides carried him to where she waited at the foot of the steps.

Eyes the color of molten silver swept over her face. "God, I love you. You will marry me this time?"

"Yes. You notice, um, that I didn't give you back your ring." She'd kept meaning to—it wasn't fair to keep it, especially when their engagement had been so brief—but somehow she kept forgetting when she saw him.

"I noticed." His smile was wolfish. "That gave me hope."

They made it inside, one step, one kiss at a time. The door had barely closed behind them when he had her backed up against it. His big hands tilted her face up so that his mouth could claim hers with sheer desperation.

He lifted his head once and said hoarsely, "Promise to slap me if I ever again try to rush you into anything like that damn house. Keep me in check."

Her heart was so full, she didn't know how much more happiness she could bear. "If I get shy, be patient with me. Won't you, Matt?"

She felt his muscles lock, as if with remembered pain. The vulnerability in his eyes shook her.

"I've learned my lesson. I swear. Before, I was too scared to be patient. I could feel you slipping away. I thought maybe, if I didn't slow down, you wouldn't have time for second thoughts. I knew better, but I was stupid enough to think that any way I could get you was okay."

"This way," she said, smiling at him with all the love she felt, "is better."

"Yeah." Matt bent his head to kiss her again. "This way is a hell of a lot better."

They'd said all they had to with words. The rest could be said with touch and passion, sighs and groans.

No, she thought later, some words bore repeating. Just as he entered her, his gaze locked with hers, he said again, "I love you, Linnea. Never doubt it."

And when they lay together in the stunned aftermath, she nuzzled his throat and whispered, "I love you."

Nothing in her life had ever felt sweeter than the way his arms tightened.

It was a miracle that Hanna had chosen them both, and

by so doing gave Linnea the courage to seize the chance
to love and be loved.

Her lips curved.

We feel like a family.

They *were* a family.

* * * * *

AND BABIES MAKE FIVE
by Judy Duarte

Despite being single, Samantha's dream of becoming a mother is about
to come true—in triplicate! Yet can her handsome neighbour Hector
convince Sam that he's her Mr Right?

AT LONG LAST, A BRIDE
by Susan Crosby

Joe knew it was past time for his now *ex*-fiancée to stand on her own
two feet. So why were all roads leading him back into Dixie's arms?

RANCHER'S TWINS: MUM NEEDED
by Barbara Hannay

Nanny Holly has already bonded with her late cousin's gorgeous twins...
and she's reluctant to let go when their rough, rugged father Gray
claims the precious babies. Yet could their future be together as a
family?

0411/023b

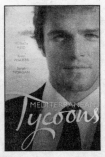

2 FREE BOOKS
AND A SURPRISE GIFT

We would like to take this opportunity to thank you for reading this Mills & Boon® book by offering you the chance to take TWO more specially selected books from the Cherish™ series absolutely FREE! We're also making this offer to introduce you to the benefits of the Mills & Boon® Book Club™—

- **FREE home delivery**
- **FREE gifts and competitions**
- **FREE monthly Newsletter**
- **Exclusive Mills & Boon Book Club offers**
- **Books available before they're in the shops**

Accepting these FREE books and gift places you under no obligation to buy, you may cancel at any time, even after receiving your free books. Simply complete your details below and return the entire page to the address below. You don't even need a stamp!

YES Please send me 2 free Cherish books and a surprise gift. I understand that unless you hear from me, I will receive 5 superb new stories every month, including two 2-in-1 books priced at £5.30 each, and a single book priced at £3.30, postage and packing free. I am under no obligation to purchase any books and may cancel my subscription at any time. The free books and gift will be mine to keep in any case.

Ms/Mrs/Miss/Mr _____ Initials _____

Surname _____

Address _____

_____ Postcode _____

E-mail _____

Send this whole page to: Mills & Boon Book Club, Free Book Offer, FREEPOST NAT 10298, Richmond, TW9 1BR